The Bridge of Now

A NOVEL

GW00578068

ALVAGH CRONIN

FLOWER *of* LIFE PRESS

PRAISE

"Alvagh Cronin has crafted a beautiful story of a family's becoming. It is a Universal story, with the love of the sacred feminine at the heart of it. Like most families, there are twists and turns on the journey that hold both terrors and treasures. You will find yourself carried away, and perhaps more importantly, also carried within, as their story offers us a beautiful window into our own becoming."

—Rima Bonario, author of *The Seven Queendoms: A SoulMap for Embodying Sacred Feminine Sovereignty*

"A gripping page turner full of insight, wisdom and mystery. If you're looking for a beautiful escape from reality—this is it!"

—Kate Gunn, author of *Untying The Knot* and *The Accidental Soberista*

"Alvagh Cronin knows the human heart and has written The Bridge of Now *straight from her own."*

—Miriam O'Callaghan, Irish Journalist

*"*The Bridge of Now *is a beautifully woven wisdom text in the guise of a magical fiction piece. This brilliant story of a family and its growth and transcendence over the generations is a page-turner! It's one of those books where the characters linger with you long after reading the book. Alvagh Cronin does a marvelous job of teaching her wisdom in this masterfully told story!"*

—Sage Solis, author of *Menopause Mavens*

FLOWER *of* LIFE PRESS

Published by Flower of Life Press
Old Saybrook, CT, USA
Astara J. Ashley, *Publisher*
www.floweroflifepress.com

Cover and interior design by Astara Jane Ashley, www.floweroflifepress.com
Cover art by Eoin Madigan, EoinMadigan.com

Library of Congress Control Number: Available Upon Request

ISBN-13: 978-1-7371839-3-8

*This book is dedicated to
Jeremy, Cailean, Aobh, and Óran.
My loves.*

Acknowledgments

I wish to thank everyone who has been on this book writing journey with me: Most especially my husband Jeremy and our three children Cailean, Aobh and Óran, to whom this book is dedicated. My loves.

Special thanks to my baby sister Nessa, who was the first person to read my writing and spurred me on to continue and be even braver. My sister Réada was my second reader and provided the practical feedback. I love you, sisters mine. Thank you, Colum for always being the best and most supportive big brother any of us girls could have.

Thank you also to my niece Aisling Maria Cronin, Colum's daughter, who brought her editing skills to my writing, bringing a more coherent story through. I also send sincere thanks to my friends Susan Reddy and Evie Hanlon who then read my first draft. Thank you also to Laura Jean Wiley Brennan who read my edited draft. Their invaluable, honest feedback went to bringing this book to a place where I felt I could publish it. I'm forever grateful to these six special women.

I was then able to bring my book to my mother for a read—a daunting prospect for any daughter whose mother was a teacher. Thankfully, my mother is also full of support and encouragement for me, no matter what I choose to do. Eternal love and gratitude, Mammy.

Deepest gratitude to Christopher and all at Glenstal Abbey who provide sanctuary, safety, and inspirational quiet time to aspiring writers and everybody else who enters the gates. Thank you to my besties Jean Kehoe and Mary Kirwan. Mary's magic Amatsu hands have brought my weary body back from the brink on many occasions. Jean, our swan, keeps us all happy to be us. They've been my partners in crime for more years than any of us will admit and are powerful healing influences in my life. They encourage me to make things happen.

To make things happen, I needed Kathleen McGowan and Astara Jane Ashley, my mentors and my publisher at Flower of Life Press. I am more grateful to these two women than I will ever be able to express. To the wonderful women who joined me on 'Divine Writing Journey' with Astara and Kathleen, I am grateful for the safe space and the great fun and creative time. We have friendships made that will last forever.

Thank you to Eoin Madigan, www.eoinmadigan.com—a supremely talented artist and friend, who listened to my description of *The Bridge of Now* and captured the feeling of it perfectly for my book cover.

But I am most, most grateful for the experience.

This is my book.

Contents

Acknowledgments vi

Family Tree ix

    Chapter One 1

    Chapter Two 17

    Chapter Three 37

    Chapter Four 57

    Chapter Five 77

    Chapter Six 93

    Chapter Seven 109

    Chapter Eight 119

    Chapter Nine 139

    Chapter Ten 161

    Chapter Eleven 179

    Chapter Twelve 197

    Chapter Thirteen 215

Afterword 227

Appendix: *The Bridge of Now* Guidebook 229

About the Author 243

Family Tree

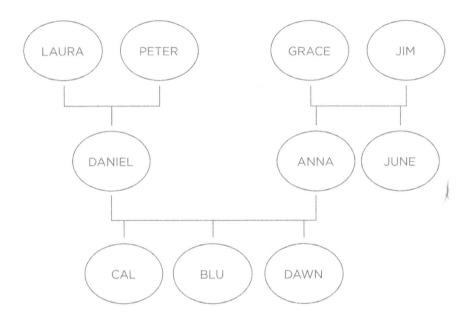

Chapter One

For Laura, the unknown future was a place of terror. Once upon a time, she had faith, but now, she was too tired. Too much had happened. There was no way back. No way to undo all that she had endured. She had hated herself and her life for so long now, and was so full of guilt and shame that she couldn't even face her own eyes in the rear-view mirror of the car.

Her body ached, yet she was sure that this pain was the only thing that anchored her to the physical plane. Her heartbeat pounded in her ears, forcing her to listen to the space she occupied and be aware of what was happening in the present. Otherwise, she was frantic. Her thoughts were frenzied and she couldn't settle on a decision about how she felt.

It would be days before she could afford to reflect on whether or not she had done the right thing.

Now, all she could manage to do was to keep the car on the road, driving as quickly as she could, to put as much distance as possible between herself and him.

She had no idea where she was going. All she knew was that she had to move fast and believe that the future would accept her.

Peter had brought mystery and excitement into her life. Nobody knew who he was at first, or where he had come from. He had seemed very taken with her, and she was flattered by his attention. She didn't remember when exactly, but over time, he had moved into her house and made himself indispensable.

He had played music on his guitar in her sitting room and made her feel safe. He had wanted to be a famous actor, and told her that one day they'd walk on the red carpet and he'd show her off to the world.

She admired his passion and ambition, but she knew deep down that it would never happen. It had been fun to listen to him, though, during those early years.

He always had some problem or other with his fellow actors. The lead never deserved the role—it always should have been him. He often told her that he suspected the female actors had slept with the director or the writer. They never got their roles on merit. They were sluts, he said. Not like her.

She never said anything about this aspect of his character. She never asked him why he didn't trust people, and he never asked her what she thought about his pronouncements. She just let him get it out of his system, and then they'd just get on with their evening or get back to whatever they had been doing.

They had some great times; he had a motorcycle and they often used it to travel to the sea or go on weekends away, where she learned how to let herself go. He introduced her to a sexual ecstasy she had never dreamed possible, and she was devoted to him and to their relationship.

He would pick her up from work if it was raining. He was thoughtful and kind to her. He didn't like how her boss treated her, and told her she was paid too little and was undervalued.

It was only later, looking back and years after his death, that she could see how unfair this was. She'd managed to buy her own house at 26 years old and had never had the electricity cut off until he took charge of the bills. How had she allowed all of this to happen to her?

He thought that her girlfriends were manipulative of her, and told Laura that she was too kind and too indulgent of them. They were fools, he said: not nearly as clever as she was. He didn't like how they giggled and behaved in the pubs with other men. They were always having relationship issues and relying on Laura to help them out. He said that Laura was mad to even listen to them, as they'd only do whatever they wanted to do anyway and she'd have wasted nights talking to them on the phone, drinking tea with them, counselling and comforting them. All for nothing.

He would sometimes come with her to Sunday lunches with her father, and was polite and even entertaining. When he asked her father for her hand in marriage, her father asked him when he was going to get a job.

He was prepared for this. He told his prospective father-in-law that his career plans were well in hand. He had a friend who owned a book-shop, and he was taking a franchise with him to expand into the city. This would allow him to continue his acting, and all would be well.

When they returned to Laura's after that afternoon in her father's house, he was quiet. They came through the door and he threw himself heavily down on his favourite chair and sighed. She asked him if he was okay, and whether her father had been amenable.

'He doesn't think I'm good enough for you,' he answered. She walked over to him and kneeled down in front of his seat, leaning her head against his knee. 'Of course he does, Peter. Dad loves you. Just like I do.'

Their wedding day was the stuff of childhood fairy tales. Laura made some adjustments to her long-deceased mother Emily's wedding dress, and got a new veil, gloves, and shoes. She looked absolutely gorgeous. The whole of her childhood village came out to see her leave the home in which she'd grown up, on her father's arm. She was beautiful, they all agreed. Stunning.

Soon after the nuptials, the couple settled into married life in the city. Laura became pregnant and Peter got a wonderful lead role in a very successful run of a play. He was the toast of the town. On the opening night, Laura thought she would burst with pride as the cast—especially the lead actor—got a wonderful standing ovation. At the after-party, he was inundated with praise, surrounded by people wanting to shake his hand and buy him a congratulatory drink. She found it difficult to get him into the taxi and back home.

The bookshop closed down. He had no time to invest in it and his friend rethought his plans, leaving with his own young family for other shores.

This meant that Peter began to lose focus, and Laura could immediately feel her tenuous dreams melting away.

He began to come home later and later, and she knew he had lost interest in their home life. She was too tired to think about what to do, and in the summer, when their son was born, she focused on him. Her little Daniel. He was the image of her own father and she adored him: her little bundle of joy, who smelled like heaven.

Peter had been present at Daniel's birth. He was to be there as a support for Laura, and it was seen as a very progressive thing to do at that time. Afterwards, however, he seemed traumatised by what he had witnessed. He told Laura that he could not go through it again, and that one child would have to be enough for her.

Over the months, a darkness would descend on the home when he was there. After returning home late, he would sleep until midday. Laura began to long for the lightness that would come at around 4 p.m., when he would leave for the theatre. He was no longer kind to her, and paid no attention to Daniel, appearing to resent Laura's love for the baby. When she asked him about it, he said he wasn't good with babies, and assured her that all would be well when the child grew up a bit and started walking and talking.

She no longer had her job. Peter didn't think it was right to raise a latchkey child and had insisted early on that if they were to have a child, Laura would need to stay at home to raise him. She had agreed to this at the time, but now felt very dependent on him; she missed having her own money. He seemed to enjoy the control this gave him and would wait for Laura to ask for money for the weekly shopping. She felt degraded and useless at no longer being able to choose what shopping to get; Peter said that the products she wanted were too dear and that she could get the own-brand products from the supermarkets as they would have to tighten their belts, now that there was a baby in tow.

During those months, the hours between when Peter left for the theatre, until Daniel went to sleep, were the hours that Laura lived for. She sang to Daniel and revelled in him. She sometimes fell asleep when he did, and would wake when Peter came home at around 4 a.m.

The first time Peter hit her, she got an enormous shock. She didn't really know what to do, and she felt so alone, she finally decided that there was nothing she could do. She couldn't leave; she had no money and a small baby to think of.

Then one night, Peter came home earlier than usual, in a very unpredictable state. There was nothing strange about this, but on that night, Laura could sense that there was something different about the whole thing. She could see that he was drunk. Again, nothing unusual there, but he was edgier than usual.

Over the months, she had employed many different methods to keep out of his way and not further aggravate him when he was like this, but some nights, she knew that nothing would work. Some nights, he would just follow her, intent on causing trouble. Some nights, he would even wake her—if she was pretending to be asleep—in order to start a row. And this was one of those nights.

When he came home, she was standing in the kitchen, having just boiled the kettle, waiting for it to cool down a bit so she could make a night bottle to bring to bed with her, in case Daniel woke up. He was mostly on solid food now, but a midnight bottle sometimes got him through until 8 a.m., and that was bliss for her.

Peter walked up behind her and whispered in her ear. She could smell the alcohol on his breath, and her skin crawled.

'Hello, wifey,' he drawled. 'Are you happy to see your husband home? I've some good news for you.'

'Go away, Peter. You're drunk and I'm tired,' she said, then tried to move away from him. He grabbed her arm immediately and went to twist it behind her back, like he usually did. She ran to escape him, but he caught up with her at the sofa and began to shower her with slaps that were getting harder and harder.

Daniel began to cry loudly just as Peter was about to lay another blow on her, and he suddenly stopped. They stared at one another, wide-eyed. Laura waited for what seemed an eternity, wondering whether it would bring Peter to his senses and stop him in his tracks.

At that very moment, she decided that no matter what happened next, she had to reach out to someone for help. This could not happen again. She could not bear to raise Daniel in this environment. She had thought, up until now, that what the baby didn't know wouldn't hurt him, but now she knew that she couldn't run the gauntlet with Peter's unpredictable temper anymore.

Suddenly, he screamed in her face, "that baby; that fucking baby; all you care about," and made for the kitchen door. She shrieked "NOOOOO," and ran straight after him, down the hall and up the stairs. When she reached him near the top of the steps, she mustered all the strength she had and launched herself at him, grabbing his collar and yanking him back.

He fell backwards with her and they tumbled together down to the turn of the stairwell. Laura landed on top of Peter. She saw that he had hit his head very hard against the stair upright, and seemed dazed. He made one big movement of his head, and she pulled her own head back—in case he was going to headbutt her—but instead, he spat directly at her and suddenly closed his eyes. His head fell back.

She couldn't move for a few moments, trying to assess what to do. He was breathing heavily, and she knew he was bound to wake up and continue where he had left off. His spittle was dripping down her face, so she wiped it with her forearm and tried to move her legs from under his body. She had never once before retaliated when Peter hit her: always opting to wait for it to be over, protecting her face and head as much as she could, stiffening her body to steel her organs from damage. She had never reacted until tonight, and suddenly, she remembered why. Daniel.

She had to get him out of here. He was quiet now, so she ran up the stairs to his room; he was sitting up in his cot, open-eyed and smiling. She quickly gathered a few things she might need for him, picked him up, and hurried down the stairs. When she reached the stairwell turn, where Peter was lying, she stopped to look: to check that he wouldn't wake up and grab her feet as she passed him. Everything seemed crystal clear to her now—it was essential that she get away from him. She had to take Daniel away. The clarity was new, but she knew she had to act on it.

From a safer place, she would have time to think, time to sort out the legalities, and time to plan for her and Daniel's future. She strapped Daniel into the car and turned to go back into the kitchen to gather some food for him. She gasped when she saw that Peter was standing in the doorframe.

She didn't know where the voice came from within her, but she heard herself say, with great force, "get out of my way." Her voice was dripping with disgust and disdain, which took him by surprise.

Incredibly, he stepped aside. She hadn't been expecting him to move, but she supposed he was still dazed and was not thinking. He seemed unsteady, but he was not her priority now.

She walked past him into the house, quickly filled a small bag of provisions, picked up the car keys and walked out past him again. He had not moved. She got into the driver's seat and drove away. She had to check the rear-view mirror to make sure that Daniel was, in fact, in the car and she hadn't dreamt it all.

After a frantic drive, she ended up outside her childhood home, where her father still lived.

Her father was unhappy about her arrival late at night, especially when he saw that she had her child in tow, but he let her into the house, quickly looking up and down the dimly lit village street as he did so. He put the kettle on to make some tea. She told him that she didn't know where she was going when she left her house, but that her childhood home was the first place she thought of.

Her father said that that was all very well, but that she couldn't stay with him. The neighbours had seen her get married, he reasoned, and she had made her bed. She would have to lie in it. He didn't ask her any details about what had happened. For the moment, he said, she could say in the shops tomorrow that she was visiting with Daniel and would be going home soon. Laura agreed to these terms and sat down at the table, trembling and exhausted.

Only now could she feel the physical effects of the trauma she had just been through. Her ribs hurt, it pained her to breathe deeply, and she had a cut just below her eye, but there was no blood anywhere. Tomorrow morning, she could patch herself up and decide what she was going to do next.

After her tea, she went to bed in her childhood bedroom. Her mind was racing, thinking about the terrible possibilities that could have come to pass. What if Peter had stopped her at the door and attacked her again in the kitchen? What if he had killed her? What would have happened to Daniel?

She knew that the friends she had lost over the course of her relationship with Peter would advise her to keep going, now that she had escaped. But there was more to it than that. The stigma Daniel would have to bear, for being a child from a broken home, for a start. Her inability to provide for them both. Her legal rights to the home she'd bought: the house that they had all shared as the family home. Could she go back?

After a sleepless night with Daniel in the single bed beside her, she got up and made breakfast for her father. He was going out fishing with his friends at the fishing club and told her that he'd be out all day. He urged her to make some decisions for herself. A week was all he could respectably say she was staying for, and he didn't want the neighbours to guess that her marriage was "in trouble," as he put it. He also did not want people believing that he was unable to care for himself, or needed the help of his daughter.

She was grateful for the space that day, after her father left with his fishing tackle, but she was also fearful that Peter would show up. She walked slowly around her childhood home, picking up items and touching surfaces. Remembering. She had grown up here without her mother, Emily, who had passed away when she was two years old. Her parents had her late in life, and although her father never said it directly, she worried that he blamed her for her mother's death.

After Laura's birth, Emily had suffered complications, and was kept in hospital for six months. During that time, Laura herself was cared for by her father's mother—her grandmother. As a little girl, she was told that her mother was "never the same" after having her, and that she slowly got sicker, dying a few weeks after Laura's second birthday.

Laura had no memory of her smell, her warmth, her touch. She grew up wondering what it must be like to feel connected to a mother in the way she saw the neighbourhood children being cared for by theirs. After school, she loved to visit neighbouring houses with her school friends. Their homes were warm and busy. There was always a smell of cooking and the fires were always lit. Then time would always come to go home to the coldness of her own house and set a fire for the evening, to be ready when her father would return from work.

She and her father had always gotten along quite well. Laura instinctively knew what was expected of her, and she did it. Life was calm and uneventful growing up, but there was no sparkle. No birthday parties or cousins or friends visiting. No picnics on her front lawn with neighbours.

Years ago—ten years or more before she was born—there had been a major catastrophe in the town. The feeling within the area, even as one approached, bore the aftereffects of this trauma. It was a small town, surrounded by rich mountains and hills of forestry. A tight-knit community had sprung up around the workers within the local forestry industry. The company had built beautiful little enclaves of houses for the workers, and life was good.

Then one day, a large articulated truck carrying an overload of logs and boulders careered down the main street and plowed into the school on the corner. It had smashed through and destroyed the outer wall of a classroom and spilled its load out into the classroom and the headmaster's office, depleting the town of a huge proportion of its future generation.

A skeletal, traumatized, grieving population tried to fight back—tried to go on—but without their children, without their future, without the love that had been obliterated in one fell swoop, they became insular and bitter. Having no one to blame scarred them and gave them no focus. Everybody knew that the trucks were regularly overloaded. When everybody knew, nobody could be held responsible.

Nothing could bring back the twenty-five children, the driver, the teacher, and the headmaster who had all perished.

The children who did survive were so altered, their security and hopes so squashed, that those who were able to, left their heartbroken birthplace as soon as they could.

At the opposite end of the village from where the old school was, there was an open field leading into the woods, where a large weir was located. Laura would often walk there, alone and sometimes with school friends. She imagined that fairies and otherworldly sprites were watching her and skipping through the trees beside her, so she would regularly sit under tree canopies and share her sandwiches with these beings. She knew she couldn't really see them, but she allowed herself to think that she could, whenever she needed company.

She gave names to about five of them. She struggled now to remember what these names were, but she thought they were probably called Bluebell and Snowdrop and other such flower-inspired names. She smiled at the memory and decided that when Daniel awoke, they would take a walk down through those woods again. She made some sandwiches to bring along for herself, and boiled a potato and a carrot to mash and bring for Daniel.

She went out to the car to check that the buggy was with them. . . and was shocked, on approaching the front door, to see Peter standing there.

"I thought you'd be here," he snarled. "Where else would you go? You have nowhere else. I've come to say I'm leaving. I've been offered a part in a big production and I'm going to take it. I was going to share the good news with you last night, before you went crazy. I was going to ask you to come with me and bring the baby, and we could start afresh somewhere new. But no, you had to be your usual stuffy, stuck-up self."

He seemed very together with this narrative, and not at all agitated. Laura wondered if he was contrite, but just unable to express it anymore. Perhaps he was just as worn out by the years of fighting as she was.

She had always tried to give him the benefit of the doubt before, but something had changed within her. She heard herself saying, "I think it's best you go alone. You should leave here now and go and get yourself organized, because I don't want you to wake my father." Inwardly she panicked, wondering whether he had noticed that her father's car wasn't there, and so she must be alone, but the words had been said now. She couldn't take them back.

The words hung in the air.

"You can return home on Wednesday, as I'll be gone by then."

Into the silence they heard Daniel let out a call from inside the house, "Mama."

Laura took a sharp inhale of breath, preparing for the effect this might have on Peter. But he didn't react. He turned, put his helmet on, got on his motorcycle and left.

She stood shaking for a number of minutes—staring unblinkingly after the motorcycle—and it was only Daniel's second, then third "Mama! Mama!" that brought her back.

She couldn't even begin to think about how she felt, so she got on with her day: dressing Daniel, giving him his breakfast and packing for their walk to the woods.

The weather was warm and bright as she wheeled the baby down through the village and out into the open field. People greeted her on the street, said it was great to see her, oohed and aahed over Daniel's buggy, and went about their business.

As soon as she was back in the woods, she felt the trees circle around her, as if welcoming her back, protecting her and calling her forward with streams of light and sparkle. The ground was uneven and she couldn't operate the buggy, so she decided to carry Daniel into one of the clearings to have their lunch, sit down, play and rest.

He made the most excited noises and gurgles that she began to wonder if maybe she hadn't imagined the sprites and elementals jumping from tree to tree alongside her as a child. Maybe the eyes of a child see so much more than we adults do, she thought, with a smile.

That night at supper, she told her father she would be going home on Wednesday, and he said, "I don't need to know any of your business, Laura. You are welcome here, but you made decisions that you must stand by, for the good of your child."

"Yes," she nodded.

She spent the next few days following the same routine: walking with Daniel in the mornings, then doing some shopping for dinner. She spent the rest of the time making food for her father and cleaning every spot in the house.

She cleaned the skirting boards and the door architraves, washed the cooker and fridge, shined the silverware and crystal that had always been sitting on the sideboard, and finally, washed the net curtains—letting them steep in the bath for hours, then wringing them out until they were as good as new.

She was sad to leave on Wednesday, and had enormous trepidation about arriving at home. But, true to his word, Peter was gone. A lot of his clothes and personal effects remained, so she spent the next few days bagging them up and putting them into the attic for safekeeping, until he returned looking for them. He had definitely taken more than would fit on his bike, so she knew he must have had help and gone with someone—maybe one of the admiring ladies she'd often met when out with him before Daniel was born.

Over the next few years, Daniel was Laura's joy. When he started school and made friends, Laura was happy; sure that his life would continue to lift in happiness. She had opted to stay at home with him as he grew, and had made curtains, tablecloths, cushions and other items for people to earn a little bit of extra money.

Daniel's development and education became her absorbing focus, and she was dedicated to ensuring he had everything he needed. Motherhood was her all-consuming passion—she never considered her life as being about anything else during this time.

She grieved her marriage—what could have been, rather than what was. They could have had a wonderful life together if Peter hadn't changed so much. In arguments, he would insist it was she who had changed and she spent a long time accepting this as fact and trying to change back to how she'd been when they were first dating. However, once he started beating her, she knew this had not been true. People were supposed to change in relationships. Grow together, become more familiar and closer. Not this. It was not her behavior that had become unacceptable. It was his.

As the years passed, and Daniel began to ask questions about his father, she always replied that he was a famous actor who had been forced to go away to follow his dream, but as he approached his tenth birthday, she knew that she could not keep repeating this same old mantra. He deserved a proper conversation.

~ Right on cue, Peter got in touch to tell her he needed the proceeds of his half of the house to pursue his next venture. He was filing for separation, suing for divorce, and expected that all would be amicable between them.

Immediately, she felt an old wound open; the old panic returned, swiftly followed by outrage at his audacity—after so many years, to just waltz back in and expect half of the proceeds of the house she had bought and had been paying the mortgage on. She knew what his entitlements probably were, but she had never thought he would come looking for them so blatantly.

She recalled the moment they had first met. His eyes dancing behind the long hair that covered his forehead. She knew now that she'd always wanted to heal the broken part within him that she could see clearly: the part that needed adulation. She knew he wasn't consciously aware of this aspect within him, so she had never discussed it with him, assuming he'd take it as judgment. But she had seen a very wounded man who had never grown up. A man who was still seeking approval from others, but who was afraid of responsibility or equal relationship.

That morning, as soon as Daniel left for school, she cycled into town. She went straight to a solicitor's office that she had often looked at and thought about approaching. After reading the letter and hearing her story, the bespectacled man told her not to worry. They would write to him and take everything out of her hands.

She left Peter's letter with him. He assured her that it would be taken into account that Peter had paid nothing towards the mortgage of the house in over nine years, that they would argue on her behalf that he'd paid nothing towards the upkeep or education of his son, and that it couldn't be possible for him to march back into her life demanding half of everything she had worked for. Laura could feel her body flood with relief as she cycled back home; glad she'd acted quickly and hadn't spent weeks letting it run around in her mind.

Daniel was doing very well at school and showed great promise. She didn't have money to educate him in any world-famous university, but she knew that he was smart and organized and would make it on his own in the world. He was sociable too, had some close friends, and seemed able for the vagaries of life.

Soon enough, within a week or two, Peter showed up at the door. Laura cursed her foresight. She had known he would turn up! From the moment his letter had fallen through the letterbox onto the doormat, she had known. She had known that he was only pretending he wanted to do things the right way, but that something else was driving his actions, and he must have run out of other options.

When she opened the door, it was as if she had rehearsed what she wanted to say to him.

"Peter, you cannot just show up here, unannounced and out of the blue."

"Laura, this is my house as much as it is yours. I'd be entitled to use my key if I so chose!"

"I don't really care what you believe to be the case, but this house is where I live with my son."

"Our son," he boomed but then seemed to think better of it. She would see him compose himself and continue pleadingly, "but look, I'm not here to fight with you. I have nothing. I have nowhere to go and nothing to show for the last nine years. Things have gone a bit wrong for me. I need help, Laura, and you always know what to do. I'm here to ask, can I stay. . . just until I get back on my feet? We were always good together, and maybe we'd find a way back to the good times."

What? He was going down this road now?

"No," she heard herself say. "Good times? No, that's not what I remember. That's not what happened, Peter. You betrayed me, you treated my love with disdain, you flaunted your love affairs and other women in my face. You terrorized me. You traumatized me. You stole my freedom from me, alienated me from my friends and options, brutalized me, and then. . . then you deserted me. I didn't deserve any of that. You left me and your child without a backward glance and now you expect me to just let you in?" Emboldened, she took a step towards him. "That's not going to happen, Peter."

"You were the one who left."

"No, I fled. After one of your beatings. You left."

He shuffled from foot to foot and looked up at her through his long dark hair. His face changed from pleading to callous in an instant.

"You know you can't stop me coming back into my own house, or into our child's life. I do have rights here, you know. Legal rights. He is my son, and this house is half mine. I've left you alone for this long and never once asked for anything, because I knew you needed somewhere to raise the boy. But now I've decided that it's time for me to get to know him. To get to know who he is. All of that is my right."

"Daniel. His name is Daniel. And I can stop you."

"We'll see about that!" he shouted.

She wondered whether he would hear the lie in her voice as she continued, "I've had a long discussion with my solicitor, and he has confirmed that to me. After all this time, you'll have to try a different tack with me, Peter. I'm not the same woman you left."

She closed the door, then put her back up against it. She didn't dare breathe, and waited to hear whether he would walk away or knock again and try to push his way in. She heard the little gate swing open and bang shut, and went to the sitting room window to see him get astride his bike. As he pulled away, he looked back at the house.

Instinctively, she stepped back a foot or two, even though she knew she could not be seen through the net curtain from the outside. Still, she felt seen and vulnerable.

What was she going to do now? What would he do?

"Who was that, Mum?"

Her eyes looked up the stairs to see Daniel on the top step.

"That was your Dad, Daniel. Come down here to the kitchen and sit down. We need to have a chat about a few things."

Laura relayed it to her son as best she could: the speech she had practiced and recited a million times in her head. She told him that after his dad had gone away to become a famous actor, she felt let down. She didn't want to stop him from seeing Daniel, but understood that he was very busy, away doing his work, and she felt that she and Daniel were getting on well as the time went by.

"But now he's back? And he wants to see me? Tell me, Mum, that you said he could see me."

"It's not as simple as him coming back and taking you out for ice-cream, Daniel. Grown-ups have a habit of making things complicated, I'm afraid. I wanted to talk to you about it. You see, grown-ups have to go through another person, who can be independent and not on anyone's side, to see what's fair for everybody. . . but especially for you, Daniel. I don't want you to be hurt or let down. So, when a mum or a dad has been away for so long, this independent person helps everyone to decide what would be the best thing. For the child especially. For you."

"The best thing would be for me to see my dad, if he's back and wants to see me, isn't that right?" Daniel pleaded, his eyes wide and seeking an answer.

"Yes, my darling, if that's what you would like, I will try to arrange that. I just don't want to arrange anything without you knowing, and without you thinking about things—how your dad might need to go away again to do another film. Then we will have to think about how you manage that in your own life."

"Yes, of course," Daniel agreed in a very grown-up voice. They nodded at one another and Daniel went back to his room. Laura's eyes followed him as he left the kitchen and she brought her hands together on the table in front of her and stared at them for a very long time.

Laura was going to be forced into arranging a meeting between Peter and Daniel. The coming years were going to be very difficult for her. Her love for her son would have to see her through.

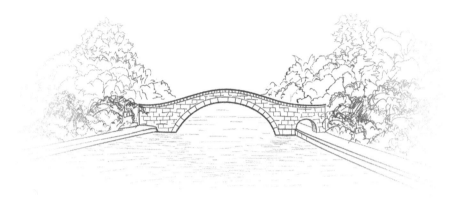

Chapter Two

Daniel was 25 years old, working in the city, when he first met Elba. He had gone to college to earn a business degree, and the company who now employed him was subsidising a nighttime Masters in Business Administration. He hoped to make it to the top of his career one day.

He was still living with Laura, but he enjoyed a great degree of freedom. They got on so well that he didn't yet have any real reason to move out.

They had moved around a lot during the previous fifteen years, all instigated by his dad having shown up when he was ten: they'd sold the house in which he'd been raised; moved to his Grandad's village; and eventually settled, six years ago, in a lovely new town about forty minutes away from the city. Laura had had no connections to the new place, and they both felt that this was an important feature, if she was to begin a new life for herself.

He had spent some very happy times in their new home, enjoying the fresh start that he and Laura had taken advantage of and brought into being. He had studied there, come of age there, and created some great memories from his early adulthood. His twenty-first birthday party was the first big event they had hosted in this home, with guests including his college friends and a few of his mother's friends from the charity shop in which she often volunteered.

The death of his grandfather had been a shocking event, and two years later, he and Laura heard that his own father Peter, too, had died. They'd been through a lot and Daniel had had to work hard to leave those memories behind him after they moved into their new home. He could see that although his mother was distressed by these events, she was now totally free, for probably the first time in her life. He was happy for her. He wanted nothing more than for her to feel completely liberated and at ease.

During this time, he found himself spending his morning commutes with an amazing old woman called Eusebia Sylvia Elba. 'But just call me Elba,' she said to him, on the morning they first met.

She, the lady on the train, seemed so wise, content, and happy. She must have been at least seventy years old, Daniel thought. Her smile seemed to hold an air of fathomless understanding, and her eyes—soft, wise, and full of humor—seemed to speak to him of faraway places: communicating a life well-lived and a heart rich with stories, experiences, and knowledge.

Daniel's commute coincided with about forty minutes of Elba's journey, wherever she was going. She always sat in the same seat, beside the window. She always waved and smiled when she saw him waiting on the platform as the train pulled in, and he always knew that the seat opposite her would be empty, as if waiting for him.

Every day, Daniel felt as though he had been centred and calmed when he got off the train. Elba was a magician.

About eighteen months into their conversations, it occurred to Daniel that somehow, he still didn't know much about her. He kept making a mental note to ask her how successful she'd been in her career, or whether she had even been allowed to have one when she was young. He had no idea how she had come to possess so much knowledge and insight. He knew only that when he spoke to her, his morning commutes went by much more quickly than they otherwise would have. During his mornings with her, he felt as though he had entered a little haven, where a woman he barely knew wove her wisdom into his mind and his heart.

He never thought too deeply about their conversations throughout his working day. There was always too much to do, too many orders to be filled, and he didn't have much time to himself. He didn't have a great deal of free time at home either, between studying, socialising, and being a son. His only chance to mull over the fascinating things Elba had said to him was during his return journeys home from work, when he found himself alone.

She was always alluding to how the impact of people's everyday choices affected the world around them. According to Elba, history was not in the past. She would always tell Daniel things like, "We are living history. The reverberations of the past are present in every moment. What we do today reverberates way off into the distant future."

Many of the things Elba said struck him as way out there, but she always spoke to them in a way that made them seem relevant and easy to accept. She was authoritative in the way she spoke—bossy, even—but her humorous smile and her warm, loving eyes made her words easy to absorb.

Daniel had often quietly pondered about philosophical and magical matters. He sometimes thought that when he was a small child, he had seen fairies and other spiritual beings, and had formed a bond with them. His mother spoke openly with him about her beliefs in another world, beyond the veil. She had told him, as an only child, to make friends with the fairies and the nature sprites who lived in the greenery.

Laura had always laughed when she said this, and he didn't think she had really meant it. But he had some distant memories of days he had spent with Laura out in nature, where he was sure he had communed on some level with beings that were just out of sight. . .

One morning, he spoke to Elba about these experiences, wondering whether she thought it possible that he had just imagined them.

"Well. . . Did you see the fairies?" Elba asked him.

"Yes."

"Then you saw them," she informed him, in a matter-of-fact tone.

"Did I, though?" he replied, with a quizzical look on his face.

"Daniel, can you see the wind?"

"No... oh! Oh, I see what you're doing there!"

They both laughed at the preposterous exchange. This was a typical example of how Elba was able to cut away excessive verbiage, theorizing, and navel-gazing. She could be blunt, but Daniel had come to appreciate her honesty. "Magic is in the everyday occurrences of life, Daniel. Make no mistake about that," she would say.

Daniel described his father to Elba as a strange man who had left him and his mother when he was very small. He had only gotten to know this man a little bit, when he was about ten years old, and didn't have a chance to spend much more time with him before he died of a drug overdose. It was such a wasted life, he said, and Elba nodded sadly.

Tomorrow, he promised himself, he would ask Elba about her life; where she was from, where she was going every day, where she had lived all her life, and how she knew so much about Atlantis, Lemuria, Ancient Egypt and all the legends—old wisdoms that had presumably been handed down to her from other times, places, and cultures.

He picked up three coffees for his colleagues—as he did every morning—and smiled, wondering what effect he would have if he arrived without them. The day was beautiful, and as he made his way into the office, he was greeted with a wonderful welcome by his colleagues. Coffee buys friends: Daniel knew this well.

He was due to find out whether or not he had been promoted today—the results of the interviews were in. Elba had told him that she felt he would get it. He felt it too. So, when his boss called him in, with a big smile on his face, he just knew that he was due to receive some good news.

The following morning, Daniel and Elba toasted his promotion with a high five.

"Well done, Daniel. I'm so pleased for you—but just remember, this is not going to be everything. It's just another event. A great event, but one of many. It's not your destination!"

"Well, Elba, today it feels like one. I've waited so long for this; it feels like a destination today!"

"That's true. It is a destination today. Enjoy your achievements. They mean so much. . . but just remember they don't define you, these labels and promotions. Remember, too, that your boss sees something in you. Always acknowledge your own worth in these things. They didn't give you the job just for your benefit, but for what they recognise you can bring to it."

Elba told him that when she was a child, she had wanted to be a dancer. She really felt free when she was dancing. She had studied ballet as a young child, and had excelled in it. Life hadn't allowed her to follow that dream, but she told him that she had taught her own children to dance, and now that she was older, she danced the steps in her heart, that her body would no longer allow her to perform.

"My memories allow me to relive everything I've ever done. What an amazing gift to have given ourselves; the ability to remember," she said looking dreamily out the window.

"Oh, I don't know about that. I've a lot of bad memories, Elba. When my father came back. . . how he let me down. . . my mum had worked so hard to keep us afloat, and yet the law entitled him to walk away with half of everything she'd worked for. My memories of that time can sometimes haunt me. Sometimes I wish we didn't have the memory faculty at all!"

"I know what you're saying, and we must never forget what we've learned through our bad times, Daniel. The bad times teach us so much. Look at what you learnt about both of your parents, about fortitude, about resilience, about never giving up. Betrayal teaches discernment, for example. We don't know it's there within us, until it's called on. We never know how brave or courageous we are, until we need it. It's the bad times that cultivate many of those strengths within us. When you're revisiting a memory, it's best to bring help," she smiled.

Daniel often privately grappled with the grief he felt for his father. The problem with death was that there was no longer any opportunity to make the relationship different. The finality and the abruptness of death stole away the possibility of ever being able to write another ending. He thought that he might have liked to have the opportunity to discuss things with his father. He would like to have met him as a man.

As he was trying to understand the meanderings of his mind during this time, Elba told him that you could access and harness great truth by watching your thoughts.

She urged him not to look at it as keeping the mind under surveillance, but to view it as being a benign supervisor in a room full of chattering children. The mind was so tricky, she said, that it was capable of turning you into your own enemy.

Elba tried to tell him that it was not his responsibility to heal his father's demons.

"But what if I could have, Elba? Helped him, I mean. Shown him a different way."

"Daniel, why would it be your job to help him or show him a different way? You were a child. His child. The responsibility was always his. In the end, as adults, we are responsible for ourselves alone. I think that's a big enough responsibility, Daniel. Please try not to take any of the blame for his decisions."

Her advice was stark, but deep down, he knew she was right.

Over that year, they often discussed the mind and its antics. Elba spoke about the dangers of spending all of our time regretting the past: wishing things had been different; wishing we had or hadn't said or done specific things, or alternatively worrying about the future: planning how we would manage worst-case scenarios; how we would afford everything; and how we'd organise all of our activities. To Daniel the future seemed daunting, even though he was excited by its call.

One morning, in the middle of one such conversation Elba said, "Daniel, let me introduce you to *The Bridge of Now*. If you master the concept of *The Bridge of Now*, you can travel to any memory safely and make the most secure plans for your future.

Now is the bridge between the past and the future, and we are always, always on it. It is always Now. And it will always be Now. Even in five years' time!" She chuckled to herself as she watched his expression change.

"The past is reachable from *The Bridge of Now*, only through memory, and the future lies before you unseen, Daniel. It is decided by you in the Now, on this bridge. It is reached by imagination. Let the imagination run free and plan a wondrous life." She sat back in her seat and continued, "Turn all of your "BUTs" into "SOs." You are always on *The Bridge of Now*, and your timeline runs through it. Life runs through us in the Now. On the bridge.

Make sure there are more SOs in this Now than BUTs."

Daniel was lost. "What do you mean, Elba? I get the Now concept. If I'm happy Now, my memories might be easier to navigate and my future might be easier to plan. . ."

She asked him to look at the sentences in which he used the word "but"—giving him an example, "I'd love to go on holidays but I can't afford to." He nodded.

Then she leaned across the train tabletop that was between them.

"Now, I'll resay that sentence, using 'so' instead of 'but'. 'I'd love to go on holidays, so. . .' She sat back quickly with an expectant look on her face.

"Do you feel that light go on, Daniel? Do you feel the universe pause to hear what your desires and instructions are?

'So' provides you with the room to come up with potential solutions. 'But' closes that door. Try not to use the word 'but', darling boy. I'd love to go on holidays, so. . . I'll take that extra overtime for the next few months. So, I'll answer that call and not burn myself out working. So, I'll book somewhere I can afford. You get it?" she asked him.

He liked that concept: *The Bridge of Now*. Turning his "BUTs" into "SOs." Creating potential.

Over the next few mornings, Elba told him a story about a distant time, when a fever had swept across a land that she had heard about when she was a child. She began her story by saying that nobody knew whether it was a future land, or a land from a time long ago, in the furthest reaches of time. Nobody knew whether it was a warning, a prophecy of things to come, or the eternal story of redemption through destruction.

It was certainly a tale of a faraway place, and it affected people who had left their imprint on all of life.

"Once upon a time, in the future or the past, this faraway place was gripped by a great outbreak of fever," she began. "During this outbreak, the people who had run society up until the onset of the disease scrambled around, trying to save what they could for themselves. While the population was busy trying to survive, the ruling classes looked for places to hide their gold," she said.

"The people in power made speeches straight to the people of the cities and towns, about how the fever was indiscriminate and they were all at risk—in fact, some of these powerful men even contracted it. Their followers were shocked and stressed that their leaders could succumb to this awful fever, just like ordinary people. Now Daniel," she whispered conspiratorially to him, "the powerful people knew that the social fabric protected them better. They had woven the fabric in that fashion, after all." She sat back in her chair.

"The public, at first, didn't realise that they didn't have the same protections as the elites. They lauded the speeches of the powerful, in a frenzy to feel safe, protected and as if they did matter after all, to the people who were in charge," Elba went on.

"But they probably did care, Elba," Daniel broke in earnestly. "The people were the workers. The voters. Surely the powerful people had to protect them too."

"Well, yes. . . you'd think so," Elba remarked. "As time passed, however, the public started to see that it was the older and the most vulnerable who suffered more severely than anyone else. The discarded, the elderly, the immigrant and travelling populations, the minorities—the ones who didn't have safety in numbers. Yes, of course, the more useful of the workforce were stronger and would be saved for the future."

"However, the nurses and doctors and other health workers perished in great numbers. Collateral damage from the front line of fighting the fever. It took the people across the cities quite a while to face this reality. Years, in fact."

"Did they rebel?" asked Daniel.

"Rebel? No. They couldn't. The fever outbreak prevented them from organising in that way. The people understood that they needed to focus very hard on what they wanted to create in the now. What did they need now? Recriminations to the ruling class always ended in civil war, and it was always ordinary people who suffered. Never the people in the high-walled buildings."

"Yes," Daniel reflected aloud. "You'd be so busy trying to survive, I suppose revolution would be the last thing on your mind."

"Many people, in their impotent solitude, found themselves living in a surreal, half-lit place. They tried to hold their patience and their faith and dreamed of easier things; remembered better, simpler times.

But as time went by and they were still out of their previous routines, they found better ways to do things, within their smaller spheres. It wasn't all bad. They communed with nature and wildlife, and had some very good insights."

"Throughout the whole time that the fever lasted, the society tried intermittently to go back to their old way of doing things. Nobody wanted this more than the elite rulers. The people tried their very hardest to return to normal, because it was the only way their society knew how to function. But during the time of the fever, so much that had been quietly discovered just didn't fit anywhere into the old way. Every time people tried to go back to it, the numbers afflicted with the fever grew, and they were chased back into their homes again."

"God, so they tried and tried but the fever kept beating them back?" Daniel asked, astonished. "Had the people decided never to let the minorities suffer again?"

"Well, that's just it, Daniel," Elba said solemnly. "What was everyone to do with the new vision that was forming? A vision where everybody was equally cared for? The vision was only in its infancy. There were well established systems in place that deliberately upheld these inequalities. A lot of powerful people had gotten rich because of inequality, and these people weren't going to let that change without a fight. They were going to do everything they could to uphold the status quo."

"The unequal nature of the society that they had lived in shamed some of the people who hadn't known, or were too busy surviving to truly see what was going on, and what they had become. But they weren't the decision makers within the systems that prevailed. They couldn't just decide that everything was going to change. It was going to take time."

Daniel nodded his head. "Yes, people automatically feel the need to get things back to the way they were after a major trauma like that. Same with the economic crashes and depressions. People always readjust quickly and get the economy back on track. . . that helps the people get back to feeling safe," he said, satisfied with his conclusion.

Elba looked up at him and raised an eyebrow. "Eh, I don't think this was just an economic blip though, Daniel. The survivors couldn't just pretend that the wisdom of the elders was lost forever, to a generation that had been in pursuit of something else. These elders had been the generation who had been born during the last big war. They'd put all of their efforts into educating their children for a time that the fever had now totally destroyed!"

Daniel looked at her, startled.

"This older generation had sat in this dismal twilight, wondering why they had been discarded. Where were their children? Their grand-children? Why were people covering their faces and staying far away from them? Where was the touch and the communion they'd come to look forward to? What had they done to deserve this? It was very fright-ening for them. The survivors, their children and grandchildren, knew this, and were upset and ashamed."

"But Elba, the old people would have known there was a fever and that their children weren't allowed in to see them," Daniel reasoned.

"Yes, some may have known, but not all. As they waited to die, the old people thought back on their own generation's time in power. They had worked hard and tried to play by the rules. They knew that there were elites—untouchables—but they didn't think they had the power to overthrow them."

"Some of them had hoped against hope that their children would. That in a huge, painful fifty-year purge, their children would tell their parents' stories: stories of civil war, abused and stolen children, illegal adoptions, mass graves, cruelty, alcoholism, murder, subjugation, control and abandonment."

"But now, instead, here they were. Alone, confused, worn out and forgotten. Their children couldn't reach them. They were the less important, spent people. Locked out. Dying. Alone. Old. Sick. Unheard. Unhelped. Forgotten. The people who had once been visited, spent time with their loved ones, received donations. Saveable. Unsaved."

Daniel cleared his throat. He thought Elba was being a bit dramatic, but he settled back in his chair to continue listening.

"As their children and grandchildren received the news that their elders had died, their only regret was not having spent more time with them. They wished they had listened to more of their stories. Absorbed more of their wisdom. 'The things I saw in the sky as a child,' one grandfather had said. He had not been asked to expand on this. However, the wisdom of what he'd seen had been handed on to his children and grandchildren nonetheless. As is the way with evolution. Everything is forever." Elba gave him a wink.

"The funerals and traditions that had been upheld for generations were no more. There was no attending to the body of the dead loved one; no putting on their favourite clothing or make-up. All of that honoring was against the government rules. Their bodies were sealed in bags and people missed out completely on coming together, telling stories, eating and drinking as a community, and honoring the passing of one amongst them."

"Everybody felt deep shame at what had become of a once rich and fertile place. What they had lost in the name of progress and convenience was clear, but what they had lost in their internal, emotional worlds was savage. This weighed heavily on the collective mind."

Suddenly, Elba abruptly ended her story. "Here's your stop, Daniel," she said, and gave him a big beaming smile. "I'll continue the tale tomorrow."

He wondered how she could be telling him such a horrible story, and yet have such light in her eyes and face. Then he remembered it was just a fable.

"See you tomorrow, Elba. Have a wonderful day," he said as he stepped down from the train and got ready to meet his workday.

The next day, as Daniel took his seat opposite his old friend, he confided that he had been thinking about the people of this fever time. "It must have been very desolate for them. Not able to go to work, their parents dying. How did the younger children and teenagers cope?"

Elba smiled at him lovingly. "Well, Daniel, the parents watched their children try to conform to the government's restrictions, and as their worlds got smaller and smaller, they retreated into their own spaces and their own inner worlds."

"The children didn't bother to speak or ask questions because it was clear to see, by just looking around them, that nobody knew what had happened, why, or what could be done about it. They couldn't go to school or college. They couldn't meet friends or socialise. They missed out on all of their big milestones and were silently growing more and more angry."

"They needed someone to blame. Their hatreds for 'others' like foreigners and strangers were exacerbated and born of fear; they knew this. Although it was an irrational fear, it had enormous consequences, drawing people back into their own communities with a sense of contraction that was deeply unhealthy for young people. They fought amongst themselves, formed gangs and groups. They broke the restriction guidelines and had no respect for the authorities or the generation that had done this to them. It was difficult for them."

"But it wasn't all bad. . . After a few years, people noticed they had stopped trusting governments and had started taking the advice of their inner selves, calling upon their soul's knowledge. They would wait for an idea to take hold; then followed the call of their souls. They drew on their humanity and their subconscious—the inner coding that made them, as an evolving species, more aware. They came into a deeper understanding in their inner silence than all of the press conferences in the world could instill."

"Slowly, they turned away from the snake oil and into the heart.

The rulers began to notice that the numbers tuning in to get their updates and new rules and guidelines were falling, so they upped the ante; they introduced tougher measures of control, travel bans, restricting people to their homes... but over time, the people learned what they needed."

Elba looked out the window, with a faraway look in her eyes, as she continued. "The structure of the day, as provided by nature, and the peace of the night, as provided by nature. The light of the moon after the streetlights had stopped working. They yearned for the world to feel peace. They thought about those in trouble, those in war and desperation, and those who didn't have as much as they had.

They wondered why the world was so unequally divided. They felt that maybe something could be done about that."

"Slowly, they began to feel their inner compasses shift and land at a place within themselves, where it felt only right that everyone should have what they need. A place where they felt that no one was greater than another. They thought about things they never thought about before."

"They wondered where their prejudices had started, and how they had fed them over the years. Who had been silently feeding them? What beliefs had been formed within them? Were they the truth?"

Elba watched Daniel for a moment, as he reflected on her words. Daniel didn't want to say this to her, but he thought that this story was very unlikely to ever have happened. He wondered though, what message Elba was trying to convey to him.

At last, he spoke. "Elba, people don't just change because there's a fever. They don't just offer everything they've gathered to other people for no reason."

"Agreed," Elba said with a nod. "Some struggled, at all costs, to get back to the life they had enjoyed before. They had had good jobs, they were on the way up, they had accumulated wealth and possessions. They found it impossible to trust that others wouldn't steal all of that away and take it for themselves. They knew this, for they were experienced humans and had seen how people fought for what they could accumulate."

"However, every time the people tried to put the previous show back on the road, the pieces wouldn't fit. . . even after years had gone by. The brilliant money-making jobs they'd once had were no longer needed. The big office blocks stood empty. Like a tree reaching up to the sky, things had broken through to an entirely new level. The majority were breathing in a new air and responding to a different sound within themselves."

"Life doesn't believe in punishment, Daniel—only lessons. The people who understood what was happening felt better in this new air. They breathed better and realised that what they were missing, they were happy to relinquish. They were content to let go of their old ways, in the hopes of a better tomorrow."

"Wait. There were office blocks in this place?" he asked.

"Oh, yes. There were massive glass cities where millions of people worked together. It had been a status symbol for each country to have these large architectural glass structures for their workers. It was a sign of success!"

"But they were all empty during the fever? Where had the people gone?" asked Daniel.

"They had mostly gone back to the towns where they were born. It was a time for hiding, trying not to catch the fever. A lot of people found that they liked the slower pace of life in the towns where they had grown up—and had strived to escape as youngsters. But now? Well, now these small towns represented safety."

"Okay, I get that. So, did they find a new way? After all the old people had died?" Daniel was only humouring Elba now.

"Curiosity drew them on to think of new ways. All that was possible whispered encouragingly to a people in mourning, and they were inspired! A redistribution of power? An examination of what truly mattered? The new comes through the passage of the old, just like always, Daniel."

"And by now, the people had already decided what was truly important to them. Clean clothes, running water, food, and companionship. Basic, I know. But vital. Nourishment for the soul came via stories of new ideas, of communities coming together to help one another."

"It sounds like a utopia, Elba. But it's not practical," Daniel remarked.

"I'm just telling you what happened, Daniel. I'm not really asking for commentary," she joked, and urged him to just listen to her.

He settled back and thought to himself that he shouldn't be so rude, and should just listen to the old lady's story.

"After more years," Elba continued, "these things seemed even more important, especially when the governments said it was becoming too expensive to keep remote homes supplied with electricity and drinking water. But workers wouldn't shut down the supply. They simply refused, and they were sacked for their trouble."

"The interesting thing was, however, those in power didn't know how to actually do anything. They had only been good at issuing decrees. They were soon mortified by their own ineptitude, and had to reinstate everybody who had been fired. That was funny! There were little wins like that..."

"The people then began to truly feel their power. They finally understood that their ruling class knew only how to rule. So, the lights stayed on. Emboldened by this, the people moved to a higher vision again. There was violence and overthrow at this stage. The void was gaping and daring a new way to begin."

"People inherently knew that when they broke a fingernail, the torn nail immediately begins to heal and even out the jagged edges. The old nail cannot be glued back on. The damage has already begun to heal, through the innate power of regeneration that still resides in the living part of the nail. Nobody has to tell the nail what to do. The nail just knows."

"Okay. . . and what happened to the people who got sick?" Daniel asked.

"Many of the people who were afflicted by the fever found that the changes it wrought within them were extraordinary. You see, they spent nights alone in their own personal hells, cut off from everything. The fever was so contagious, they had to rely on themselves alone. They had to ask all those they loved to stay away from them."

"In their fevered dreams, they saw demons and walked down long hallways filled with filth and grime. The walls oozed septic liquid and deafening noise. They saw faces of people they recognized, but did not know, hurtling towards them in the darkness. They scaled the slippery outer walls of old castles, trying to access the castle's inner warmth. They were chased by unseen enemies through the thorny forests and woods of their minds. They were shot in open plains by snipers just outside of their view. They ran from burning houses naked, and having lost everything, reached out for rocks on stormy seas. They scrambled for safe ports in raging oceans. They killed and were killed. They ran the gauntlet and didn't know one reality from another."

"When the affected people were awake, they instinctively reached out for comfort and company, but no one was there. They could hear only the distant sounds of happiness in other rooms of their houses or in other homes on their streets."

"This seemed to last an eternity. When the fever was finally finished with them, and had wrung out every last memory they had, it left them hollowed out like a shell. They were vomiting, cold, lost in their reality, and unsure on their feet. They hobbled around and walked in circles through the rooms in which they were confined. They had no ability or power, and wondered whether this was the 'dark night of the soul' they had once heard about."

"During the time they had the fever, they didn't feel any emotion, or any sensation, other than feeling like a rag doll. They didn't seem to be in control of their bodies. They felt betrayed by life itself: as if they had been possessed by something so horrific, they'd never even conceived of its existence. Some wished they would just die and the horror would stop.

It left them shell shocked: emotional husks. They dared not hope that it had passed. They didn't believe it could ever come to an end, or that anything could ever be the same again. They were changed forever. Nothing they had seen could be unseen, and nothing they had experienced—with no one there to help them—would be forgotten."

"Silent and alone, they had been reborn."

"When they started to feel better, they wondered why—with so many people dying—they had been spared and given another chance at this life."

Daniel leaned across the table to Elba and gently said, "Elba, I'm watching you telling this story, and I can see in your eyes that you believe it's real. I'm sorry that I was so dismissive earlier."

"Thank you, Daniel. I'm not finished, you know." She laughed ruefully and commented, "Wait until you hear the rest of it! One man dreamt about being the last man left on earth. Can you imagine his horror? Can you imagine being the only one who was witness to the aftermath of whatever this cataclysmic event was? He dreamt that he had gone everywhere in the world during that night; it was as if time was frozen. He saw people and animals frozen in time. He felt utter desolation and loneliness, like an unknowing child that had been abandoned in a huge, vast wilderness.

Nothing responded to him—no person or animal. He felt no warmth or life coming from anything. Utterly helpless and bereft, alone and unsupported, he had never known a feeling like it before. He didn't know at the time that it was a dream. He thought he actually was the last man left alive. He never fully recovered from the reality of his dream. His townspeople did their best to bring him back to their reality, but he was lost forever to them."

"This is a terrible, terrible story," Daniel whispered, "but I can't wait to hear the ending. . . what happened then?"

"The fever lasted about ten years in the final analysis," Elba told him sombrely. "Everybody was utterly changed. Everything was over! At the beginning of this time—as the rich got richer and consolidated all they'd earned in the old world—the people felt powerless. They thought, this is just another power grab by the elite. Nothing new here in this for the workers or the poor."

"But by the time the decade was done, everything had changed. The past had been purged by the souls who had been willing to speak of their truths, give their testimonies, demand accountability where it was possible. The people instinctively knew that the only way they could heal from the trauma of their experiences was to share them, talk about them, acknowledge them, voice them. They needed to hear themselves speak. As they came back to the community, they reached out to one another easily. Their memories of being social creatures and needing one another were so deeply ingrained in their nature."

They listened to one another with empathy and compassion, allowing everyone who spoke as much time as they needed to process their feelings. As they listened to their neighbours, their own inner distress eased. They heard their own voice echoed back to them in the experiences and testimonies of others."

"The time given to each person who wanted to speak was crucial. Every story was valid, and everyone was truly recognized by the attention and respect they showed to one another. The pain and confusion they had suffered was etched on their faces, and on the collective generational groups."

"The elders who had survived knew that the anger of the youth needed to be released and expressed in a safe way: a way that wouldn't cause that generation of future leaders to be destructive and punitive during their years in power."

"The value of the crisis was that it allowed a rebirth. All birth is traumatic and painful, but there can be novelty, a feeling of expansion, going beyond what the realms of what possibility had been previously. It made sense that the young people had felt robbed of so much: the milestones, the acknowledged rites of passage that had been obliterated in the panic of the fever. They felt ignored. The elders knew that even in the worst place ever, when all appears lost, even then there's hope."

"Especially when you consider that our consciousness is eternal and that we are eternal beings, with the timeline flowing over our Bridges of

Now. Life experience shows us how quickly reality changes and shifts—back to your original question, how could they help the youth to find the safe place within that concept?"

"The teenage years had always been about looking outward, seeking a way to make an impact. The group who had come into those years during the fever time came to learn—too soon, perhaps—that nothing exists outside of the self. What, even, is real? They often thought, as children, 'what if I'm the only one who is real?' Life was now teaching them that their imaginings weren't too far from the truth: not in a sociopathic, nobody-exists-but-me way, but in the final realisation that I came in alone, I'll go out alone, and during all of the life in between I can only exist within myself. That starkly puts into focus where my power is."

"That's a bit heavy for kids, but I know what you mean. So, what happened?" asked Daniel.

"What happened?"

"The place you're telling me about."

"Oh," said Elba. "Nobody knows if it was myth and legend or factual history. But a wind of change had come and people listened to the messages on that wind."

"They are said to have made choices that gave birth to a civilisation that was to last for an indefinable length of time into the future. They created something different. They didn't waste time on recriminations and judgment. People knew what one another was thinking, and with this telepathy, they understood the core desires that people had."

"Pretence and ego fell away. The dysfunctional aspects of mind disintegrated, and the lands prospered once again. People learned from what they had lost, and vowed never again to lose sight of the shortness of their time lived on Earth. They saw eternity and the assistance that was available to them from all of creation. They spoke of legions of angels and warriors of Light. The people danced and celebrated and a Golden Age was born."

"Oh Lord! Was this a new Atlantis? A new Utopia?"

"I'll tell you the rest of what I remember tomorrow, darling boy. This is your stop."

Daniel disembarked, got the coffees and went to work, shaking his head at the tall tale Elba had related to him. She was usually much more practical and helpful.

He stood at the door of his office building and looked up at all of the floors above. This glass building housed the potential for his future.

"All of that mad stuff could never happen here," he confirmed to himself, and walked inside.

Chapter Three

Weeks passed without Daniel seeing Elba again. He had noticed, the last time they met, that she appeared tired. Her crazy fever story had probably indicated to him that she wasn't at her best. He hoped she was okay, and cursed the fact that he had never gotten her number or address. He wished he knew what had happened to the people with the fever. Had they created a new Atlantis? Even though he knew it was just one of Elba's far-fetched tales, he still wanted to hear the ending.

He looked for Elba every day on the train, and really missed the company of this lovely old lady. Every day as the train drew into his station, he closed his eyes and sent a silent prayer that when he opened them, he would see her smiling and waving at him from the train. He would get aboard, nonetheless. He walked up and down the carriages day after day, and felt an emptiness within him when he couldn't find her.

However, time soon began to fly past, and Daniel became very busy with work. He didn't have much time to think of Elba during his hectic days of gathering data and attending Monday morning sales target meetings. He was promoted again and began overseeing his entire section.

The weeks turned into months.

Then he met a beautiful woman called Anna, through a college friend whom he had gone to visit in a city about 100 miles away from home. They soon fell head over heels for one another, and began to meet every weekend. Daniel bought his first car for his frequent journeys down to Anna, and Anna came up to stay with him at least once a month. Anna worked in a large hotel, where she and Daniel would spend weekends together getting to know one another.

He loved her dearly: he felt that they were soulmates, and had known one another always.

Laura and Anna got along well. When Daniel told his mother that he wanted to go and live with Anna, Laura couldn't pack his bags quickly enough.

He started applying for jobs in the city closest to Anna, and found that he had his pick of employment offers. He attended the interviews alone, and one weekend, he and Anna walked around the business district of the city to get a feel for where he would most like to work.

When his company got wind that he was looking to move, they offered him a position in their branch in that city, along with relocation expenses and a package to match what he had been offered by the other companies. He felt obligated to them for having funded his further education, and happily took up the new position.

This offer enabled him and Anna to buy their first home together.

Their new home—a large, detached house—stood about half an hour away from the city. It had a large wrap-around garden that boasted a beautiful old water pump in the corner. The estate agent explained to them that this pump had once served the surrounding area, when the house had been surrounded by nothing but countryside. Nowadays, the local area was a thriving suburb, full of young families starting out on their life adventures together.

Anna drew out the softer elements of Daniel. She didn't laugh at him when he cried at their wedding—in fact, she cried too. Their wedding was small: they held the party in an old castle hotel, with about thirty guests in attendance. Laura beamed with pride that day, as did Anna's parents, Grace and Jim. Anna's sister June was her bridesmaid.

During the first year of their marriage, sadly Anna miscarried two babies, but she was so focused on becoming pregnant, she put her feelings to one side and kept going. Her doctor confidently announced, "Anna, you're ovulating, fertilizing, implanting. . . it's just a matter of time before you have a successful pregnancy." She wrung her hands together and focused on that.

Their first son, Cal, was born two years after they married.

After she gave birth to him, Anna found herself floored by unexpected grief for the babies she had previously lost. She was swamped by a deluge of emotions she had been holding back for the previous two years. . . but she kept them quiet, believing that nobody would understand how she felt.

She listened to what people around her were saying. Yes, she had a new baby, and she was delighted—but what about the babies she'd lost? Well-meaning visitors and friends told her that if she'd had the other babies, she wouldn't have given birth to this beautiful child. She suppressed all of the anger she felt when people said things like this, because she could see where everyone was coming from.

Friends spoke words of comfort to her, and she was grateful, but she still felt empty.

It had all happened so quickly, she thought, trying to reason with herself that what she was feeling was natural: meeting Daniel, falling in love, buying their house, getting married. Every moment of that had been wonderful, and she wouldn't have wanted to change a single thing. But the miscarriages had been painful and difficult to accept in the fairytale few years she'd experienced.

On the day she and Cal were discharged from the hospital, there was great excitement. Daniel brought the car up close to the entrance and two of her favourite nurses, two who had been especially kind to her, walked her to the door. She asked Daniel to take a photograph of her with them. They then helped her to put Cal's new car seat into the back of the car, and she got into the front. Daniel clucked around her—even putting on her seat belt for her—but as they drove home, she felt bereft, lonely, scared and on the verge of tears.

The truth was that Anna was sure that she would not be able to look after this baby. She was shocked that she was allowed to keep him—this beautiful child—and just walk out the hospital door with him, no questions asked. She could not believe it. She just wanted to cry.

At home, everything Cal would need was set up and ready. Anna's parents and sister were there, bearing streamers and champagne. A Moses basket had been placed beside the bed, and Daniel had set up a bed in the spare room, to allow him to sleep before going out to work. Anna herself was thoroughly exhausted, and would have loved nothing more than to sleep.

The days after their return from the hospital passed by in a haze. Anna lazed around with the baby, feeding him and watching him sleep. She changed him and bathed him and sat by his side all day and all night. She couldn't believe nobody had called in to pick him up: to take him away from her.

Daniel did the washing up when he came home from work. He made her tea and toast and spoke kindly to her, but Anna could sense that they weren't communicating properly. She felt like she was slipping away into another place within her mind—a place no one understood, not even her—and she would never have the words to describe it to anybody.

She avoided Daniel's eyes; in case he could see how hollow she felt. She had nobody to talk to, because she was sure that if she told the visiting district nurse how she felt, they would definitely take the baby away, to live with somebody who knew what they were doing. She didn't want to tell her friends, as she feared they might judge her. Many had had children with no issues, and they would think her weak.

She phoned her mother on a number of occasions, asking her not to drop in and telling her that she was very tired, but that she would be up and about soon. She never expressed the blackness of the hole into which she had slipped.

Yet Grace, her mother, could sense it. She asked Anna's sister June, who lived nearer, to call in, check up on her, and find ways of sussing out how she was doing. June reported nothing strange: just a tired new mother who was a bit overwhelmed, but would ultimately be okay.

One night, Daniel woke up to hear Cal crying. As he stood by the bedroom door, he saw that while the baby was crying, Anna was sitting upright in the bed, staring into space. He tucked her into bed and gently took care of Cal.

The next morning, he sat down on the bed next to Anna and peered at her with some concern.

"Are you okay?"

"Me? Yes... why?"

"I came in last night. Cal seemed as though he had been crying for ages, so I thought you must be asleep. He woke me up. When I came into the bedroom, you were just staring into space. Are you sure you're okay?"

Anna searched her mind, and had no memory of any of what Daniel was describing. "Oh, I don't know. Maybe I was just tired. I don't remember that..."

"Do you want to see if we can get some help for you, with the baby? It's very stressful."

"No. I don't need any help. I am more than capable of minding my own baby, don't you think?"

"Yes, I do... but I also know that sometimes it can be tough on new mothers, trying to get everything right. If you need any help, please tell me."

Anna felt found out. She vowed to herself never to let him find her like that again, feeling that she would now have to prove herself a capable mother, to Daniel and to everyone else. After that incident, she became hyper vigilant and jealously protective of Cal. She wanted to prove that she was coping.

She couldn't allow herself to think back to the delivery of her beautiful baby: this child she had longed for. She couldn't bear to remember it. When she had heard the nurses say that his head was stuck in her pelvis, and he was going to come early—prematurely—she had assumed that he would be damaged.

After the delivery, they had briefly taken the baby away to check that he was maintaining his temperature. They had assured her that he was fine, but she couldn't allow herself to believe that. Surely, they would come back and tell her that there'd been a mistake. They would tell her that her child had not survived.

Daniel accompanied the nurses, to be with his son, and when he returned to her bedside, she searched his wan face for her fears. He gently told her that their baby was safe, alive, breathing unhindered, and that all would be well.

The relief that flooded her body hadn't gone all the way to her beliefs, though. Sitting here now, in the darkness, she thought that she might still be expecting him to die. Did she really deserve a baby? A healthy baby?

Who would understand any of this? They'd think she was out of her mind. A counsellor she'd attended many years ago had given her some tips on how to manage her thoughts but right now, she simply could not access the information or the memory of what she'd been told. She couldn't find the beginning of the thread she needed to follow to unravel the jumbled thoughts within her.

Cal had different ideas to his mother. Maybe different beliefs had been embedded in him. He was not hindered by any of his mother's worries: he was thriving. After he began to demonstrate that he was his own little person, Anna began to trust a little bit more. She'd waited so long for "her baby", she had almost forgotten that he would grow to be a fully functioning human being in his own right. She was growing to trust him, but she still did not trust herself.

You see, Anna had been raised in a paradigm in which you would be fine "when"... when your exams were finished, when you got a good job, when you got your car, when you got a house, when you got your new cushions, when you got married, when you had a child...

She had been longing for so long now to feel fine, good, complete, that she was giving up hope, and believed that life was just an endurance test. She had achieved so many "when" milestones, without feeling an iota of accomplishment. She now decided that the whole thing must be a conspiracy. Everybody was just pretending. Other times, she felt as though she had been left out of some big secret that the rest of humanity seemed to understand.

The following year, Anna and Daniel had another son called Blu. Anna appeared to cope much better this time, from what Daniel could see. She was back at work; Grace had been minding Cal. The birth was easy, and Cal seemed thrilled to have a brother. Blu was like a replica of Daniel as a little boy.

After the second labour, Anna felt a little better: a little less like a failure. She'd managed to go full term with Blu, which meant that he was immediately stronger than Cal had been after his birth. Anna felt the happy hormones of her second pregnancy helping her to recover from the dark period she had endured after Cal was born.

But she knew that she had unfinished business with what had happened during that time. The memory of it was like an enormous, scary recess within her mind. She felt that if she could get herself right first, then she would safely be able to travel back and release the fears and stresses of the miscarriages and Cal's birth, but not yet.

Her mother came over a few days a week, after Daniel had gone back to work. They would spend a few hours chatting, Anna might have a nap, her mother would put on a wash or two for her and she would just keep an eye on Anna.

This time, her mother Grace and sister June had devised a plan to ensure that Anna was not left to drift into a depression. They knew they wouldn't be able to stop it from happening, but this time, they were going to be around more often, to see whether it made a difference. They developed a habit of visiting Anna at least once a week, to sit and eat a lunch that Grace would lovingly prepare beforehand.

Anna knew why June and Grace had taken to calling around so often, but she appreciated the company so much that she was not going to look a gift horse in the mouth. She was greatly touched by the care that her mother and sister were showing towards her.

Daniel got another promotion, with a healthy pay rise. He and Anna then decided that Anna would not go back to work at the hotel, after her maternity leave. This relieved Anna of the stress of thinking about who would mind her babies and she was not inclined to return to the city anyway.

When Blu was one month old, Anna asked Daniel whether his own mother would like to come and stay for a few nights. Laura lived over an hour away by car, and Anna knew that she must want to see more of the boys. Daniel was very touched, and called his mother immediately.

Laura was initially hesitant. "I don't want to be in the way, Daniel. If Anna needs time..."

"It was her idea, Mum. She would like you to come. If I feel she's getting stressed, or if you feel she's getting stressed, we will act accordingly. I don't think she would have suggested a visit if she didn't want you here."

Laura happily accepted the invitation, and arrived at their home the following week.

Anna was deeply moved by the mountain of presents Laura brought with her: little teddies, cosy blankets, building bricks, toys and clothes. It was obvious to Anna that every time Laura had left her house in the last month, she must have picked up a gift for her two grandsons.

"You're so kind, Laura. This is all too much."

"Nonsense," Laura exclaimed. "What's a grandmother for, if not to spoil her grandchildren?"

Anna went to bed early that night, once she knew that Cal was settled. She took Blu to her bed, so that he could rest in the Moses basket beside her. She hoped to get a few hours' sleep before the next feed.

While Anna and the children slept, Daniel and Laura got to sit down for dinner and a good catch up.

"How's work, Daniel?" Laura asked, as they sat back after their meal.

"Delighted with the promotion… but… it's work, Mum. It's a means to an end at the moment. I don't find it particularly inspiring, but I'm not looking for anything else right now. They're looking to expand and franchise in some new areas. I'm thinking about how I could position myself to be involved in that. I'd like to get my teeth into something new, but for now I'm happy to manage my team and make sure everything here settles down.

It's hard for women, it seems. Really takes its toll on you. This "having babies" lark isn't as easy as us men make it look," he joked, smiling at her warmly. "It must have been very difficult for you—what with my dad, and you being on your own."

"Times were different then, Daniel. Men were just starting to come into delivery rooms… and I'm afraid Peter wasn't cut out for that," she remarked, smiling broadly. "Thankfully, I never had a moment of baby blues. All women are different. I was just lucky I guess."

"You didn't have time for postnatal blues, I suppose, Mum."

Laura looked at him, shocked. "I don't think it's about having or not having time for… I don't think post-natal depression is a self-indulgent thing or a thing you can decide to have or not have…"

"Oh no. Oh my God, I didn't mean it that way! Of course, I know it isn't. I witnessed how it just crept up on Anna. Trying to cope with too much. That's what I really meant. If Anna heard me say that, she'd be perfectly within her rights to have me tarred and feathered!"

"Yes, she would!" Laura laughed. "And I'd bring the feathers! All women are different Daniel; all pregnancies are different and all deliveries are different. All circumstances are different too.

By the time I had you, I already knew deep in my bones that the dreams I had for my marriage were built on sand. Your presence in my life reminded me I had so much else to live for. I knew I was responsible for protecting you. Look at Cal and Blu and you'll get a sense of what I mean."

"I know what you mean. I just can't imagine how you had the courage to face all that alone."

"I wasn't alone. I had you. You were my guiding star." Laura's eyes looked upwards, as she remembered back to how Daniel had given her the strength to carry on during the hard times. How he'd eventually been the catalyst to her finding her freedom and independence.

"Well, I wasn't very good at putting the bins out or mowing the lawn for you," he chuckled.

"No. You were useless at that."

They both laughed and began to clear away their dinner plates. Daniel put the baby bottles in the sterilizer and they went to sit down and have one last cup of tea.

"I'm so glad you're here," he confided in his mother. "I have a very long day tomorrow and I probably won't be home until after 9 p.m., so I'm very glad you'll be here. I'm sure Grace and June will be popping their heads in throughout the day as well, so there'll be plenty to keep you occupied. You won't be waiting for my heroic return from work."

His mother giggled and Daniel gave her a wry look.

The next morning, Laura woke at around 9 a.m. She heard Cal babbling to himself downstairs, followed by Anna answering him as if they were having a full-blown conversation.

She was smiling as she got dressed, listening to their little chat; Anna was ascribing full sentences to Cal and answering him accordingly. She supposed every mother did it.

She went down to the kitchen and greeted Cal with a big "hooray!" He was sitting in his highchair, and appeared very excited to see her. She strode right over to him and planted an enormous kiss on his forehead, then looked over at Anna with a wink.

"I couldn't help but hear the very intellectual conversation you were having with your son. Between you both, you'll sort out the crisis in the economy and have a cogent plan for world peace in no time."

"That's the idea! Did you sleep okay, Laura?"

"Really well. Like the proverbial baby, Anna. I'm so glad to be here. I want to be of help to you if I can, but also, I can stay out of the way too. I've brought books and I can just sit and read them, if you'd prefer."

"Laura, you're really welcome here. I wouldn't have invited you if I'd just wanted you to stay out of the way," Anna said. "You did such a good job raising Dan, I'd really like your skills to rub off on me!"

She gave a big smile to her mother-in-law and scrunched her nose.

"I feel so much better this time, though—maybe because Blu is much more able to hold his own than Cal was. I'm not sure why, but I'll take it!"

"'Hear, hear, sister," Laura replied heartily, as she crossed the kitchen to switch on the kettle and put some bread in the toaster. "So, tell me the ground rules. Any rooms I'm not allowed into?"

"Ha! No. The rules are that you're allowed to go anywhere you like and do anything you like. If you want to do anything, do it; eat anything, eat it; say anything, say it."

"Ah! Carte Blanche. Just the way I like it." Laura wiggled her eyebrows.

"Sit up at the island beside Cal and I'll make the tea and get your toast."

The two women talked for an hour or so, with Laura tending to Cal as Anna made a new batch of bottles. Eventually, Laura asked whether she could take Cal outside for a walk. She hauled him out of his chair, changed his nappy, dressed him and wrapped him up well for a walk down to the local shops.

She wanted to get milk and bread for the house. Anna had told her that Grace was bringing dinner later, so she just picked up some chicken and salad for their lunch.

She knew Anna had everything she needed for the babies, so she took her time walking back, venturing down a different route through the neighbourhood. The atmosphere of the place was that of a very self-contained suburbia, from which people commuted to the city and families began their lives together.

There were creches for children, a vet and dog groomers, hairdressers, grocery shops and chemists. Everything that was needed was within reach.

When she got back, Anna and Blu were snoozing on the big nursing chair, so Laura went to change Cal and put him down for his nap. She wandered into the kitchen and put together a light lunch for Anna and herself, then sat down with a book, waiting for whatever would happen next.

Anna was so grateful to have Laura in the house. She never felt as though she had to put on a performance for her mother-in-law. She knew that Laura had been through so much herself—as a woman and as a mother—and she never felt judged by her.

She wolfed down the chicken salad and artisanal bread that Laura had brought back, then looked at Laura—startled by her own speed—after she had completely cleared her plate. "Oh my God, I had no idea I was so ravenous," she laughed.

"That's why it's important to have the option. And it was delicious," said Laura. "Yum."

Anna brought out some clothes that had been drying, and they started to fold little vests and baby clothes, chatting easily and making little piles of each boys' clothes.

"I'd forgotten how many little things babies have, how washing for them is like washing for a football team! And before you ask, yes, we did have washing machines when I had Daniel. I did not have to go down to the river and smack the dirty clothes off stones," laughed Laura.

Anna smiled. "That's not the way my mother tells it, Laura!"

Afterwards, Laura went up to her room to give Anna a bit of space. She sat for an hour or two reading her book, before hearing Grace arrive. The first indication of Grace's arrival came in the form of boisterous squeals from Cal, who was overjoyed to see his other grandmother. Laura felt a slight twinge of loneliness then, knowing that she lived further away than Grace did. It was inevitable that Grace would know the boys better that she would over the coming years.

She shook her head, brushing the thought aside. This was her mind again: always catastrophising and imagining things that were not important.

After a moment or two, she heard Grace call up the stairs. "Laura, I'm here. The boys are both up. Come down. Let's see you."

Laura and Grace had not seen one another for over a year, so Laura smiled and skipped down the stairs, giving Grace a warm hug and remarking that it was lovely to see her again. "Aren't we the luckiest women to have two such beautiful, healthy grandchildren?"

"Oh, we certainly are, Laura. You're looking fabulous as always: ultra-chic. You'd win the Glamorous Granny competitions hands down over me. Easier seeing the ten years I have on you every time we meet!"

"Ah now Grace, you're no shirker in the glamour department yourself. We are neither of us spring chickens, but we both have plenty of life in us yet."

Anna listened to this exchange with a smile on her lips, throwing her eyes up to heaven at Cal. Cal was very excited to have so many people in the house. They all spent the afternoon chatting and showing him how to play with the gifts that Laura had brought. They sat on the floor, making car noises and building towers with blocks, only to knock them down and build them all over again. Cal couldn't get enough of it. When they knocked the blocks down, his laughter rang through the house. All was right with the world.

In the early evening, Grace set about heating the dinner she had brought for the women, and Laura and Anna bathed the baby in a little plastic bathtub. The smell of lavender made them all dreamy. While Anna took Blu to his nursing chair, Laura bathed Cal, got him into his bedclothes, and gently laid him down in his cot. Anna came to the door and put on the music that he liked, then smiled at Laura, indicating with her head that they were off duty and dinner was ready.

Grace had set the table. She and Laura sat opposite one another while Anna sat at the top of the table, in between them. They talked about different things throughout dinner as the music from Cal's room floated in their direction from the baby monitor. Blu was in his Moses basket on a sofa across the kitchen. Both boys were sound asleep.

"I'm so blessed," Anna exclaimed suddenly.

The three women smiled. "We are all blessed!" agreed Grace.

"I never thought, after my miscarriages, that I could be sitting here with two sons and their two grandmothers. Isn't it wonderful for us to have this time?"

Anna was feeling strong and supported in this loving female space. She was ready to address how she'd been feeling after her miscarriages.

Laura nodded agreement and looked over to Grace, who had put her face down to look at her hands. The other two women realized that she was sniffling. Anna reached out her hand, covered her mother's hand and asked, "Mum? Mum? Are you okay?"

It took Grace a moment to speak. "Yes darling. I'm just emotional, I suppose. It is indeed a blessing that we are all here. I know how you fought to have your boys, and how brave you were to keep going after the miscarriages... It just suddenly brought back memories of the baby I lost before you were born, and I just got caught in the emotion of it all."

Anna had always known that there had been another pregnancy between June—who was seven years older than her—and herself. Growing up, they had often lit a candle for their "sister who didn't stay", but nobody in the wider family had ever discussed it. Certainly, Grace herself had never brought it up so directly before.

Laura stayed glued to her seat, wondering whether or not it was appropriate for her to be here for this special moment between mother and daughter. Anna, as if sensing her hesitancy, looked at her, nodded to her and patted her hand, indicating that she should stay put.

Grace went on. "Laura will have some memory of what it was like at the time. I was just the age you are now, Anna, when I got pregnant. She was our second child. She was to complete our family... Oh, I'm not saying we wouldn't have had you, darling... or anything like that. Please, I don't want you to think..."

"I never thought that for a moment, Mum," Anna said gently. "And anyway, this isn't my story. It's not about me. This is your story. About what happened to you and what that painful experience was."

"It was a horrible time for women. Oh God, you have no idea how horrible. I mean, I know it's far from perfect now, but back then, it was the Stone Age. There was no light at all."

Grace broke down in tears, while Laura went to the kitchen counter to get some tissues. Anna stood up and leant over her, wrapping her arms around her mother. Her mother sobbed and sobbed, letting out a cry that seemed to come from the very depths of her soul.

Anna had never seen her mother like this before; the practical, loving, devil-may-care woman was shifting something massive within her. Anna wasn't frightened by this. She was just taken unawares that this storm had been brewing within this lovely woman, who had raised her and cared for her, given her everything in her heart.

Grace began to regain her composure, and soon signaled to Laura to sit down. "Sit, Anna. Sit, Laura. I'm sorry. I was just overcome." She looked directly across at Laura and shook her head. "Do you remember how difficult it was? How austere and cold, how shamed we were as women, how. . . how awful."

Laura silently nodded her agreement.

"I went into the hospital to have my baby, just like when I'd had my first baby, June. I was expecting a lot of pain, a lot of blood, a lot of discomfort, and a lot of days sitting on a swimming ring.' She looked up knowingly at her two companions, and they all let out a low laugh of understanding.

"I was not expecting what happened," Grace went on. "All of a sudden, my plans were shredded before my eyes. A doctor told me straight to my face that my baby was dead, and that I'd have to work extra hard to get it out of me, as it wouldn't be able to help me." She gave a little whimper and bit her bottom lip until it appeared white. Neither of the other women spoke. They just held space for her to go on, if she were able. Eventually Grace looked up at her companions and back down at her hands. "He meant that during the labour, the baby helps by being alive and going with the contractions of the mother's body. . . mother and baby are in harmony for this part."

She looked up at the other two women and they both nodded, indicating that they understood exactly what she was saying. "I laboured for nearly thirty-six hours to deliver my beautiful daughter. A nurse went home, had her night's sleep, lived her day and came back. And I was still there. In the same spot. Imagine that."

A tear trickled down Anna's cheek as she listened to her mother relay her experience of giving birth to a sister whom she would never know.

"I'm not telling you this for any real reason. I mean. . . I don't want pity. Just. . . isn't it so hard to make sense of? After she was born, they wrapped her in a blanket and gave her to me for a few moments. I don't know what I was supposed to do, or what they were thinking or hoping I'd do. I was exhausted and out of my mind with pain and shock. I felt so alone. I felt as if I'd done something wrong. I'm sure they weren't, but I felt as if everyone in the hospital must have been talking about me and wondering what I'd done to deserve such a horrific thing to happen."

"I can remember her perfect little nose and her lovely long eyelashes. She had chubby little cheeks. She looked just like a perfect little baby, fast asleep in my arms. Her image is imprinted on my mind. . . but when I try to look at the little parts of her face, it's like I can only see the outline. Like it was brandished on the back of my brain for reference, but I'm not able to examine it."

Laura and Anna looked at one another with concern.

Grace spoke again.

"And your dad never saw her. My beautiful Jim. My best friend. Here was his little daughter and he was never to see her. Then they just took her away, and that was the last I saw of her or heard about her.

I've heard that nowadays, they give mothers little imprints of their baby's hands and feet, a lock of their hair, some little photographs. . . and that seems so much more. . . compassionate. . . or fitting. At least these mothers have something to validate their experience. It might be something that will help them to grieve. Nothing is going to make up for what they've gone through, but it's a gentler way to deal with a grieving mother. In my day, we were just left to wonder whether the whole thing had really happened."

"They kept me in for a few days, because I was bleeding. They were afraid I'd haemorrhage or get very ill. Then, when they were satisfied that I wasn't going to get worse, they sent me home. Just like that. The doctor told me I'd have to be quick if I wanted another child, as I would be considered an elderly mother at this stage. I was thirty-five."

The women remained in silent communion for a couple of minutes. Laura broke the silence with a single word. "Brutal."

"Mum, what happened then?" Anna asked. "Did you have a funeral? I've often meant to ask where her little grave is, but I haven't wanted to put you through reliving this tragic time."

"No. There was no ceremony for stillbirths back in those days. They just took the babies and buried them in the Angels' Plot of the cemetery. It was all very archaic when you think about it. There was no closure. Nowhere to visit. No headstone. The hospital sent a bill then, for the cost of burying her."

"Barbaric," said Anna. "So where did they bury her? Did they not tell you?"

"No, Anna. I have no idea exactly where she is. One of the bigger cemeteries, I'd expect. Maybe it was on the bill. I don't remember. I'm sure there's a record of it somewhere. But nobody encouraged you to do anything about things like that. What would be the point? Nothing was going to bring your baby back to life. You were just expected to get on with your own life. People didn't speak about it—and if they did, every-one just told you to have another one."

"I was told that I was lucky I already had a child, and not to be look-ing for anything more than that. . . as if I was greedy or something, for having wanted a second child. My own doctor examined me after a few months and told me I'd be fine: to just get on with raising June and not push myself to replace the baby I'd lost. Replace. My God, it enrages me when I think of it now, but at the time, I just took what he said to be the way it was to be for me. It sounds so insensitive in today's world. But that really was just the way it was."

"What did Dad do?" asked Anna after a few moments, when she was sure that her mother had finished.

"There was nothing your father could do, Anna. Poor Jim. He just continued to do what he'd always done. But I felt like such a failure. All of the women in the area were having their children, and I wondered why I was being punished. There were women who were just having child after child, with no issues—or at least that's what I saw. That was all I saw."

"June was a focus for me, for sure, and she kept me going. She was such a sweet little girl, only three years old. She had no idea what had happened to me. She just accepted that the little brother or sister who was going to come decided not to come, and she didn't distress in any way about that."

Laura sat listening. She was quiet, then looked at Anna and said, "There were no support groups or refuges or any of that then for women in trouble or in pain. There wasn't the same sense of sisterhood that there is now. Women were more separate from one another. Women were not encouraged to talk about those things. 'Women's problems', they were called. You went through your trials alone. Women didn't even talk to one another about these things. Social life was for men."

"Yes," agreed Grace. "That's so true. Social life was for men. Pubs, golf, fishing, sports. All for men." She shifted in her chair to face Anna. "But it did all end well for me, Anna, my gorgeous girl—with your birth. I was well and strong by then, nearly forty years of age. I heard whispered that I was very old and there might be something wrong with you, if you survived at all, and. . . all that kind of stuff was milling around in the atmosphere. Everyone asking me if I was sure. Sure? I was sure alright! Sure that I was pregnant and sure I was coming home with my baby this time."

Grace shook her hair back and looked up at the ceiling for a few moments.

"I was defiant. I knew. I knew that you were going to be perfect and I knew you were going to live. The only time I had the slightest doubt or fear was when I arrived at that big maternity hospital and found myself retracing my steps from four years earlier. The long corridors and high ceilings gave me the creeps. The same noises, the smells, the sound of babies crying. . . I froze in place until I could feel you wanting to be born. There were no injections this time. You were coming, my body reacted, and we performed the perfect dance of creation that women and babies have been doing since time began."

Grace looked lovingly at her daughter, then at Laura. The three women spontaneously reached out their hands to one another and formed a silent circle of support. They let the energy flow between them and felt their hearts filling.

At that moment, Daniel arrived home, stealing into the house to avoid waking the boys. He walked quietly through the hall and came to the kitchen door. There, he took one look at the three women, and immediately crept back out. He stood in the hall for a few moments, wondering what he should do.

The women looked as if they were in prayer. He knew that they hadn't noticed him, but he had to do something to announce his arrival home, without waking the boys. He caught his reflection in the hall mirror, smiled and made a face to himself, laughing inwardly at this farcical situation he found himself in.

After a minute or two, he heard a kitchen chair scrape the tiled floor, so he opened and closed the front door again. Anna moved in his direction. "Dan? You home?"

"Yes," he said, coming into the kitchen and reaching to give her a hug.

"Hi darling, hi Mum, hi Grace. . . good day?"

"Perfect," the ladies said in unison.

Chapter Four

When Cal was five and Blu was four, Daniel and Anna brought them on their first family holiday. They traveled to the Mediterranean, drawn to its warm climate and its difference to home.

They decided to hire a chalet next to a beautiful vineyard. A section of the vineyard's land had been specially designed and prepared for campers. It was beautifully laid out with a mixture of camping spots for tents, pitches for travelling camper vans, parking spaces for caravans, and lovely little wooden chalets—one of which Daniel had picked out for them.

The boys were excited by the bunk beds in the rooms. Even though there were three bedrooms, they insisted on sleeping in the same room, taking turns each night to sleep on the top bunk. The site boasted a swimming pool, play areas, a small supermarket, a restaurant and a bar. It was like a little piece of heaven.

For the first couple of weeks, the family stayed on the campsite, appreciating how they could live so simply with so little. They met many lovely people. The children made friends in the pool and on the slides, and their parents were brought together through these childhood alliances.

After the first two weeks, Daniel decided that he would take the car out of the site and travel around the environs, to see whether he could find somewhere new for them to visit the following evening.

One of the parents on site had told him that there was a little town about ten kilometers down the road. It was an old, gated town with a warren of small streets and shops, and was well worth a visit.

After dinner that evening, the boys went to bed, while Anna went outside to sit on the deck and relax. Daniel told her that he would go and look at the town, so he could plan a day out for them there. Anna thought it was a great idea, adding that she really wanted to sit and take in the atmosphere for a while. She urged him to take his time, and let her know by text how he was getting on.

When Daniel got to the town, he found that there was a one-way driving system in place. He followed some signs that led him to a parking lot, where he could leave the car and then explore the town on foot.

A buzz of noise surrounded the town, with people coming and going through a large gateway. After traveling along with the flow of people for a few streets, Daniel came upon a thriving marketplace, which stocked every kind of product imaginable: food, jewellery, toys, ceramics, clothes and so much more. He spent some time wandering from stall to stall, marveling at this carnival of colour and diversity.

Many little cafes and restaurants were dotted throughout the town. Their seating spilled out onto the square, where shoppers were taking some time to pause, chat and be together.

Daniel was greatly enjoying the experience. Everything at home was so different. Shops shut at 6 p.m. He had never come across this kind of night-time market activity in any town in which he'd lived.

It was as he made his way through this evening market that he spotted Elba. As clear as day. He couldn't believe his eyes. He was sure he was imagining it. He heard her distinctive laughter first. Looking in the direction of the sound, he spotted her talking to a young lady holding a dog.

He immediately made his way over to greet her, and she smiled at him, wide eyed and welcoming, as she saw him approach.

"Daniel! Oh, Daniel—how wonderful to see you!" she exclaimed.

He embraced her warmly. "Where did you go? Where have you been? Are you on holiday too?" The words were out of his mouth almost before he reached her.

"I'm from here, Daniel," she said. "This is where I was born. Come. I'll show you. Come up and have some food. Are you alone?"

"Yes," he said with a nod. "I'm alone."

Elba said goodbye to the friend she had been talking to, and beckoned Daniel to follow her. "This way."

They walked up the medieval steps, away from the market square and into a narrow warren of streets. Daniel was speechless, and could not take his eyes off her. He was fully expecting her to disappear into the ether.

"Elba, you look twenty years younger. I was afraid you had. . ."

"Died? Oh no, Daniel, I wouldn't die and not tell you—or at least haunt you," she guffawed. "How's your job? Did you stay in the same job? I want to know so much about how you've been. I've thought about you so often, and wondered how life was treating you. Whether you'd met a girl, gotten married. . . there's so much I want to hear!"

They arrived at a big double gate and walked into a small courtyard. He followed her up a stone stairway and into a lovely, welcoming room, where he sat down as Elba prepared some coffee.

"I missed you so much, Elba," he exclaimed. "I never thought to ask you what your plans were, or what you were going to do. Where did you go?"

"I always come back here, Daniel, no matter how long I've been away. This is where I'm from. It's part of who I am, and I can never stay away indefinitely." She moved across the room to where he was sitting and sat opposite him. "Well, did you stay in your job?"

"I did," Daniel confirmed. "They made me offers I couldn't refuse, at times when I needed them to. I moved to a different city, but I'm with the same company."

"Life's funny that way. . . the offers you can't refuse," Elba laughed. "So, you're happy?"

"Very," confirmed Daniel. "I am so happy. I love everything I've created. I'm married to a wonderful woman named Anna, and we have two beautiful sons. I'm so hopeful for the life ahead of us."

"But. . ."

"No—but nothing. . . well, I know that my wife Anna struggled with baby blues. She won't discuss it—she believes I'm judging her, I think. But I'm not. I would just like her to be happier. She's a bit distant sometimes, and I can't seem to help her. It's frustrating. She has started doing yoga now, and she likes it. It seems to calm her. . ."

Daniel trailed off, then shook himself. "But look, here I am again, just after finding you, and I'm already going on about my woes! I should be celebrating our reunion. Enjoying your company again. I'm thrilled to see you, Elba. I hope you know that."

"Of course I do, Daniel. I'm pleased to see you again, and I'm honored that you view me as a safe person. It's a privilege to know that you can discuss things with me so readily. What else is friendship for, if not to mull things over?

Believe me, Daniel—I know that women are strange." Elba gave a loud throaty laugh, and Daniel couldn't help laughing along, albeit a little nervously.

"Tell me something I don't know, Elba," he quipped, and settled down with his elbows up on the table. "I'm all ears for your wisdom though, so please talk. I'm open to listening."

"Women generally don't need a lot of help, Daniel—except maybe to lift heavy objects!" she joked, with a wink. "If Anna is anything like you, she goes deep, she shifts big old karmic loads, and she needs a lot of quiet time. Women tend to do this on a deeper level, and not at the same speed or level that men do. Women carry so much global pain subconsciously. We have a different place within our minds that we are not sure anybody else has, so we tend not to talk about it. Some women don't even know it exists. They just think they're sad for no reason. Then they hear about a tsunami or an earthquake. . ."

"Then, I also know women who have a hard time with contentment. Why should she be so lucky as to have a loving husband and beautiful children and family? Women—we can persecute ourselves sometimes about such things, because we have an unspoken awareness of the pain on earth, particularly the pain of other women. This can make some women feel that we don't deserve our pain, if we are lucky and safe. It can feel like a minefield, the female psyche."

"Yes, a minefield," Daniel muttered under his breath and shifted in his chair.

"We also hold within our cellular memory—our bones and cells— the memory of the whole female story, down through the ages", Elba continued. The persecution of the Divine Feminine, the demonization of beauty, the burning of the witches, and the destruction of female wisdom. . . it's a long story. Anna doesn't need you to do anything other than what you're doing. Love her. Be there for her. We can't carry anybody else's load."

"But we can help, surely."

"I don't think so, no. Not really. We can just be there. Of course, we shouldn't add to somebody's pain, but no more than that can be expected. If you were to know exactly what to do to take away somebody else's pain, of course you would do it, but we can't know what another is going through."

"We can only know our own pain, and that is our work. It sounds like your Anna is strong, Daniel. Think about this: why do you consider it a failure for you, if you've decided she's not happy, or if she's not as you would have her? That's your question, isn't it? Why is it up to you to have her any other way than how she is?"

"Elba, I think most men would consider it a failure if their wife wasn't happy."

"There you go again, Daniel. It's not about you. It's not personal. Her mood is about her, not you—especially if you're not doing anything to cause her pain."

Daniel felt the old, familiar sensation of being simultaneously schooled and calmed by Elba's words. Whenever she had spoken to him like this in the past, he had never felt scolded. He just felt as though he had learned something real.

"I don't know, Elba. It's frustrating when I don't know what to do, when I can't fix something, when I just... don't know."

"Really, Daniel," Elba said gently, "you have to trust yourself. You actually always do know what to do, if you listen to your inner knowing. Do you think you would have come here without everything you need? Sometimes the mind can hide the solution from us; distract us with how we think things should be; but if we wait and listen to our true voice... we know."

She smiled at him, then moved to the back wall of the room, to get something from a dresser. She soon returned to the table and handed him a basket of bread and olives. "How do you always do this?" Daniel marveled. "How do you make me feel so calm, as if I can handle anything?"

"Oh Daniel, you know you can do anything. I just remind you of that." She smiled warmly at him, then went on, "when I was a little girl growing up in these streets and alleyways, my grandmother used to tell me that we were all born under our own star. I've never forgotten it."

"She used to take me out at dusk some nights and ask me to pick out my star. I tried to pick the same one every time. She told me that attached to that star was my angel. This angel would walk with me on the Earth unseen, and guard my spirit... because she knew that the star under which I was born gave me a specific life purpose, and gave my life a special meaning."

"This angel would never judge me or try to coerce me. The angel knew I would have no conscious memory of what we had planned before my life began. She helped me swim through the Waters of Forgetfulness of the birthing process. If I didn't do what the Star Angel and I had planned for my evolutionary journey, well, we'd just be pulled back to the star to make another plan. The Star Angel didn't wonder whether I was wrong or right. She just sat beside me and walked with me, no matter where I went."

"She admired the fact that I was brave enough to be human and to breathe oxygen! She was never going to leave me." Elba chuckled. "Of course, I have no proof that anything my grandmother said was true. It might sound quite childish, but it's served me well."

Noticing that Daniel had now finished his coffee, she smiled as she got up to put his cup away. "How long are you here for?" she asked him when she returned to the table.

"Three weeks in total. This is the last week of our break. Could I bring Anna and the boys to meet you, Elba? Not here—we couldn't invade your home. The boys are very noisy! But maybe we could treat you to a meal somewhere in town?"

"Yes, I would love that. Please do. If you're here for the next week, I'm available anytime you want to pop into town—are you out at the campsite?"

"Yes."

"It's a wonderful set up they have out there. This town has owed a lot to that old vineyard over the years. It's provided us all with a lot. . . and I don't just mean wine," she giggled, before walking over to a nearby press and producing a bottle of wine. She waved it in his direction, raising an eyebrow to suggest that they share it.

"I'm driving," Daniel mock-scowled. "Believe me, there's nothing more I'd prefer than to sit here, getting mellow on wine and talking to you."

"You are such a darling boy. I think I'll drink some," she said happily and gave him a large grin, as she fetched herself a wine glass.

They looked out the balcony window and ate the bread and olives Elba had put out on the table. The balcony overlooked the courtyard they'd walked through, and Daniel felt like he was on a very elaborate set of a Shakespearean-era play.

Elba spoke to Daniel about her childhood in the town. She told him that when she was a girl, they were told that the truth was held in these streets: that the truth was simpler than they could ever have imagined.

"I was brought up here just to be. I was told that the truth was known, and that I didn't have to worry about what it was. It wasn't until I went to the city and fell in love and started to live outside of these streets that I felt the need to worry. Here, in this town, we had every type of person. In every community of people, humanity will show itself in all its guises."

Daniel loved spending time with this old woman. He had missed her so much in his life. Her wisdom touched his heart and soul, and he felt safe and content in her company. They sat for another hour in silent companionship interspersed with bouts of conversation and friendship. The decade since they had last been together melted away into the ether.

When Daniel returned to the campsite, Anna noticed he was flushed with excitement, and his eyes were lit up. She was sitting on the deck with a glass of wine. "I thought you'd left me," she scolded him, laughing. "Where on earth were you?"

"Oh Anna, I met my Eusebia Sylvia Elba tonight. After many, many years. I haven't seen her in over a decade. When I first started working with my company, I spent well over a year travelling with her every morning on my way to the office. Then one day, she was gone, and I never saw her again. . . until tonight."

"The old lady on the train?" Anna's eyes widened in astonishment. "You told me about her when we first met."

"Yes. She would like to meet you and the boys before we go home."

"Ah, I'd love that. Yes, do arrange for us to meet her. You used to talk about her a lot. I'm so glad you found her again."

"I'll set up a time, Anna. I'm so excited for you to meet her," he enthused, then sat down and exhaled deeply. Anna could see how happy he was, and the sight of his joy gladdened her heart. Eventually, he spoke again. "I love it here. I really love it. This has been the best holiday."

She beamed at him and sat back, stretching her legs out in front of her and faced her head skyward to look at the moon.

The next day, Daniel went back to the town to meet Elba while the boys were snoozing. She told him that she would bring him to a very special bakery, where he would taste the most divine bread he had ever eaten. She spoke the truth—it was mouth-watering.

Over coffee, Daniel again found himself spilling out all of his worries to Elba. What was it about this woman? He told her that he was worried about the future: what life would be like for his sons, how they would look back on their childhood, how he could be sure he was doing enough for them. He was worried about the planet. Pollution. Climate change. Everything was such a mess, he said. What would they do about it all?

"Things are as they are," Elba replied softly, "and plenty of things in this world are none of our concern, Daniel. For example, worrying about how or why things got to where they are is a distraction from any solution. Just looking for who and what to blame and keep us distracted from our own part and from rectifying action. There are as many versions of history as there are individual human perspectives, and trying to find the "correct" version of events only brings you down the road of recriminations. Remember *The Bridge of Now*."

"If you're doing your best for your children now, that's all you need to be concerned about. You can't organise their future for them. What kind of a future would you organise if you could? You have no idea what they're born for! Why would you worry about what they'll create? Trust them to create and build something for themselves. They hold the blueprint for their futures. Your generation was here to break down the old structures, not to know what's coming next. That's your sons' job."

Daniel looked out at two swans gliding along the river. Wow. His sons' job is to create new structures. How exciting. How terrifying! Elba interrupted his thoughts.

"I had a beautiful friend named Floyd who lived here in this town with me until he died five years ago. He had been the Master at the school when I was a little girl. He never left here to find his fortune or considered this place too small for him or his wisdom. He was the wisest man I ever met. He once told me that we needn't concern ourselves specifically with the Divine plan."

"Until the moment we are expressly entrusted with all of the secrets of the universes—how to hold up the moon, how to command the tides, how to direct the intelligence of an ancient symbol or the seed of a sun-flower—we need have no concern about the march of the universe, other than playing our own part in it, to the best of our ability."

"When I was a child, he and my grandmother instilled in me a great trust in the universal laws, and I have never lost that trust, even during times of distress. Neither of them ever left these tiny streets and this small community, but they had the wisdom of the ancients."

She smiled at him and squeezed his hand. "Oh, darling boy, take the massive responsibility off your shoulders. That over which you have no control, you cannot be responsible for. You're only responsible for yourself and your reactions. Lay down your sense of betrayal when the earth moves in a way you don't like."

"Your concern is always your inner life, then your actions and reactions: your way of framing your thoughts, the way you pay attention to your feelings. This is the only place in which your power resides. Even if you were able to plan to the finest detail what the future would be like for your children, who's to say they'd even like it?"

"Well, Elba, they're too young to know what's good for them," Daniel said, with a hint of desperation in his voice.

Elba's eyes were filled with understanding as she spoke again. "I remember, as a little girl, stoutly defending my different positions to Floyd. Believe me, I wasn't a shrinking violet: "I have opinions," I remember shouting at him! "That's okay. Of course you do," he would answer gently. "And if you see your life as an act of service, you must have these inner directions and be ready to act. However, if your opinions are injurious to your inner life, lay them down. If your opinions take you away from how you can help, take you away from a place of compassion and acceptance and understanding of other humans, change them." I will always remember the morning he said that to me. I had my arms folded defiantly and was telling him that one day, I would change everything. It seemed like big advice to a little girl, Daniel, and I was unsure whether he knew what he was talking about or not."

"Was he saying activism isn't important?"

"No. Quite the opposite, I think. He was saying we should confine our activism to where we can make a difference—that when, or if, you become the opposite of what you're fighting, you run into the danger of becoming the same thing in the other extreme. That's injurious to the soul."

"The ego feeds on that "I'm right" notion that we tend to hide behind.

Just make it easier on yourself. Do what is practicably possible. Recycle. Be energy aware. Love nature. Respect animals and all living things. Tread gently on the Earth. Allow your children to do what they came here to do, even if you don't always approve."

"The true power is ours, and it is at its most powerful when we are working in love; the minutiae of the Divine plan, whatever it may be, is not our direct concern in this life. We will never find it all out in a conscious lifetime, so don't get distracted down blind alleyways."

"Expect miracles around your children, Daniel. I mean, really expect miracles. When you're expecting visitors, you get ready for them. You change their beds. You lay the table for them. Actively expect that everything will be fine for your boys in their time, and for their time."

"That's a gorgeous thought, Elba," Daniel said dreamily. "They are such special kids. I adore them."

Elba nodded now, happier that he had ended the tug of war within his mind. "Remember that the factors that go into informing our generations are different. The new comes through the passage of the old, remember. Why would we restrict the new people—the children—to our old, outdated ways? Each little human being is informed by different things in their lives: their socioeconomic circumstances; their nationality; the history of their people; experiences of their ancestors; likes, dislikes and ambitions and opinions. It's all too complex for us to understand and master. The more you can say, 'I don't know', the happier your life will be."

She was smiling now. "And each generation is of their own time. Stars align in ways the human brain could never understand—let alone believe—to give them access to the consciousness they'll need to carry out their Divine contracts and duties. How could we have arranged all of that, with our limited human awareness? The answer is, we couldn't."

Elba gestured to the waiter to bring them another bottle of water. When he arrived with it, she smiled at him, and they exchanged a few sentences in their own language.

When the waiter left, Elba looked back at her companion. "Daniel, give your children everything they need, then stand back and watch them. Trust them, as you trusted your own generation. Each generation despairs at the new one, or is exasperated by them; but life is constantly evolving, as is consciousness. Each person is of their time."

"We are not privy to anybody else's life purpose and need only concern ourselves with the evolving story of our own. Again. Our only point of power. There is nobody on the planet—not the most highly acclaimed gurus, your teachers or parents—who know exactly who we are or what we are doing here. They can have great theories, but they don't know. All idols have clay feet, therefore, so never rely on anybody else's opinion of you. If people, parents, or society have an expectation of you, weigh it up with how true it feels to you. Tell your sons the same thing. Empower them. Don't talk to them constantly about all the things that are wrong, in your opinion."

"Elba, I'd love to agree with you or see things the way you and your school teacher saw things," Daniel said, "but doesn't structure bring order to society? People need to pass on the rules and the accepted norms. And I mean, we have to denounce mass murder, genocide. . . we can't just let people get away with things. . . go around doing whatever they like. . ."

"Well of course, there is justifiable and unjustifiable war, there is sacred rage being acted out in many troubled places on the planet. Hate breeds hate, though, and the history of the human race is a good demonstration of that. An eye for an eye and a tooth for a tooth has never led to a resolution unless all die, and even then, nothing is achieved. You can be right without telling everyone else they're wrong!"

"There are many deplorable aspects to the human story. But great heroism too. I ask you again, who knows what any soul came here to do? Yes, we probably do need rules—if we don't trust people. We only require structures and rules because we have allowed things to get so far out of control and we don't trust that other people know what they're doing."

Daniel was silent for a few moments as he tried to digest this. "Seriously though, Elba... are you telling me I can't have an opinion?"

"No. I'm suggesting that feelings are probably better than opinions. I've found that opinions are rigidity in another form. Having a fixed position in a changing world... well, the ground is always shifting beneath your feet! Feelings give you room to change. They give you room to grow and evolve."

"It's my opinion that one should not murder another, Elba."

"That's not an opinion, Daniel, no matter how you argue that it is. It's an admirable trait in your character, but even then, you must see that it only applies in a perfect set of circumstances. Circumstances where you are never attacked, those you love are never hurt, your tribe are not destroyed, your people are not vanquished. If you had your land stolen and your friends starved, you might feel differently."

"Well, yes. There's war, like you said, justifiable war," conceded Daniel.

"But you just told me that it was your opinion that murder was wrong. Are you saying now that murder is not wrong in war?" she teased him.

He looked ruefully at her, and she shook her head, still smiling. "Daniel, I'm simply saying that my opinion is we sleep easier with fewer opinions. Remember? The more you can say 'I don't know', the easier life is."

He grinned, feeling the urge to tease her back. "My opinion is that today is Tuesday. In fact, I know today is Tuesday."

Elba chuckled. "That's a safe opinion to have in this spot. In Australia, at this exact point in time and evolution of consciousness, you'd be considered yesterday's man."

Daniel couldn't help but laugh at this, and Elba regarded him with a great warmth in her eyes. "Here is the problem with rigid opinions, Daniel," she went on softly. "We are so far away from feeling happy and safe inside ourselves, we build structures of how people should behave in order for us to feel that this is okay. We are safe."

"Take, for example, looking back on the good old days. That's only from a viewpoint of perceived safety, isn't it?

THE BRIDGE OF NOW

Listen to people now talk nostalgically about decades in the past; the fashion, the music, the social life. How wonderful and simple it all was! Living through those decades was a different thing entirely from the memory of it—I can promise you that! Memory can be safe, because of the distance, or because in the telling of the memory, a certain filter can be used."

Daniel nodded, sat back and said, wistfully, "I'd just love to know what happens next in my life. I'd like a map!"

Elba's eyes twinkled with mirth. "Having a map is great, but you'll often have heard that focusing only on the destination makes you miss out on aspects of the journey which we should pay more attention to in the *now*. This society that we know now is only 2000 years old or so. The calendar we use is set from the time of Christ. . . yet humans have been here for eons: evolving, changing, exploring since time immemorial. Nothing began at the time of Christ, irrespective of what the Julian and Gregorian calendar would have us believe. Prehistoric! Preposterous—there's no such thing."

"Despite the rules that we set down—norms, as you call them—my grandmother once told me that the human animal develops in the way the species has always developed. It happens in seven-year cycles. Let me give you one of these maps. . . the map my grandmother gave to me during our time together."

"The first seven years of a human's life are known as the mother time—or chakra, as the yoga people like Anna call them—and is when, in older, better functioning societies, the child would have spent most of their time around the women of the community. They learnt about softness, warmth, how it feels to be fed and feel hunger leaving the little body, yieldingness, comfort, and safety. As babies and toddlers, they are very much still in a theta brainwave state, and they are carried everywhere, totally reliant on others for safety and support."

"Their experiences at this stage can, of course, have massive repercussions for how they evolve later in life. Their brains are not yet developed enough to rationally debate right from wrong. Everything just is the way it is. I am. I exist."

"The second stage is known as the time of the father chakra, and is typically a time when a child will move away from the women of the community. They will move towards action, as opposed to being."

"Their attention moves to their father and the men in the community. They ask, "Who is he, where does he go, where does he get the things he brings back, how does he get them?" They learn about consequences: if you do this, that happens. This chakra, or development stage, lasts from the age of eight to fourteen. The child begins to develop sexually, and learn that this is the womb of all creativity within the male and the female. The child comes to know the sensation of *I feel*."

"By the age of fourteen, a child knows everything they need to know about the feminine and masculine aspects, through their exposure to their parents and the women and men of their communities."

"You may have heard the expression, "Give me the child until he's 14, and I will give you the man." There is an awful lot of truth in that, since our foundations are set during these years. The old people knew this."

Elba paused to laugh at the distant expression on Daniel's face. She knew he was applying this theory to his own life, and had traveled away to some distant place in his mind.

She pressed on. "During these years, we must be conscious that the child is more or less a prisoner, in many ways—a hostage to their circumstances. They have neither the ability, nor the wherewithal to move away if there is something going on in the home that they don't feel right about. A child can't just up and leave and go to the city to find a job at nine years of age, if the homelife is troubled."

"Children have no direct decision-making power. This is why it is especially damaging to all involved, to harm a child. If you agree that it is sociopathic to harm something that has no power, then you must understand that a child can never be the cause of, or take the blame for, anything that happens in your life. When an adult is shouting at a child for any reason, it is not the child who is in trouble. It's the adult. Always. Irrespective of what the child has done. Parents need to understand this."

"My God," Daniel exclaimed, "I love this, Elba! This theory of yours is magic. It explains so much of what childhood is about, doesn't it?"

"It's not my theory, Daniel," she laughed. "It's a story that was well-known when I was young and developing, and it was used as a guide to help us interact with every member of the community, according to where they were in the development cycle. Everyone knew it, so there were no surprises for us. We just tried to go with the flow and understand other people. Will I continue?"

"Yes please," Daniel urged her. "I've just been thinking about my childhood. But also, about my children."

Elba reached for a drink of her water and continued, "The next phase of development is from the age of fifteen to twenty-one. In these older, better functioning societies that Floyd cited to me, the community would come around the child at this stage and ask them who they were, what they could do, what were their interests, and what they wanted to add to their society"

"The community would give the child ample opportunity to show them. They would offer the teenager apprenticeships in the shops and factories and creative pursuits of the town, offering them creative expression and power."

"Through this process, the child grows into the realm of *I do*. Now, of course, we have structured a system that stifles this creative time for the teenager. We dress them the same, put them into stuffy rooms, teach them the same boring dogma, judge them by the same examination papers. How mad is that? If that isn't a set up, I don't know what is."

"How is school a set-up, Elba? Doesn't it give every child the same chance?"

"Well, Daniel, think about it. The children who are most likely to be at the top of society's structure blossom best in this organised and structured environment. Hence, change moves very slowly through the generations, and the societal structure stays the same to the outside world. Imagine if every fifteen-year-old truly had the same chance in life? Bliss."

"Bliss indeed for everyone. Happy teenagers are a good thing," Daniel laughed, thinking back to his own youthful years.

He could well remember the different fights and dramas he and his friends had created; how they had gotten into trouble and let off steam, how they had stressed about exams in subjects they cared nothing about, but had to pass if they wanted to make anything of their lives. They were told this very clearly in school, and it had been very destructive to his self-esteem. And he was lucky. He liked the structure of school and exams.

He had known as a young child that Laura couldn't afford to send him to university. Until Laura had received an unexpected windfall from his grandfather, he would never have been expected to go to university. He was from a "broken home", he had been lucky just to get an education, and the best he could have hoped for was to get a job somewhere and work hard at it. The money had changed everything.

"During the next stage of development, the growing human winds their way through the tricky roads of the heart," Elba continued, breaking his concentration. "Twenty-one to twenty-eight. We meet others, fall in love, and develop strategies to get into good stead with the person of our desires. We feel the pain of rejection, we have our hearts broken, we experience betrayal and the gut-wrenching treachery of people we considered friends."

"Yet we also come to know the pure joy of connectedness, love, empathy, compassion and care. People begin to truly feel what it's like to say and feel, *I Love. . .* Our thoughts turn to partnership, to common goals and ideals. The heart chakra is the bridge between the feminine being chakras—the root, sacral, and solar plexus—and the masculine doing chakras that are yet to develop—the throat, third eye, and crown."

Daniel frowned, a little bemused. "Hold on, what?"

"Shhh. Listen," Elba admonished him, with a wink. "When we are between twenty-nine to thirty-five, we are led into a very active and vocal phase of our lives as humans. This period covers the phase of finding our voice, and is related to the throat chakra. *I speak.*"

"Society listens to who we are, what we have to say, how we express ourselves, and rewards us accordingly. The throat chakra is the conduit through which we express our inner selves."

"Of course, you've guessed that the next stage of development is the third eye. This is where you are now, Daniel. This is your current stage."

"Between the ages of thirty-six to forty-two, we seek to bring our dreams into reality, seeking a higher vision. *I see.* Most of us are busy raising children or interacting with nieces and nephews. We are seeking a higher vision for them and for ourselves, through our intellect. This is a time in human development when society tends to regard us as the leaders, the strong people, the people who are doing the work, paying the taxes and keeping the show on the road."

"Our parents are usually getting on in years. We are thinking about them, processing our own childhoods, and getting an opportunity to heal the wounds of our childhood relationships with our own parents— sometimes through our own children. We see our parents begin to inter- act as grandparents, and this enables us to see a different, perhaps softer, side to them."

"We, of course, are now in the pressurised roles of having to earn the money and provide everything. It gives us a different perspective of what our parents went through while raising us. We see things differ- ently through our third eye. There is a new wisdom."

Elba looked at Daniel and waited a few moments before she spoke again, because she could see he was thinking about what she had said.

"I honestly never thought of things this way, Elba," Daniel mused at last. "This is really helpful to me, actually, because I can relate what you're saying to Anna, and what she's going through as a mother. She talks about how she understands her father a bit better now, as she sees him so much in Cal. This is so interesting, Elba."

"Yes, the old people have always said that the first son is like the mother's father." Elba smiled. "Interesting, isn't it? How the genes work their way through."

"So, the last big energy chakra is the crown. This develops between the ages of forty-three and forty-nine. It brings with it a connection to higher thought, and a relationship with the great sky and God. *I under- stand.* So, by the age of 49, Daniel, we are said, as humans, to have lived through the 7 ages of man."

"And then we're on the scrap heap. Oops, sorry Elba!" Daniel smiled and reached out to squeeze her hand.

She guffawed at this, and tenderly touched his face with her other wise old hand. "Oh no, Daniel, don't you believe it; we are only just beginning to come into our true wisdom during our fifties. We are the elders, the seers, the champions of the children, and the champions of all of those who struggle. We see the futility of what we spent younger years worrying about, and we pick our battles. We are the wise ones."

"Let's walk," Daniel suggested, after a few moments of reflection. They had finished their meal, and he was feeling the urge to move. "Can you walk for a while?"

Elba nodded, so they got up to head off down a sunny boardwalk by the river. Daniel indicated to the waiter that he should keep the change from the notes he left at their table.

"How old is this town, Elba?" he asked her, as they meandered down the boardwalk.

"Twelfth century, Daniel. Long before you and I were a sparkle in the dust."

"Still standing."

"Built to last."

Daniel offered her his arm, and they walked in happy companionship for nearly half an hour.

She asked him whether he was free tomorrow, as there was somewhere very special that she wanted to bring him.

He said he could be free tomorrow. He would check with Anna, but didn't see a problem. She asked him to bring his car into town, to pick her up. He said he would.

Chapter Five

That night, Daniel was restless. He wanted to remember everything Elba had told him: the seven ages of man, chakras, energy system of the body, yoga, ancient wisdom, old people, development...

He tried to explain it all to Anna, but she was none the wiser when he had finished. Though she was a little bemused by his jumbled words, she smiled and said, "I love the effect this old lady has on you. I always saw how happy you were when you used to talk about her. I'm so glad you found her again. What are the chances? Meeting up with an old lady you knew years ago, on a camping holiday with your family... there must be some meaning to it, Dan."

"I really believe there is. Would you mind if I went to see her again tomorrow? She's asked me if I can pick her up—says there's somewhere special she wants to bring me."

"Fine by me. If you could go in the afternoon when the boys will be tired and keeping out of the sun, that'd be great."

They smiled at one another and settled down for a relaxing evening of doing nothing but listening to the crickets.

The following morning, Daniel took the boys for a swim and played some ball with them. They went back to the chalet to rest before lunch.

"You go see your old lady now," Anna urged him. "And take your time. We really will be fine." She enjoyed the afternoons, when the boys stayed out of the heat and she could laze around with nothing to do but read, do some yoga, or admire the view of the vineyard.

Daniel set off happily to Elba's house. Once he was there, they both ambled back to his car through the old medieval streets. Elba pointed out some of the main attractions of the town. They stopped in the old church to light a candle and admire some of its ornate statues.

The church was small, but its walls seemed to echo centuries of prayer and supplication. In the last century, this building had served as the central church for miles around. Here, generations of local people had come to present their newborns, get married, and take leave of their elders.

Daniel and Elba soon arrived at the car. From the passenger seat, Elba directed Daniel out of the town and into the countryside—telling him, as she did so, that when she was a child, she and her friends would cycle down this road, carrying picnic baskets and wine.

When they had traveled about eleven kilometres beyond the town, she indicated that he should take the next left, to travel down a small laneway.

They arrived at a makeshift overgrown parking area. As they got out of the car, Elba asked Daniel to carry her bag. She said she would need all her wits about her to get her bearings and lead him to their destination. "I haven't been here for. . . oh, it must be fifteen years or so," she remarked. "But I'll bet this place hasn't changed."

Daniel let her lead the way, looking around at the scenery as he walked. He thought he could hear her talking under her breath, so he instinctively fell behind enough to give her some privacy. It sounded as though she might be praying, and he didn't want to intrude.

She soon stopped at an old stile into a field and asked him whether he could help her over it. He cleared away some brambles that blocked the small stone structure, and then easily climbed over it, putting his hands out to help Elba follow him. She flashed a huge smile at him as she made her way over the stile, and he couldn't help but smile too.

They walked on a bit further, and as they reached the brow of a little hillock, an enormous vista opened up before them. Daniel breathed sharply as he took in the huge meadows before them: it was like a painting, or a picture out of a fairy-tale book. On the horizon, he believed he could see the point where earth met heaven. The colors before him comprised the entire spectrum of the rainbow. The fields nearest to them were yellow, red, and green, and he could also see lavender fields in the distance.

Little huts stood out as specks on the landscape—Daniel knew they had been built long ago, to shelter the lavender pickers of this enchanted valley from the midday heat.

Daniel suddenly and unexpectedly felt as though he could cry. The view was so breathtakingly beautiful: he had really thought that a place like this could only be viewed in the imagination.

"What an expanse, Elba," he marveled. "What beauty. What a place to live. Imagine having a home here and looking upon this every single day. You'd never leave... or get any work done! This height is just perfect. It lets you see everything."

"We ran through these fields and hills as children," Elba said in a faraway voice. "We picked flowers and dreamed big dreams. You know, Daniel, the story goes that there was once a big cathedral here, which served all the counties for miles around. People would come here to be changed and healed by the wise women and men of the valley, or just to get a different perspective.

"The basilica was said to have been razed to the ground in the Middle Ages, but this place has always held an energy of peace and healing and love. Once you've seen this place, it never leaves you. I may not have been here in many years, but in my mind's eye, I am a regular visitor."

She pointed across the fields to a grove of about six or seven trees. "There's a little side chapel in the trees over there. They call it the Nun's Chapel, but who ever saw a birthing stone in a nun's chapel? I suspect it was somewhere quite different, in its time, than a celibate nun's place of prayer." She raised a quizzical eyebrow at him, then grinned. "We'll go there soon, but first, let's eat."

They made their way to the grove and found a soft mossy spot where they could have their lunch. Elba sat down on a tree trunk covered in ivy.

"Eusebia Sylvia Elba, Queen of the Forest," Daniel joked. She radiated a smile that made his heart shine.

He handed Elba's bag back to her, and she set out a snack of cheese, olives, and bread. They ate and talked for some time. Daniel told her about his job: how it had been satisfying for a long time, but how, once he met Anna and had the boys, they had become his main focus.

He told her he had been thinking all night about what she had related to him the previous day, about the energy system of the body and the developmental stages of humans. He said that he was fascinated to reflect on where he was now, and what could be coming next for him and his family. He asked her whether she could explain the whole thing to Anna, as he himself had made a mess of explaining it to her. Elba promised she would tell Anna all about it when they met.

She listened easily as they ate, offering him no opinion or words—just her presence and attention.

"I feel better, I think, now that I'm older," Daniel mused. "I feel more able to manage my life. I know it's a pressurised time—paying the bills and keeping body and soul together—but I like it. I think childhood is difficult for some people, especially given what you were saying about children being a hostage to their circumstances. Hearing that will make me a better father, I think. Well. . . I hope."

He fell silent for a few moments, before continuing. "My father, as you know, was absent most of my childhood. Does that give me a disadvantage, do you think? At being a father myself?"

"No, Daniel, I wouldn't think so," Elba replied gently. "You saw men in the town where you grew up, you watched men in the community, you witnessed your mother doing the typically masculine work of bringing in the money for food. I would say you were an intuitive little boy, who knew what was really going on." She smiled. "Will I tell you a little bit more about the theory that might help you piece it all together?"

Daniel nodded.

"The lower three energy centres that are developing up to the age of twenty-one, or adulthood, were considered by the old people to represent the feminine or the being within," Elba shared. "The top three energy centres they said contained the masculine, or doing aspect. The heart, they considered to be the bridge. And they are all related."

"You alluded to this yesterday, but I'm a bit lost," Daniel chuckled. "Related how? What does that mean, Elba?"

Elba nodded, understanding. "Okay. I'll try to explain it as we were taught. The root represents Mother Earth, and its corresponding masculine chakra is the crown—Father God/Father Sky. The sacral area is the womb of all creation, in both men and women; it provides the hunch, the gut feeling. All ideas, all birth begins here, and then the third eye provides its corresponding masculine by bringing the idea to fruition. It thinks up the necessary steps to bring an idea to life."

"So, my gut tells me I'd like to paint a picture. I see it in my mind's eye, then I set about getting the paint, the canvas and all the brushes I'll need. Now the two corresponding feminine and masculine energies within are working in perfect harmony on a common project. All should go well."

"If someone tells me that they can't think of a way out of something, or they're blocked in some way, I always ask them to clear the sacral chakra in order to allow the third eye to see clearly. The internal work or struggle is usually in the lower chakras, to allow the higher chakras to flow freely.

"The solar plexus—the power center—is expressed through the throat. This is where we speak who we are within. You will see people at funerals barely able to get their words out, so deep is their grief. It's not their throat chakra that's in trouble; it's their solar plexus; their power center. It's the solar plexus that shuts down when we get a fright, like after the death of someone close. The proverbial 'kick in the stomach'. A nervous voice means a nervous butterfly in the tummy."

Elba laughed. "Think of yourself at every interview or exam you ever did. If you felt confident in what you were saying, your voice was clear, or the words flowed out onto the page. If you felt unconfident, your voice probably gave you away, or you wrote drivel onto the page that even you couldn't understand."

Daniel mulled over what Elba was saying. He knew she was extremely wise, and he didn't always comprehend what she was saying, but he felt it was important that he understand this fully. Anna had once confided in him that she had struggled with exams, even though she was the most intelligent woman he'd ever met. Could this have been the explanation?

"So, you don't ask or answer a question with your throat, Elba?" he chuckled. "I'm finding that a bit hard to square in my mind."

"Oh no, Daniel, the throat and voice box will answer, alright. But it will only deliver what's in the solar plexus. Anger and frustration come through in the voice, but they're felt in the power centre. The lower chakras are very closely associated with the emotional body, the inner child, and how we feel, while the upper chakras are associated with action, speaking, thinking. And your poor old heart is the bridge, the interpreter!"

Her eyes twinkled with humour as she watched him absorb her words. "I'll leave it with you. You're here for another week, aren't you? You know where I am." She winked as she began to clear up their lunch. "I'll draw you a picture, if you like."

Once the food had been cleared away, Elba smiled brightly and asked, "Nun's Chapel?"

"Nun's Chapel," Daniel agreed. "Let's see it."

They walked back towards the road from which they had come. As they got close to the roadside hedges and trees, Daniel saw the side wall of an old grey ruin.

"Here?" he asked.

"Yes, that's it. Take your time, please; it's very overgrown. I might need a hand."

Ivy had grown so far up the side of the old wall, it almost obscured the whole structure. Daniel followed Elba to where she said the entrance porch had once stood, and they walked into the inner chamber of the building.

The space was just a little larger than the ground floor of a modern-day house. Daniel could see there had once been some little rooms off this main chamber, but they had long since been reclaimed by nature. Arches appeared every few feet on each wall—Daniel supposed that doors must once have stood in those spaces.

As Daniel stood still—absorbing the energy and atmosphere of this ancient place—he found himself hearing a low hum he couldn't quite explain. The building seemed to be making a different noise to anything he'd ever heard before.

No roof remained on the old walls, so Daniel looked up to the sky for a moment, then brought his gaze back down to the floor beneath his feet. The old walls were made of granite. Some walls seemed more marbleized than others, but one detail that particularly struck him was that the lower stones were very large. He wondered at the strength, vision and effort it would have taken to carry and deliver these massive rocks to this place.

"How old is this place, Elba?" Daniel asked.

"Sixth century, Daniel. It's a very old building indeed."

They walked up to the top of the building, where an altar would generally be in a church. There, in front of them, was a low stone table with a large hollow indent, forming a shallow sink.

Daniel heard himself say, "Yes, this looks like a birthing table to me. . . or somewhere you'd bring babies to be blessed or baptised. This doesn't look like an altar, where they'd conduct a religious service. Besides anything else, the celebrant couldn't see the congregation."

"That's true—although I think in those times, the celebrant would have his back to the congregation—but yes, they would have been very short people to use this as their table altar. This is too low for little old me, Daniel!" Elba guffawed as she flamboyantly sat on the large stone table.

Without a word, Daniel sat down beside her. For a long while, neither spoke as they looked out at the large, open room in front of them.

A lone butterfly flew in for a few moments. They followed its journey with their eyes, watching it land here and there, before making its way out through the roofspace.

Daniel was saddened by the idea that this place just sat unused, year after year, with no one to witness or celebrate it. No one to reconstruct it or return it to its former glory. It was just an old building, lost down some by-roads in the middle of nowhere. There was no population to have kept it going over the years, leaving him and Elba here today, speculating about what it had been used for.

He stood up on the table and looked out through an opening in the back wall, which must once have been a window. As soon as he did so, he was treated again to the fabulous view of the valley.

The experience was breath-taking; he truly felt as though he had been brought to somewhere very special. He felt the great loneliness of this chapel, but he was also deeply grateful for having experienced its silence and peace.

Elba craned her neck and looked up at him. She was gratified to watch a beam of light touch his head, and knew that he had been touched by the spirit of this holy place. She was glad she had brought him here.

As she rose, she gently patted the table, as one would a faithful horse that had safely carried them both on a long journey to a treasured destination.

As they drove back to town, Daniel felt as though his whole body was emitting the low hum of the nun's chapel. He felt that all of his cells had been blessed.

He and Elba traveled in the blissful silence of two people who had experienced something they could never explain to anyone else.

When Daniel and his family arrived in the town the following day for their date with Elba, there was no sign of anyone. The parking spaces that had been at a premium on Daniel's first visit to the town were now a dime a dozen. The stalls were gone and the square was empty.

In the corner of the square, Daniel spotted Elba sitting in front of a small restaurant. A kind-looking gentleman sat beside her. As they approached, Elba stood up and clapped her hands with glee. The boys instinctively ran to her and gave her skirt a little hug.

"Oh, I'm so glad you're here, Elba," Daniel exclaimed warmly, and went to embrace her. "Where has the market gone?"

The man who was with Elba answered, "the market travels around the region on a weekly basis. It only visits here on Monday nights, Tuesday mornings, and Friday evenings during the tourist season."

"What a lovely life," Anna breathed wistfully.

"I prefer to stay in one place," the man remarked, with a grin. "My name is Rolo. This is my restaurant and you are all very welcome here."

Daniel introduced Anna and the boys to Elba. Rolo ushered them into his restaurant, leading them to a large round table at the back, beneath a large bow window. The vista overlooked the river to the front of the town. They settled down, Daniel ordered some drinks for the children, and Elba asked Rolo to bring them some menus and nibbles.

Elba beamed a beautiful smile at Anna. "I'm so glad Daniel found you, Anna. We were travel buddies for a long time, and Daniel never thought he'd fall in love during those years."

"I had much more cerebral concerns, Elba," Daniel laughed.

"Sure. Like all men in their twenties." Elba winked conspiratorially at Anna.

"I think we were just lucky to meet one another," Anna responded with a smile. "Do you have a family, Elba?"

"Yes, I have two boys, just like you. And then I had a girl. They all went to the city many years ago. They come back in late summer, when their businesses have closed and they want to recharge. They own a house outside of town, down the river. They rent it out for a lot of the year, and go there themselves for August and Christmas. It means we see a lot of one another, but also have space. It's ideal. I love spending time with them, and with my grandchildren."

Daniel felt ashamed that in all the time he'd known Elba, he had never asked her any questions about her family. Yet here was his wife, and it was the very first question she had asked. Women were amazing.

"Where were your children at the time that I met you, Elba?" he asked now.

"I went to your country to be with my sister," Elba replied. "She had married there many years ago, then her husband died and she became very ill. They had no children, and she needed me to help her. I visited her every morning in the hospital and cared for her animals in the afternoons."

"You never told me," Daniel said—thinking, as he did so, that he had never asked. "You must have been so lonely."

"No." Her voice was gentle. "I wasn't lonely. I met you most mornings, Daniel, and you reminded me of my boys when they were younger. That helped me. I met many other people during my daily return journeys from the hospital to her house. I watched you grow up over those years and attain what you wanted at that time. I wasn't lonely. I spent mornings with my sister, and my afternoons caring for her animals and getting to know your people. It was quite a gentle time for me. It was bliss, really. Nothing was mine, and I was just being helpful. It was great."

"Why did you go? Why did you disappear, Elba?" Daniel asked her now. "One day you were there and the next you were gone. I never saw you again. Well, until now. . ."

"My sister was discharged from hospital. I stayed with her for another month, but obviously didn't have to travel by train anymore."

Daniel understood now.

"Before I left for home, I did travel the train to say goodbye to you, but for some reason the mornings I did, you were not on the platform. But I knew I'd see you again someday," Elba said matter-of-factly.

She then looked directly at Anna. "I know how hectic these years are for you, dear Anna, raising babies. There's not enough time to complete everything you want to do."

Anna laughed. "Are you reading my mind, Elba?"

"No. I just remember. Even in a small town like this, that period of a woman's life is difficult. If I could talk to myself at your age, I would be very, very gentle."

Daniel got up to help Rolo, whose shirt had gotten caught in a door while he had both of his hands full with plates.

"I worried too much when my children were born," Elba shared with Anna. "I worried that I was doing everything the wrong way. I assumed that everybody was judging me. I expected too much of myself. It was my grandmother who took me aside one day and told me to begin to trust my children."

She laughed at the memory. "I remember screaming at my grandmother that things were different these days—that these were helpless infants who didn't ask to be born, and now I had such a huge responsibility to them. 'No,' my grandmother insisted. 'Don't be so arrogant! They are starlight incarnate! A flash of intelligence all their own. Your only responsibility to them is to love, feed, clothe, and nourish them. Not ask to be born? Don't make me laugh!'"

She chuckled at the memory, then looked deeply at Anna. "Soon after we stop nursing our babies, we realise that they are people. Just people, like you and me. With their own star to follow."

Anna looked at her, startled, and instantly felt freed.

"You're not responsible for everything that happens to them," Elba concluded. "That was the greatest piece of advice my grandmother ever gave to me."

Anna looked at her boys. Daniel had returned to the table and was feeding bits of meat to Cal. Blu was just sitting in his seat, smiling directly at the two women. He looked like an angel. The sun shone in the window, and Anna was transfixed by the beauty of the scene.

She looked back at Elba and said, "They're not mine."

"No. They just chose to come through you. I think my grandmother was probably right. How could they be born if they hadn't asked to be? Wouldn't make any sense." Elba stole a glance at Anna, to see what was registering with her.

Anna felt a sense of deep relief flooding through her, as she truly recognized and let go of how difficult it had been since the birth of her children. She released her growing sense of not being good enough, of doing wrong by her children, of letting them down. She allowed herself to let go of her fear of being found out to be a charlatan, who wasn't fit to be a mother at all.

"What else did your grandmother tell you about your children?" asked Anna suddenly, turning her attention back to this beautiful old woman.

"Oh, lots of things." Elba gestured with her hands. "They have a path of their own. Our only responsibility as parents is to help them to reach their potential, without trying to define it for them. After all, who are we to know the higher vision of another, or to make any judgments on it, or to put moral constraints on it? She said that we should allow them to express themselves so that when they are adults, they are confident enough to master their own lives and make manifest whatever they are here to do. Things like that: simple things, obvious things."

Anna nodded. These things didn't sound simple at all to her.

"What do you think about miscarriage, Elba? We lost two pregnancies. I'm not sure if I was too sad, or frightened, or in some way not able to be a mother to them. Why would such a thing happen to a young and healthy woman? I've racked my brains as to what I did wrong, what I had eaten, what could have happened, and why those children didn't make it. I worried for a long time that I wasn't fit to be a mother. That Nature or God or the Universe. . . or whatever. . . was trying to tell me something." Anna blurted out this fear she had held within her for a long time, but had never put into words until now.

"Oh my goodness, dear Anna!" Elba exclaimed. "It's tragic to hear you speak this way of the suffering you went through at that time. But you know, Nature or God or the Universe. . . or whatever. . . clearly decided that you'd be a beautiful mother. Look at how that was proven."

Her eyes travelled to Anna's beautiful sons. Anna's eyes followed hers, before they looked back at one another and smiled.

"Anna, I have a feeling that the souls of those babies you lost are not lost at all and are very, very close to you," Elba told her earnestly. "I have a feeling it is always the soul's choice whether to be born or not. Maybe they were just meant to come into your life for that short time to prepare you—give you a wave, say hello, kiss you from another place where you know them very, very well. Otherwise, the grief for our lost babies wouldn't be so acute, would it? I have a feeling they stay with you. Stay with this beautiful family you and Daniel have created. Did you do anything to acknowledge their short stay in this life?"

"I've a little box with my pregnancy tests and the hospital bracelet from when I had my D&C," Anna answered. "Morbid, I suppose..."

"You should plant something. Two apple trees, two rose bushes... something hardy that will last." Elba touched Anna's hand and smiled warmly at her. "You could dedicate these living things to the spirits of the babies who didn't stay here with us in this dimension at this time, but whom I have a feeling you know very well, and will meet again."

"That's very comforting, Elba, thank you. We will do that. I was so lucky. I did have my boys. My heart breaks when I hear stories about women who never go on to have children, despite years of trying and miscarriage and fertility treatment. It's all so hard to understand: why women go through so much. And the partners, too. Our second miscarriage was what was called a 'missed' miscarriage. We were sixteen weeks along... or so we thought. When the consultant looked at the scans he said, 'There's no baby growing there. At sixteen weeks, there should be a big one sloshing around in there.' Just like that. Well, Dan fainted! When we got him up off the ground, he was as white as a sheet. Poor Dan. It's so hard on men."

"What a shocking bedside manner that doctor had, Anna," Elba remarked disapprovingly.

"Yes. He did my D&C, but we found a lovely woman who delivered the two boys."

"I'd say you did!" Elba praised her. "Well done! What do men know anyway about having babies?" Elba muttered under her breath. "Men. They have to be in the middle of everything!" She laughed now and leaned her head across to touch Anna's shoulder. Anna instinctively laughed along and reached her arm around Elba's head, leaning her head in to touch hers. Then they looked at one another and smiled.

Anna looked out the large window, and saw two swans on the river. They were just gliding along, and looked as though they were effortlessly floating, even though Anna knew they were paddling furiously under the water. The sun glistened on the water, sending dancing sparkles of light across its surface. A few people had lined up alongside the river, occupying tables at the riverbank cafés. Anna suddenly felt very much a part of this scene. An active player in a beautiful afternoon.

"I think I would like to talk to Dan about trying for a girl."

Elba nodded immediately. "Yes. Girls are lovely."

After dinner, they all had coffee. Daniel asked Elba to explain the seven cycles of development to Anna, and the two women chatted happily about them for quite some time. It seemed that Anna already knew about the different colours of these chakras—he assumed she had heard about them through her yoga practice.

When Daniel came back from paying the bill, he overheard the women talking about the colors of the rainbow: seven, of course. Elba remarked to Anna, "and of course, all those colours together combine to make white. . . it's just how we appear through the 3D prism. We are really white light."

"Yes." Anna was nodding.

He might ask her later what they were talking about.

Elba walked down to their car with them. She gave the two boys a little crystal star each, telling them that they were magic stars, and that every time they had a worry, they must tell the star and allow it to take the worry to the magic star station as they slept. Here, the worry would be dealt with by the star people, who were very wise and understood little boys' fears and concerns.

She turned and handed another star to Anna. "For you, Anna. . . or, you know. . ."

Anna smiled and gave her a warm hug. "Thank you, Elba. It has been the highlight of my holiday to have met you."

Once Anna was in the car, Elba turned to Daniel. "Safe home, darling boy," she said softly.

Daniel found himself becoming unexpectedly choked up. "Thank you, Elba. I really don't know how you do it, but yet again, you've brought such order to my life. I will miss you so much. I think I'm clear on where we go from here. I have such hopes for our future. . . I'm worried though, that we won't achieve it back in reality. Everything seems so magical and possible here. But it's not the real world."

Elba squeezed his hand. "Daniel, you decide what's real. What do you want to create? That's your only question now. *The Bridge of Now*, remember?"

Daniel nodded in recognition, before suddenly remembering the fever story she had told him long ago. "Oh, Elba—I've always wanted to know. About the people with the fever. Is it the right time for you to tell me about them?"

Elba's eyes sparkled with humor. "It must be the right time, since you're asking!"

Daniel smiled wryly at her, remembering her old habit of cutting through unnecessary navel-gazing and speaking simple truths.

"After the fever had passed. . . did they create a new Atlantis?"

"No. It wasn't Atlantis or Lemuria. I believe that time is cyclical in nature. Everything that goes around comes back around. So, it's as likely that the whole story is yet to happen, as to have happened in the past. Don't worry. You'll know what to do if it comes around in your time."

"That's all I'm getting?" he asked coyly.

"That's all you're getting, darling boy," Elba answered.

They embraced, and he left.

Chapter Six

Like a miracle, she arrived. She was about to change everyone's life forever, and she seemed to know it.

Anna woke Daniel late one night, saying she thought she was in labor. They went to sit together in the kitchen. When Anna vomited up her tea, they rang Anna's sister June to come and mind the boys, while they headed to the hospital.

On examination, the midwife decided to keep her in. Three hours later, a beautiful baby girl was born. Weighing in at six pounds and five ounces, she was tiny—born two weeks early, but with that old, silent wisdom that all new babies have.

Anna was sick and sore, so Daniel sat with her into the day, mesmerized by his baby daughter and the strength of her mother. When the evening fell, a nurse came to tell him that she would be taking the baby to the nursery for the night, and that he should go and allow Anna to rest.

Daniel looked at Anna, shocked, and asked her whether he was in the way. She smiled and said no—that it had been great to have him there all day, allowing her to rest—but that she was very tired now and wanted to settle down for the night, knowing their baby was in expert hands.

He gathered his bits and pieces together and got ready to leave.

"What will we call her?" asked Daniel before he left.

"Dawn would be a nice name—and as she was born at 6 a.m., it would be apt, too! Dawn Laura Grace."

"Dawn Laura Grace," repeated Daniel.

Dawn shifted her head in the cradle, and Anna picked her up to feed her but first handed her to Daniel and asked him to give his daughter her first goodnight kiss.

"You might walk this one up the aisle, Dan. Like Jim did me. He's told me it was a very proud moment for him. Your little baby girl might one day get married," Anna said jokingly to him and emotional tears sprung into Daniel's eyes.

He lifted Dawn and whispered in her ear. "Dawn, my little lady. I promise you now that before I walk you up any aisle, I'll give you the option to abscond to the airport with me. Whoever stands at the top of any aisle waiting for you had better be the best man on the planet!" Anna squealed with laughter at hearing this and lay back into her pillow.

Daniel thought he would probably burst with happiness and pride as he left. He looked back from the door and was sure that in Dawn's profile, he caught a look of his own mother.

His heart swelled as he went out to the car to phone her.

"Mum, you've got a granddaughter."

"Oh, how fantastic. Oh my God! That is amazing news, Daniel. I'm so pleased. I hope everything went well?"

"Yes, tiring. . . and that's just me. But Anna was fabulous. I don't know how you women do it! How are you feeling? Will you be able to get down to see her? We've decided to call her Dawn. She's Dawn Laura Grace."

"Dawn is a beautiful name Daniel. And thank you so much for including her grandmothers. Oh, I'd love to see her, but I think you'd better check with Anna and let me know when she's up for a visit. I need only stay a night or two and I'll try to be helpful and stay out of the way. But maybe I could bring the boys for a walk or do something helpful for you, while the new baby is settling in?"

"I'll talk to Anna, Grandma," he joked "and I'll come back to you. Thanks."

Laura felt her heart flutter with pride and happiness as she put down the phone. A beautiful little girl—her granddaughter—had been born. She burst into tears of joy. She reflected on her own journey, and thanked heaven that things were different for Daniel than they had been for her. Hopefully, things would improve again for little Dawn.

She thought back to the woman she was when Peter had returned. The terror she had, the loneliness she felt. When the court found that he was entitled to half the value of the house in which she had raised Daniel, Laura was devastated. Of course, Peter then disappeared with a substantial sum of money, from a house she had bought and paid for, leaving her and Daniel in a rented two-bed cottage back in the village where she had been born.

She had been bitter about this for a long time, and spent days ruminating on the injustice of everything. It enraged her to think about how much had been robbed from her son and herself, for the benefit of Peter aimlessly roaming the country, pretending to be someone he wasn't.

During the course of the divorce, she found out that Peter had had two other children, with two separate women. Two girls. Daniel had two half-sisters whom Peter never thought to tell them about, and no matter how often she tried to convince the teenage Daniel that it wasn't the case, Daniel believed that Peter was living a happily-ever-after life with these two girls. He believed it was only he, Daniel, whom Peter hadn't wanted.

This belief was largely put into his head by some of his new classmates—the village curtain twitchers' children—who knew how to hurt him. She lost count of how many afternoons Daniel arrived home with knees scuffed and hair tousled, unwilling to talk to her. He would head straight to his room to recalibrate.

He did have some friends, but there was a group in school who loved to pick on him, and Laura worried that he was too sensitive to handle it. During those years, she often felt lost and hopeless: a failure. The one thing that she most wanted to avoid—the pain of her child—was happening daily in front of her eyes, and there was absolutely nothing she could do about it.

She had no friends left back in the village of her birth. Her school friends had all grown up and left, just as she had. Her father was intensely embarrassed by her marriage breakdown, and didn't really want her mixing with other people in the neighborhood. He never expressly said this to her, but she knew it in her heart.

Laura's father did have a great relationship—insofar as he was capable—with Daniel. She was grateful for that small mercy. They got on well together and seemed to understand one another. "It's not the lad's fault. None of it. Nothing is of his doing," he would say to Laura. Laura would nod, wordlessly; taking on the blame for the predicament everyone was in.

Her father even taught the young man to fish, spending weekends down the river with him while Laura seethed at home, becoming more and more distressed about the future and her plight.

During this period of her life, she couldn't understand the places she went within her mind. She knew that she was safe from Peter now, but that didn't prevent her from revisiting an old place of deep dread within herself, where she would hear the door click closed and know that she had no way of escaping the blows to come. She often relived that old feeling of having to resign herself to an excruciating fate. She supposed women were used to surrendering in the face of brute force.

She had given herself an awfully hard time over the years. Why hadn't she fought him off all those times he savaged her? Why hadn't she screamed the place down? Called the police? Reported his brutality? Gone to one of his plays and stepped up on the stage to tell the audience exactly what the star of the show was like in his own home?

Maybe because like most women, she knew she could endure. She had often survived those years by hoping that he might change.

She wondered whether she had left a part of herself in all the trauma—was she searching for reunion with aspects of her own being that had become frozen in the terror she had experienced? Was there a very scared, timid part of herself that had felt complicit in her own imprisonment? Did she blame herself? Like her father blamed her? Could she ever forgive herself?

The "you've made your bed" comment that her father made years earlier still haunted her.

She knew Peter had deliberately separated her from her many friends: punishing her for all of his own inadequacies and broken dreams. He had turned into a monster through his desire to own her, her money, her home, her body.

These experiences had taught her that the deep-down rage and shame of her gender was justified. But undeserved. Women mostly did what they had to do to survive and to keep their children safe.

She supposed she could have used the beauty of her youth to her material advantage within the patriarchal structures that existed at the time. Play the game, get the job, sleep with the boss, get the promotion, keep herself safe, turn a blind eye to the corruption. Be a bit-part player.

Was this what the suffragettes had fought for? Women in board-rooms, implementing the same tired old policies? To Laura, the whole thing seemed like such a sham.

She had chosen to leave and go it alone, with all of the pain that had ensued: a time of hardship, penny-pinching, and trying to be everything for her only child.

Could she move beyond her fear now? What opportunities had her experiences presented her with? Even when she had been at her most desolate, even when she had thought that all was lost, there had been a learning within it. Maybe everything she had been through had taught her resilience.

Having Daniel to live for had certainly been crucial to her survival at some junctures. His very presence, or his need for dinner, had brought her back from many a dark cul-de-sac within her mind.

Even in her thirties, she had known that diamonds and pearls were not found on the open road, but were found within, deep down and hidden in the darkness, where they'd been formed. She was just looking for a way to simplify herself and let go of her past.

Then, two days before Daniel's seventeenth birthday, Laura's father suddenly died. She found him when she was dropping his dinner by, sitting in his chair with a blanket over his knees: head drooped, eyes closed.

He looked as if he had simply fallen asleep after a big meal. The doctor thought he must have had a heart attack.

This seemed to jolt Laura out of her psychological self-torture. It wasn't just that she now had to organize the funeral; it was an utter shock. She realized that—as preposterous as it might seem—she had never, ever imagined that her father would die. She had genuinely never considered what she would do when her father was dead, while she was still alive.

Maybe this was because she presumed it would only happen far off into the future, when he was a wizened old man in his 90s. She had just never conceived of a time when she would be an orphan.

She had always truly felt alone in the world, but somehow, her father had been her partner in that loneliness. They had been bound together by a tragedy about which they never spoke. Their stoic, non-emotional relationship was a direct result of what was missing in their home: her mother, Emily.

Her father's funeral was small, dignified, and undemonstrative, just like the village itself. She and Daniel walked behind his coffin to the back of the church, then out into the graveyard, where they watched his casket being lowered into the ground. The villagers had come out to offer support, but Laura had a sneaking suspicion that they were just enjoying the spectacle.

Afterwards, she discovered that her father had left her not only his house, but also a large amount of money. She was floored when the solicitor told her the exact amount. Her father had never given her, nor anyone else, the impression that he had this much money. In fact, he had always been frugal and even afraid to spend what he earned.

Laura's jaw was on the floor when his solicitor read her the will.

"Where did he get all this money?"

"Well, I'm afraid I don't know the answer to that question," he answered stuffily, looking at her through round spectacles perched on the end of his nose, "but there are three accounts, the proceeds of all of which are to go to you. In the execution of my duties, this is all that is required of me. You are, of course, welcome to discuss these matters further with the bank, should you so desire." He nodded to her and closed the file, indicating to her that it was time for her to leave.

"Indeed," she replied faintly.

For the next few weeks, Laura really struggled to make sense of it all. She cried tears of frustration and shame at the memory of her sparse childhood, when she had presumed there was no money for nice things.

Her father had always given her the impression that there was no money for heat in rooms that weren't occupied. Every radiator was turned off, unless the room was in use, or somebody important was expected. The spare bedroom, the front sitting room, the hall and the landing were never heated. Every light in the house was switched off before bedtime, so that electricity and oil would not be wasted.

There was no swing or slide in her back garden. There were no treats at Christmas or birthday times. There were no cream cakes on a Friday. No holidays, no expansion, no release, no dreams of anything better. And now, she learned that her father had nearly half a million pounds in the bank?

She wondered at the mindset of a man whose life bore witness to his being a poor man, when this had never truly been the case. What lack existed within him, that he had to live such a lean life, devoid of joy and pleasures?

In any event, the death of his grandfather earned Daniel reprieve from the constant bullying he was suffering on the school bus. Word had gotten out among the local curtain twitchers that there was money in the family, and all of a sudden, Daniel was considered a cool guy.

Laura had also become a very welcome visitor to any of the shops in the town. She was greeted warmly and regaled with fond stories about her father: how he had come in here every day, stood in that very spot, and been an absolute gentleman, who always had a kind word to say about everyone. A bemused Laura was informed that her father had always considered his fellow man, had been such a stalwart of the community, that nothing had ever been too much trouble for him, and he had done such a good job raising her on his own and never looked at another woman, so devoted had he been to her mother Emily, who had been a lovely lady, even if she wasn't from around these parts.

Laura didn't recognize this man whom everyone was now pretending to have loved, but she nodded and smiled politely when she was treated to these tall tales. She agreed that it was indeed very tragic, that her father had indeed been a wonderful person, and that she would miss him dreadfully.

That much was true: she would miss him. Just his presence. Just the knowledge that while he was alive, she would always have somewhere to go. There would always be someone who was in charge.

And she would grieve. She would grieve her father's wasted life, and his unexpressed, unfulfilled potential. She would do her very best to deal with the rage she felt within.

When she went to the bank to transfer everything into her name and account, she asked the bank manager how long the money had been accruing, and whether he had any idea how her father had come to have so much.

The manager informed her that her father had always had money; he had inherited quite a sum from his own parents, and that the bank was very proud of having managed her father's affairs. Each year, he had gained interest on some very wise bonds they'd chosen for him, and they were now willing to do the same for her.

She smiled ruefully and thanked him.

Her pauper days were behind her. She returned home and turned on every radiator in the house and called the oil man to deliver a full tank. She opened the windows and let the heat out. Daniel was smirking at her childishness as she turned on every light in the house and insisted the landing light stayed on when they went to bed. Over the coming months, she often thought about what a blessing in disguise it was, that she had managed to get everything sorted out with Peter. She shuddered as she reflected on how, if they were not already divorced, she would now probably be forced to make him quite a rich man.

For some reason, she felt obliged not to sell her father's house too quickly, but she knew that she would eventually have to do it, in order to gain some measure of freedom from her past. She wasn't ready to do that at first: she thought that when Daniel finished school, it might present an opportune time for both of them to leave this sad place and create something else for their future.

She felt like a boiling cauldron of unexpressed emotions, and she wanted to give herself some time before she moved away. She was deeply conflicted between being grateful to her father for having assured her financial independence, and feeling bitter about how arid everything had been throughout her life to this point.

She couldn't help but think that she would have made better decisions earlier on in life, if she had known that she was going to inherit so much money. Which decisions they might have been, she wasn't sure, but she felt very angry that her father had never told her that her options weren't as limited as she imagined them to be.

After receiving the unexpected windfall, one of the first things she did was tell Daniel that their money worries were over. She wanted to enable him to make more imaginative plans for himself and his future. She had enough money, for example, to fund a college or university education. She had enough money to pay for his student accommodation if he wanted to move away, and enough to purchase anything else he would need.

Daniel told her that he was more relieved for her, now that she didn't have to worry so much about the future.

They had a long discussion at this time about Peter. Daniel told her that his father's absence had greatly affected him, but that her own steadfastness had always provided him with all the love and stability he needed.

He revealed that during the brief period of Peter's return—when Daniel was ten years old—he had hoped against hope that Peter held sincere intentions of being a real father to him. Deep down, however, he had sensed that this wasn't Peter's true reason for coming back. He wanted to be wrong about that: he just wanted, more than anything, to be like the other children in his school.

Peter had spent just enough time with Daniel to appear as though he wanted to establish a relationship with his son. In court, he used the time he had spent with Daniel to argue that he was entitled to half of the value of the marital home: that he needed to be able to afford a home in which he could continue to develop the relationship with his son.

Once the court granted him the money he wanted, he was gone in a flash.

Daniel looked his mother straight in the eye and said, "Peter used me, his son, to get money. Imagine. Money from you. Who had so little. I couldn't take it all in at the time, as I was so young and I didn't want to see it. But after you sold the house and he immediately disappeared. . . well, I really knew then. I just couldn't face it for a while. It was easier to blame myself—or you, for having done something to upset him."

Laura's eyes were brimming with tears as she listened to him. She remained silent and nodded, indicating to him that she understood completely what he was saying.

Daniel told her that he knew—now that he was older—that it had been neither his fault nor Laura's fault that Peter had left. He could now see that his father had had his own demons. He told her he had been thinking about how awful Laura must have felt, to have this man return and try to take away everything she'd built.

He told her that if his father's behaviour had taught him anything, it was how not to be as a man, a father, or a husband. "I promise you, Mum, that if I ever meet a woman and have children, I will never do anything like what my dad did to you and to me," he assured her.

Laura had embraced him then, overcome with pride at the thoughtful, compassionate young man she had raised.

And now, here they were. She was prouder of him than she had ever been, and couldn't wait to meet her little granddaughter. A few days with Daniel and his family was exactly the tonic she needed. She smiled to herself and decided that the very next day, she would go shopping for Dawn and pick up some little pieces of clothing for her.

She told every shop assistant she met that she had a new granddaughter. She told anyone who would listen that her son already had two sons and a beautiful wife, but wasn't there something very special about a daughter? Wouldn't it be a wonderful addition to any family to have a little girl? She ambled from shop to shop telling everybody her good news and when she got home that night, she spent hours wrapping her granddaughter's gifts and she released tears of happiness and joy.

The following week, Laura arrived at Daniel and Anna's home.

She was immediately smitten with Dawn, just as she knew she would be. She sat holding her, marveling over her sheer perfection, touching her little button nose and raising a prayer to the heavens for her. She wished her a life that was blessed. She wished her courage and tenacity. She wished her grace and ease.

She collected the boys from school, took them for ice cream, and spoke to them about how exciting it was that they now had a new baby sister they could love. She sat with them as they did their homework, and relished the beautiful feeling of relaxing in the home that Daniel had created. She was so proud of each member of this wonderful household. They were a beautiful, happy family, and this was a golden time for them.

Blu was identical to Daniel; it almost scared her at times. Sometimes, when Laura looked at him, she was transported back in time, and would have to shake herself back to the present.

Cal and Blu went everywhere together. They were the perfect counterbalancing partnership. Cal was serious and earnest, careful and methodical. Blu was a walking disaster: constantly getting himself into some scrape or another, but so funny and charming that he was inevitably able to get away with it. Together, the unlikely duo was an unstoppable team. Laura asked Anna whether they had their own language. Anna laughed and confirmed that sometimes, she thought they did.

Over the next few years, Dawn's two brothers took every opportunity to show her how deeply they adored her. They spent hours putting on shows for her in front of her high chair, and she learned to laugh by watching them play.

The little crystal star that Elba had once given to her mother went everywhere with her. She carried it like a talisman.

One day, Daniel heard Cal talking to her about the lady who had given the stars to them. He was nine years old now, and was able to tell Dawn all about the time they had gone on holidays and met a good witch. The good witch had given them all a star to take their worries away.

As he heard his son's excited chatter, Daniel thought fondly of Elba. He yearned to see her, to talk to her, or to spend time together by the river, eating the melt-in-the-mouth bread in that fabulous bakery they had visited. He would love to have another meal with her in Rolo's restaurant. He hadn't appreciated just how lucky he was to have her company every day on his old train commutes.

Youth really was wasted on the young. He smiled as he remembered this phrase that Elba had often used.

Daniel never felt more appreciated or loved during the years that followed, as his children grew and he and Anna settled into parenthood. Now that their family was complete, he progressed further through the ranks at work, by now managing a very large team.

Anna found herself rediscovering her childhood love for painting. She began attending an art class each Monday night, once Dawn had started playschool. She and the other women in the class began showing and selling their works at local fêtes in the district. Anna used an emblem of three little stars somewhere in every painting, as a signature of her work. The local newspaper did a feature on her, and all of a sudden, she began getting commissions from people to make little gifts for their loved ones.

Daniel was relieved that she seemed content.

Despite what Elba had said to him, he had always felt responsible if he thought she was unhappy. He wondered whether this was because he never quite believed that she loved him as much as he loved her. Did he believe that he wasn't good enough for her? He often felt strangely unnerved when she was happy—delighted, at first, that he had pleased her in some way, but worried that it wouldn't last and he'd have to keep upping his game. Anna wasn't demanding unreasonable things of him, he reasoned with himself, so where had this worry come from?

He sometimes thought that he might be trying to overcompensate for his own father. Maybe his father's fecklessness had made him overly cautious in the other extreme? Maybe he was just trying too hard, and judging himself by an impossible standard?

He often wished he could have another conversation with Elba about all of this.

Anna, on the other hand, was very happy. This was the most content she had ever been. She was completely oblivious to Daniel's mind wanderings. Watching her daughter growing up gave her enormous pleasure.

Dawn took part in everything. She was emotionally self-sufficient, dressed herself from the age of three, and enjoyed being alone or with other people equally.

Anna and Daniel built a fairy garden in the corner of their garden, right next to the old water pump that still sat on their property. They hoped this garden would introduce some magic into their daughter's life, but they needn't have worried—Dawn had an inherently magical way with life.

The fairy garden came to life under the protection of three large trees that provided shelter for Dawn's fairies. Anna made a sign at art class that read "Welcome to our Fairy Garden", and completed the aesthetic with some fairy doors, toadstools, and tiny picnic tables and chairs.

She and Daniel got a miniature tree trunk for Dawn to sit on when she was in the garden. Dawn insisted that they get two more for Cal and Blu, as she envisaged that they might also need to spend some time there. Anna tried to explain to Dawn that they were big boys now, so they might think that the whole fairy garden notion was silly.

"Well, Mum, that's no reason why they cannot see if they like it or not," Dawn retorted matter-of-factly. "The Easter Bunny might leave eggs there. . . and what if there was no space for the boys' eggs?"

Nobody had an answer for that conundrum. So, they got two bigger tree trunks for the boys.

Anna and Daniel picked out two apple trees for the garden, too, as Elba had once suggested to them. They decided that now was the appropriate time to plant them, in memory of their miscarriages. They positioned these commemorative trees close to the fairy garden, so that their energy would be close to Dawn.

If ever Dawn was missing for any length of time, they'd inevitably find her in her fairy garden, having long, detailed discussions with imaginary beings. Anna then worried about how she would interact with other children in school, but again, she need not have been concerned. Dawn was a natural with both fairies and people.

She enjoyed great popularity in school, as she cared deeply about her classmates. She instinctively knew when another child was unhappy or worried for some reason. Her teacher told Anna that she had a natural ability to distract and help them.

The teacher often tried to overhear conversations to ensure she was not taking on too much, but again, Dawn showed absolutely no sign of stress or overwhelm. She was adept at her classwork, sport, music, and drama. She was also ethereal: strongly connected to a different place, yet so knowledgeable about Earth's history. She listened avidly to anything she could about past kingdoms and old cultures, eager to hear as many fairy stories as her parents could make up or remember.

Dawn was brimming with innocent exuberance, and Anna sometimes felt that she just wanted her to stay that way. She didn't want Dawn to launch herself on life, only for life to let her down. She had once been told that by raising daughters, mothers got a second chance to speak with their own inner child. Raising boys was different to raising girls.

They had often talked about working with the "inner child" during yoga classes. The teacher had told them that the inner child is closely associated with the emotional body, but that she was also a wise being. Yes, she would love fairy gardens and ice cream after school, but it was also important not to patronize her.

The teacher had said to them, "she's closer to your inner core and life purpose than the persona you've cultivated in order to fit in with your social surroundings. She has the key to your ultimate healing. She's the gateway to, and the gatekeeper of, your subconscious—watching and surviving everything in childhood, long before you began to refer to the conscious mind. She knows. She will reveal her secrets and her wisdom only when she feels safe, understood, and useful to what's unfolding for you at this time."

Inner child, eh? Until Dawn arrived, Anna had no idea she even had an inner child—no idea that she liked pink and cream as a paint combination for a bedroom, for example. She had no idea that she loved little pink cushions and cuddly toy elephants dressed in tutus. But she did. She thought her inner child would be studious and nervous, as she had been. But no. It was liberating: she got to be girly, and had the perfect excuse.

Now, by going to check on her actual child—who was sitting under the tree, exclaiming loudly—she was about to find out that she, too, could talk to fairies if she wanted.

"Hi Dawn, dinner in ten minutes," she said brightly. "Are you hungry? It's getting very chilly out here."

Anna sat down opposite her daughter, on one of the boys' tree trunks.

"Yes, I am. I'm just finishing up here. I'm talking about my feelings. I have to listen until I have finished. My 'majory friends told me so, Mum."

"Imaginary, Dawn."

"Yes. 'Majory."

"They give you good information, good advice?" Anna humored her.

"Well, they're not really living here like we do, so they say different types of things. They tell me not to worry, to mind nature and then nature will mind me. We don't always talk. Sometimes we just laugh and play. Sylvia the big tree fairy minds us all."

"That's lovely, Dawn. And it's time well spent, let me tell you."

"Mum, you can come here if you're ever sad or worried." Dawn's little face was deeply earnest as she addressed her mother. "Even if I'm not here or I'm busy at school. The 'majory friends told me you can; they say that sometimes you seem sad, but you shouldn't be. They said to tell you don't be embarrassed to speak to them, even if you can't see them and you only see trees. They said that you're a very lucky person."

Anna smiled. "Dawn, you're very kind to let me have access to your friends like that! Thank you."

"But you're my mother. I'd share everything with you. You gave me my magic star and it was the star that brought me out here one day to meet the 'majory people. They have stars too."

"They have stars?"

"Yes, of course! We all have stars, Mum," Dawn chided her.

"Oh. . . well, will they talk to me if I don't have a star?"

"Yes, because you gave me mine and you always put them in your paintings. You believe in stars. They see you looking at the sky."

"A very special friend of your daddy's gave those three stars to us, Dawn. She handed one each to the boys, and gave one to me. I knew it was for you."

"Oh yes, the good witch. Why didn't she give it straight to me?"

"Oh, you weren't born yet," Anna said, then smiled at Dawn's astonished expression. "But I think the lady knew you were coming to us. She was a very wise, clever and kind old lady. She was 'majory in her own way."

"I would like to meet this woman, Mum. I think I would get on very well with her. It's not many old people believe. . . you know. . . in magic. My teacher doesn't. She says fairies and magic don't exist. She's wrong though, but I don't tell her."

"Maybe you will meet Elba one day, Dawn. Maybe we will all see her again someday."

Anna shuddered. "Come on in, Dawn. It's getting cold now. Say goodnight to the fairies."

The next day, while Dawn was at school, Anna was at the kitchen sink, gazing out at the fairy garden corner. She was sure she could see something twinkling.

"Twinkle, twinkle, little star. . . how I wonder what you are. . ." she hummed to herself, then dried her hands and walked out towards the little magic corner.

It was a cold spring morning, and she soon realized that the twinkle she had seen was the snowdrops that they had planted last year. The tiny flowers had sprung up, seemingly overnight, in little clumps that had caught her eye.

Anna smiled to herself, noting her disappointment that the place wasn't strewn with stars from the 'majory people. She sat down on Cal's tree stump and leaned back against a tree. She closed her eyes to rest and soon fell into a dream.

Chapter Seven

In Anna's dream, a beautiful woman walked towards her out of a background of slowly-swirling mist. She wore a deep purple and violet hooded cloak, lined with silver, that seemed to flow from her. It shimmered like a reflection on water. Anna noticed that the cloak was fastened with a pearl and turquoise silver buckled brooch, just above the woman's heart. The woman's dark auburn hair was long, escaping out of either side of her hood to frame her face.

The woman looked straight at Anna; her eyes were hypnotic and drew Anna in, like deep pools of love. The woman stretched out her hands, and instinctively, Anna reached out to hold them. Their grasp was gentle but secure. The woman smiled; a smile that evoked such a feeling of safety in Anna's heart that she didn't care that she could not feel any ground beneath her feet.

"Look," the woman said gently, nodding to Anna's left. Anna looked around and saw the moon, hanging right beside her in space. It was so close to her that if she had wanted to let go of the woman's hand, she could easily have touched it. Up close, it was silver, not grey. It seemed to be lit from within, like a gigantic light bulb, reflecting the light of the sun. It didn't hurt the eyes to look at and Anna stared into it for some minutes.

It had a magnetic pull and pulse emanating from its inner core that felt so familiar to Anna. It was like a tide; pulsing towards her, then away from her, until she found her own body reacting in unison with it. She closed her eyes, relaxing into the sensation.

Suddenly, she found herself walking barefoot on soft grass. Her feet were cushioned by warm moss, and as she looked around, she was awe-struck to behold an idyllic countryside scene that stretched before her for miles. She could see the horizon off in the distance beyond acres and acres of rolling grassland and colourful fields. The beautiful woman was gone, but Anna did not feel alone.

The expanse before her held the most stunning array of trees and flowers Anna had ever seen. The soft warm light of the sun fell upon her shoulders, making her feel very warm and comfortable.

She noticed that about a mile into the distance stood an enormous rock. It looked out of place in the middle of the rolling flatlands and large expanse, yet it was inexorably drawing her towards it.

As Anna came closer to the mysterious rock, she witnessed a lot of mayhem taking place at its base. She quickly took refuge behind a nearby tree, peering out to assess what was going on and decide whether or not she should get involved.

From this perspective, she could see people milling around the base of the rock, throwing grenades and other war time devices, fighting with one another and screaming battle cries. Many people were wearing full chainmail battledress, carrying swords and shields, and some were on horseback. A number of people were trying to scale the rock, but kept slipping back down.

In the bizarreness of her dream state, Anna also saw another group of people with clipboards tucked neatly under their arms. Many of them were sitting on stacks of folders, and surrounded by filing cabinets that had been crammed full of papers. These people, too, were shouting at the top of the rock, trying to get the attention of whatever was up there.

Her eyes slowly travelled up the rock, and she could now see that from this ancient stone bloomed a large castle. It had at least thirteen storeys, and was immense. She could see that the castle must be inhabited—she noted a few candles burning in the windows—but she couldn't see anyone moving about inside.

She didn't want to draw attention to herself, but she could see that a little further ahead of her, there was another, larger tree. If she could make it that far, she might be able to make more sense of what was happening. Slowly, she crept forward, willing herself not to make any noise or alert the warriors or the strange office people to her presence.

Once she made it to the next tree, she was able to gain a much better sense of the sheer size of the castle, and what was going on around it. Everybody wanted to gain access. They wanted to elicit some response from its inhabitants. Her gaze again travelled up the rock that morphed into the castle, then moved up further, to take in the castle itself.

At the very top of the castle, below the battlements, there was a massive round room. She could see, from the light in the windows encircling the space, that these were all windows of the same room. She supposed that there were other windows of the same circular room on the opposite side of the castle, but she couldn't see them from this vantage point.

In the very instant that she realized and decided this in her mind, Anna was transported to the interior of this very special round room.

Yes, there were twelve windows, six on either side—this was the first thing she noticed when she got her bearings. In front of her was a large stone fireplace, bookended by two large candelabras. The candles were lit, emitting a strong but soft glow. To the left of the fireplace, there stood a small doorway.

Even though it had been warm outside, the fire, too, was lit; red, orange and violet flames danced around a large wooden log, continually forming new shapes and rhythms. The effect was mesmerizing. Anna stood and watched the flames move for quite some time.

Then she noticed an enormous gold gilt mirror positioned over the fireplace. Some ornate writing had been inscribed on the wall above the mirror, near the ceiling.

Slowly, she walked over to the first window and looked out at the landscape before her. It was enchanting: like something a Renaissance painter would portray. Suddenly, she remembered the hullabaloo she had seen at the base of the rock.

She peered downwards, straining a little to see the scene below her. Sure enough, even though this was the opposite side of the rock to that from which she'd approached, there were large crowds gathered at the base of the rock, seeking her attention. She locked eyes with a young man, along with many of his followers, and instinctively shook her head and mouthed "no." She held her face expressionless.

With that, she averted her gaze and moved slowly to the second window.

The view was slightly different here, and the people at the base of the rock were slightly different too. They seemed to be from a different era—their clothes were unlike those worn by the first group, and they seemed to want something different from her than the other group had. Again, she caught the eyes of the people who seemed to be leading this group, and again, she shook her head and mouthed "no."

She moved on to the third window and did the same thing, then again at the fourth window.

She had no idea what she was doing, but she noticed that the people were beginning to walk away and fade into the landscape. This left the base of her rock clear, and the muck and dirt that had been created by the crowds gradually began to give way to soft new grass and meadow flowers of many different varieties and colours. They were sprouting before her eyes and making her heart sing.

She was now near the back of the room, at the fifth and sixth window. The sun was warm, shining in on her face but she did the same thing again. She engaged the people with her eyes, mouthed "no," and moved on, freeing the people to leave, and freeing her to be in control of her time in this sacred space.

She got a sense that had she started to engage any of these people outside, they would have returned fire, there would have been more trouble, and she would have brought it on herself. Here, she was safe. She had noted from the outside that there was no way in—no matter what the various groups of people were trying, none of them were gaining access.

This awareness spurred her on to finish the twelve windows and clear the territory around the castle, so that she could be at peace.

It was as if word had spread at the base of the rock. By the time she arrived at the ninth window, people were already beginning to walk away. She looked back into the room, and for the first time, noticed that a large chair was positioned in the very centre of the room. It was a silver velvet chair with elaborate beading on the feet and legs, and it looked like the most comfortable chair she had ever seen. She knew it was for her.

A low table had been placed at each side of the chair. She couldn't quite make out what was on them, but she decided there and then that as soon as she was finished clearing the land, she would sit and watch the fire.

The eleventh window was the window where she had seen the people with the files and filing cabinets. Now, there was nobody there. She watched as the files melted into the earth below, giving way to a beautiful burst of colourful flowers. The warriors she had seen at the twelfth window were also gone; in their place stood only the horses, grazing on the lush grass.

Satisfied, she moved to the centre of the room and sat down on her chair. It immediately enfolded her, as though it had been made for her. She looked at the low table to her right, and saw that her favourite meal of patatas bravas, soft broccoli and succulent chicken was right there, waiting for her.

As she began to eat it, she could taste each bite: the picante sauce was the perfect strength, and she had never tasted anything so good. She sipped on a delicious drink that had also appeared on the table, and her tastebuds sang. She finished the entirety of her meal, then turned to the low table to her left.

On it was an embroidery piece that she must have started at some point, and was now halfway through. She picked it up and saw that the picture she was embroidering was that of a phoenix. "Ah," she thought aloud, remembering an old Cervantes quote she loved. "The phoenix

Hope can wing her way through the desert skies, and still defying fortune's fate, revive from the ashes and rise."

She looked directly into the fire and thought about the symbology of the phoenix, and how fitting it was for her now, that having sent her enemies home and called a truce with those who would do her harm, this was what she was engaged with for the day. She spent some time winding spools of thread into the orange, purple, gold and red of the phoenix. A long period of restful time passed, until she was almost finished.

She noticed that the fire needed some more wood, so she looked around for some fuel. She saw some down to the right of the fireplace and got up to put it on the fire. Her eyes looked up the wall, where she had glimpsed the inscription earlier. Now, she read:

You Own and Master a Sovereign Space into which No One Can Intrude. You Are The Beloved Daughter of an Ancient Peace You Can Never Lose.

As she moved to refuel the fire, Anna's eyes fell upon her form in the mirror. She was unsurprised to see, reflected back at her, the beautiful face of the woman in the cloak.

She awoke with a start. Befuddled as she was to find herself back in the fairy garden, she immediately jumped up and walked back to the house. She entered the kitchen and quickly looked around to find a pen and paper. "You own. . . and master. . . a sovereign space. . . you are the daughter of. . . oh!. . . of an ancient peace. . ."

She continued to think about the dream all afternoon, even as she was picking up the children from school. It had all felt so real to her. The woman. Her cloak. The moon. The rock and the castle. The round room. The mirror. The chair. The food. My God, she could still taste the food!

When Daniel came home from work, she told him all about it over dinner, and asked him what he thought.

"I think you're being asked by your subconscious to check your boundaries and pull your power back into yourself and rest," he said gently. He then asked her whether he had ever told her about the advice Elba had given him on boundaries.

"No, I don't think so," she replied.

Daniel went to put on the kettle, trying to recall exactly what Elba had once said to him.

He could well remember that morning on the train. He had been telling Elba about how he had overstretched himself with his plans for the weekend. He had promised one friend that he'd go to an event with him, and had promised his boss that he would do something else. The problem was that even though he would prefer to go with his friend, he felt that he'd better do what his boss wanted.

He allowed himself to drift down memory lane for a while, thinking back on the conversation he and Elba had shared that morning. . .

Elba asked him to think of all the people with whom we interact every day. "People on this train, on buses, in shop queues. Some people we don't even see, don't notice, and don't interact with. But our energy lines criss-cross over and back. We meet."

She had smiled at him and continued. "Then, there are the people with whom we actually do interact. We talk, smile, exchange gifts and loving embraces. This group comprises the people we nod a cursory nod at, to those with whom we share meals. From the people on our street to our close, intimate relationships—our parents, our lovers, our children, our siblings, our friends. The interactions between us and them all are very varied."

"The group that are made up of who I call the 'garden wall' people, are the ones we speak to over the fences. They see our heads. We pull into our driveways, they're in their front garden and we can't avoid interacting with them in some way. These are 80% of all our human interactions."

"Now, in this precise situation, we can pretend we're on our phones, avoid their eyes, make no connection, or we can shoot them a wave of acknowledgment, gesture to the phone—implying the imaginary conversation—and move to the safety of our own home. Or we can genuinely be delighted to see them, hop out of our car, engage them, have a lovely friendly chat over the fence, discuss many issues. . . even sit on the wall, talking with them for hours. You can have hundreds of relationships like this."

"Secondly, there are the 'kitchen table' people. These are the people who see more of you than your upper body!" Elba chuckled. "They can even be the 'garden wall' people who you've invited into the heart of your home, to sit down as equals at your table. They've qualified as closer than just acquaintances. You see more of them. You see their heart and their power center and they see yours. You know who they are and they know you. They bring gifts, food, and companionship. You value them. There is a bond, a relationship, an ebb and flow between you."

"These are your friends, your family, your trusted advisors, and confidantes, and they reflect back to you what you give to them. These form 20% of your human interactions and relationships."

"Lastly, there are the 'fireside' people: the special people; the ones who know you intimately. They share your inner world, they know everything about you, and they often know you better than you know yourself. They love you in spite of your faults and failings. They may even love you because of your faults and failings, as you perceive them. You can fall asleep in front of your 'fireside' people, and they won't be offended. They won't judge you; they won't change the channel on your TV, they won't spill red wine on your white carpet, nor will they tell you if they don't like your curtains. They won't lie across your couch, leaving no room for you. They won't stub their cigarettes out on your cushions. They will never tell you that the flowers in your vase are past their best!"

Daniel had laughed out loud at this, and Elba winked at him. He couldn't help but wonder where the old woman was going with her tale.

She continued, "These relationships form a minute fraction of the relationships you will have on this journey, in this plane of existence. If you can count five 'fireside' people in a long lifetime, you are a very lucky person."

"Problems occur in our lives when we have 'garden wall' or 'kitchen table' people in our fireside room. Sometimes, people just barge their way in—they bypass the kitchen table initiation and protocol entirely, and just move themselves in. They have opinions on everything. They sit and pontificate and make us feel worse. We think they're right and we're wrong—because they act as if they're right and we're wrong! They feel entitled to voice their opinions and demand that you serve them in some way. We feel hollow around them—very aware that our boundaries are out of kilter."

"Sometimes, though, we invite these people in. Sometimes, we deeply admire these people. They're our gurus. Our teachers. Maybe even our boss!"

She had looked up at him at this point, and he smiled. He always knew that Elba's stories would help him in some way with a current predicament.

"We apply great weight to their opinions," she went on. "Their opinion of us is important—too important, maybe. We can even define our opinion of ourselves by our perception of what we think they think of us. . . as opposed to knowing that their opinion of us is none of our business! We move the fireside room furniture around, so it will look the way the guru wants it to. We change our curtains because the guru doesn't like them. We change the colour of the carpet, throw out our little side table that was such a comfort to us, remove our old comfy cushions that had formed the perfect shape for our bodies. . . all in case the guru thinks they're shabby."

"After some time, we realize that we don't recognize this fireside room anymore. It's full of strangers. It's no longer our safe place, or our inner sanctum. It has been invaded by gurus. Whose fault do you think this is, Daniel?"

"The gurus?"

"No. Of course it isn't the gurus' fault! Gurus just do what gurus do! It's our own fault. The gurus were only ever supposed to pass by at the end of our streets. We were only supposed to give a cursory nod to them, but now, instead, they've moved in. Don't complain about someone burning your house down, if you were the one who invited them in and gave them firelighters, Daniel!"

Now, Daniel looked at his wife and smiled. When he recalled a conversation with Elba, he always strangely felt as if he'd met her again. It was almost as if reliving the memory of being with her brought her closer to him in his current space. She had such a wonderful aura about her.

"It took me a while to understand what she was saying, Anna. But she was right. I reassessed all of the relationships I had at that time. Garden wall, kitchen table and fireside. I became much more discerning about whom I allowed into my kitchen, let alone my fireside room. In fact, that room was empty for a long time, until I met you. I watched my own awareness and didn't make a big drama out of it. It was an internal change: I didn't have to issue any eviction notices or cause any disruption."

"What did you do about the weekend?" Anna asked him.

"I told my boss that I had some plans I'd forgotten about, but had made a commitment to. He was fine with that—there was no problem at all. The problem was within me."

"How interesting," Anna mused. "So, who would be your fireside people now?"

"You, the children, Mum—that's it for now. My kitchen table is full of healthier relationships and my front garden is chock-a-block with lovely people."

He smiled at her and they sat in easy companionship.

"She's a little genius, that woman, isn't she?" Anna laughed.

"That she is, Anna," he replied warmly. "The great Eusebia Sylvia Elba."

They both sat in quiet reflection for a while, feeling a renewed sense of respect for their sovereignty in their own inner place of power and peace.

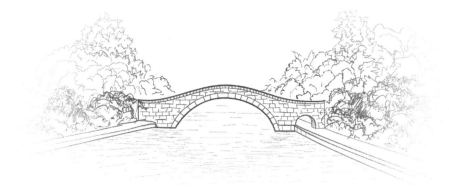

Chapter Eight

Just as he had once told Laura, Daniel had known from a very young age that if he was ever going to be a father, he wanted to be the best father he could possibly be. He remembered the anticipation that had crept over him every birthday, every Christmas, every Easter. He had always hoped against hope that his dad might come home.

In Daniel's imaginings, his dad would show up, collect him from school and take him to play football in the park. They would eat ice-cream, go for burgers and chat about manly things. Daniel would forgive his dad for not having been around when he was younger, and they would just look forward to the future and be friends. He wouldn't ask him where he'd been during his time away, or how he felt about his mum.

They would plan camping trips away, and his dad would teach him how to kayak. Maybe they would even climb a mountain together, or go for long treks. They would spend weekends camping. They would gather wood and set a campfire and roast delicious marshmallows above the flames.

He now knew, of course, that being a father involved so much more than that. It wasn't all about treats and days out. It was about love and consistency—neither of which his father had seemed capable of delivering.

Daniel could vividly remember the fateful day Peter had come back, when he was a young, impressionable, and hopeful ten-year-old.

He had been astounded to catch sight of his father at the door, talking to his mother. He was too shy to approach them directly, so he hung back, watching them from the top of the stairs. He couldn't make out what they were saying, but when the conversation ended, he could tell that his mother wasn't happy by the way she was breathing and standing with her back up against the door.

His dad had gone, but he asked Laura to arrange for them to meet. He would wait.

About a week later, he saw his mother crying in the kitchen. He hated it when she cried. He knew, from past experience, that it was probably about money and not having enough. He was well accustomed to thinking of ways he could ask for less from her. He knew that his life was different from the life of other boys in his class, but he also knew that his mother was the best, and he'd prefer to be here with her, than to live at Luke's or Michael's house... even though they both had dads as well as mums.

"Why are you crying, Mum? What's wrong? Can I help you?" he asked, a little anxiously.

Laura shook herself as soon as she saw him. She hurriedly wiped away her tears and smiled. "Oh no, darling; it's good news. Really. Your dad wants to arrange to see you, and the intermediary man I was telling you about thinks it's a good idea, too."

Daniel's eyes lit up. "Oh wow, Mum, that is the best news ever! I'll see him and maybe he can help us... you know, with money and everything. I'll talk to him. He's a famous actor."

"We are okay for money, Daniel. We have enough. But yes, it would be good for you and your dad to spend some time together now and get to know one another."

"So why were you crying? Were you crying?"

"Yes. Sometimes mothers cry." She smiled again and brightly added, "but it's nothing to worry about. We always feel better after a good cry. We're funny like that!"

Laura couldn't help but resent Peter, with every fiber of her being, when he came to take Daniel out the following week. She was expected to dress and hand over her sweet, impressionable little boy to this monster, who hadn't cared for years whether they'd sank or swam without him.

She knew, in her heart of hearts, that Peter was back for one reason, and one reason only: to get something. He wouldn't care that divorce would leave her and Daniel in a very precarious position, because over the previous few years, he had demonstrated, over and over again, that he cared about nobody but himself.

He arrived at the exact time he was supposed to. He looked superb: his hair and face were clean and shining, and he was beaming a big broad smile across that gorgeous face that Laura just wanted to smack.

Nevertheless, she opened the front door, and Daniel walked out in front of her to stand before his father. The excited, hopeful look on his face almost broke her heart.

"Hello, Dad," he said quietly. The butterflies in his tummy were nearly too much for him. His joy at finally seeing his father—there to pick him up and take him out, at long last, just as he had always yearned for—was too much for him to bear. He couldn't contain himself. He rushed forward to hug Peter, who immediately lifted him up and swung him around, laughing heartily.

Laura felt as though she was about to vomit on the spot. She didn't think she would be able to stop herself. She leaned her hand up against the doorframe to steady herself and hoped the nausea would pass. She could feel the beginnings of that rash on her neck that showed up when she was distressed and always gave her away, so she turned to go back inside.

Peter placed Daniel back on the ground and casually said, "Thanks, Laura. See you later. We'll be back at 6 p.m." With that, he ushered Daniel down the narrow driveway and through the little gate. Laura didn't trust herself to say anything in response. For Daniel's sake, she had wanted to say, "Have a great time." But the words refused to form in her mouth.

She went inside, taking some deep breaths and trying her best to calm herself. She put her two hands to her neck and breastbone to try to calm the angry rash, and stared into her own eyes in the hall mirror. She had prepared for this moment. She had a number of ingredients laid out in the kitchen, so she could immediately start baking bread and cakes for the afternoon. She wanted to keep herself busy and focused. Daniel would only be gone for a few hours. . .

Fears swirled through her head as she baked. She couldn't help feeling terrified that Peter might harm Daniel, just to hurt her. Maybe he would kidnap him and take him away, and she would never see her son again.

Maybe she should just pretend that it was okay for Peter to move back into the house. Then at least she would know where Daniel was at all times, and wouldn't have to worry about him disappearing.

She knew, deep down, that her fears were irrational, and that Peter had no real interest in Daniel. The last thing he would want to do was run away with him. That would leave him with far too much responsibility on his hands, and would certainly cramp his style.

She put the bread into the oven and continued making the little cakes, still making a conscious effort to breathe as deeply as she could.

Daniel, meanwhile, was having a great time. All of his carefully planned dreams were coming true. Peter had taken him to a pub restaurant down the road from home, where Daniel had always watched happy families having lunch and playing in the grounds, wistfully, and wishing it was him. It was wonderful.

Peter told him he could have whatever he liked, so he ordered an enormous burger with onion rings and chips and a variety of sauces. His father told him all about how it felt to be on stage: how amazing it was when the big light shone on you, and you couldn't see the audience properly but you knew they were there. It was exhilarating, he said, and Daniel thought to himself that this was a great word, and sounded like a great feeling to have. He could imagine how his father must feel, being a great actor.

After Daniel finished his burger, Peter bought him a huge ice cream sundae. Then they went to play pool in one of the smaller side rooms off the main restaurant—Peter showed Daniel how to chalk and hold a cue, explained the rules to him, and they were off.

They laughed and joked together for a long time. Peter told Daniel that he was quite a pool player, and that he would be able to make a great amount of money from being the best little pool player in town. He said they could tour the pubs of the area and hustle all the other pool players out of a lot of money. Daniel knew he was joking, but he laughed along, bursting with pride to think that he had been successful at the very first thing he'd done with his dad.

Many of the other men in the restaurant seemed to know his dad. They kept nodding at him and asking him how he was. Daniel was deeply proud to be there with him. His father was a famous actor—that must be how everybody knew him.

When he got back home, Peter left him at the gate, then he walked up the driveway alone and knocked on the door.

Laura had been waiting at the other side of the door, but didn't open it for a few moments. She wanted to make it seem as though she had been doing something other than peering through the curtains, waiting for them to round the corner. As soon as she opened the door, Daniel waved goodbye to his dad and scooted in past her and straight up the stairs.

Laura didn't look at Peter as he nodded curtly at her, then left. She just couldn't.

Daniel was very excited that evening, telling her that he loved being with his dad. She didn't ask him where they had gone or what they had done. Daniel told her that they'd had a great time, his eyes were shining with joy, and that was good enough for her. He was thrilled that she had baked the bread and cakes he liked—exclaiming that all of his favourite smells were in the house now, but that he was too full to eat.

He ran back to his room, still in a state of high excitement. When Laura next saw him a short while later, he was fast asleep. She stood in the doorway for a long time—feeling a lump in her throat—and watched him sleep.

Two days later, she got a letter from her solicitor, agreeing the terms by which her son would see his father: twice a week for the next four months, then for overnight stays every second weekend.

Her solicitor had initially objected to this, but ultimately ended up telling her that there was no basis for her to refuse Peter's demands. These were his rights as father to his child. Peter's solicitor argued that his client had been requesting a reconciliation with Laura, but that his efforts had been dismissed out of hand.

Laura had no choice. She had to agree to everything until she got Peter out of her hair.

Peter continued to show up on time for his appointments with Daniel. Daniel loved telling his friends all about his adventures with his dad, and soon began to make up elaborate stories about what they had gotten up to. His friends were enthralled by his stories of abseiling and rock climbing and making preparations for upcoming summer camping expeditions.

In reality, they had never got any further than the pub. They didn't always eat. Sometimes Peter had already eaten before he arrived to pick up Daniel. On those days, Daniel got a basket of sausage and chips to snack on while they played pool. Then, as the weeks went by, his father started playing pool with the other men, winning all the money that they gambled.

Daniel was too young to play darts, but his dad seemed to be a champion darts player, as he won all of his darts games, too. Peter's darts games in the pub became a regular routine, with all of the local men waiting for him to arrive so that they could try their luck against him. At first, Daniel loved admiring Peter's darts prowess, but after a while he began to feel left out.

His mother began mentally preparing him for the upcoming overnight stays with his dad, saying that the court—the intermediary man she had referred to before—would make sure he had a safe place for Daniel to sleep. She told him that while his home would always be with her, maybe over time he could have two homes: one with her and one with his dad.

Laura had to admit to being very impressed with Peter's scrupulous timekeeping, even though she still loathed him and resented having to dance to his tune with regard to Daniel. She still suspected his motives were not as honorable as he was keen to show the court.

Daniel soon became a bit distant towards her when it came to Peter, and didn't want to speak to her about what he did with his dad. So, she just decided she would just take a watching brief. Though she would have loved to be proven wrong, she still felt, deep in her bones, that this would all end in tears for Daniel. She wanted to be there to catch his fall.

Before long, the separation agreement came through. Peter was granted half of the value of the family home and joint custody of his son. It was then that Laura found out that he had two other dependents; two girls, with three years between them. Peter was currently living with the mother of his youngest daughter and was—by all accounts—the model father.

Laura's world came crashing in around her. Joint custody? Was the court so gullible? She couldn't believe that Peter was coming back into Daniel's life with a ready-made family, and a sister he could visit every second weekend. When she read about the two other children, she came out in that rash on her neck again. The fear that overcame her took her by surprise. Was he planning to seduce Daniel to go and live with him and his ready-made family? Was he really going to try to take Daniel? Had this been his plan all along?

Why had he been pretending that he wanted reconciliation with her, if all the time he had another woman and child with whom he was residing? Her solicitor surmised that maybe, once Peter had realised that she wouldn't countenance taking him back, he felt he needed to use another angle with the court. Well, she'd fight him all the way, to keep Daniel.

He needn't think he was going to get away with this! She was ready for war, if that was what he was declaring. Her heart was racing as she left the solicitor's office.

When she got home, she closed the front door and made her way shakily to the kitchen table and sat down heavily. Then, she just broke down in tears and cried for a long time. The stress of the previous years finally tumbled out of her. She felt very alone and scared.

Laura seethed over her ex-husband's duplicity, and her powerlessness in the face of it, but she voiced none of this to Daniel. She wanted, above all else, to put him first.

The following Sunday, they both waited for Peter to arrive. Laura's concern mounted as the scheduled time for Peter's arrival came, then went. She tried, at first, to reassure Daniel—telling him that his father might have gotten delayed, or was perhaps stuck in traffic, but she was sure he would be with them soon.

They waited for over an hour.

Daniel slowly limped up the stairs to his room when it became obvious that Peter wasn't coming. Laura rapped on his door and tried to talk to him, but he tersely said that he was okay and didn't want to talk. The next day, he told his school friends that his dad had been called away to star in a very special film, and would soon be a famous Hollywood film star.

It was then that everything changed in Daniel's young life. Laura sold the house she had bought when she was 26 and she moved home to a rented two-bed forestry worker's cottage in the village where she had been born. Daniel felt confused and hurt but glad of the omnipresent company of his mother.

Peter was given two weeks to come and collect the items he had left there years before, but he never turned up to collect them. The one thing he hadn't forgotten to leave with the solicitors was his bank account information.

Now that he had his own family, Daniel was determined to be there for his children as much as he could. He knew the damaging effect his father's absence had had on his own self-esteem, and his ability to feel the same as his peers.

He made an effort to attend every one of his children's football matches and basketball games and school plays and choirs. Any time he wasn't able to make it, the absence weighed heavily on him. He told his children that it would always be the exception, rather than the rule, if he were unable to make it to one of their events.

He often spoke to Anna about his fears. She tried to calm him down: telling him that there was no such thing as a perfect father, and all he had to do was his very best. She loved her husband's earnest nature, but she could also see the stress he put himself under, trying to be all things to all people. The perfect son to Laura, the perfect husband to her and the perfect father to the children. These, after all, were his 'fireside people', she reasoned with him. They loved him anyway. She expressed this to him as well as she could, thanking him for providing a loving and safe home for the children and assuring him that their children were secure and weren't judging him. The only judgment of him was coming from himself.

Anna had experienced what would have been considered a very traditional upbringing by comparison, with both of her parents present in the home.

Her parents loved one another very much, and everyone in the house felt it. They were on the same page about most things, so there were seldom arguments or raised voices in her home.

Anna's sister June was seven years her senior, and had adored her when she was a baby. After tea, she would take baby Anna into the sitting room, play with her and sing to her. As she grew into a toddler and went on to start school, June would teach her about everything she herself was learning.

She would read to Anna from her books and help her with her homework to such an extent that Anna ended up being academically far ahead of other children in her class.

June showed her how to draw maps of countries and taught her the correct flag for each one. June told her which languages different people spoke, and what their cultures were like. As a result, Anna was able to read and understand words way beyond her age range, and could do sums she wouldn't have been expected to do, while other children in her class were still struggling with the concept of tens and units on the abacus.

June wanted to be a teacher, and Anna desperately wanted to please her older sister, so she worked hard to remember everything June imparted to her and what she most wanted was to be a good student. Their mother, Grace, let them get on with things and didn't see anything wrong with June's behavior until, one spring, she attended a meeting with Anna's teacher.

The teacher was concerned that little Anna could read the time and draw maps and knew flags. At first, Grace thought the teacher was being a little over dramatic when she raised her eyebrows disapprovingly at Grace and said, "We must allow the children to be children." Surely it was a good thing that her Anna was so academically gifted?

But the teacher's words and facial expression stuck with her, so she decided to keep an eye on June and Anna over the Easter holidays. She noticed that at the end of each week, June was setting tests for Anna, which alarmed her somewhat. She decided to talk to her eldest daughter one night after Anna had gone to bed.

"June," she began gently, "I don't think that Anna needs to know all of the things that you're learning just yet. She's only six years old and really doesn't need to know yet about all of the things you know. She probably can't grasp the concepts that you can grasp."

"She can, Mum. Anna is very bright and she needs to be challenged, so that she can reach her full potential." June was very firm and matter-of-fact as she said this. It struck Grace—as she examined the deeply serious expression on June's face—that her eldest daughter already looked every inch the stern school teacher.

"June, she's six," she pressed on. "She has plenty of time to learn all that you know, and you have plenty of time to learn all that your teachers know. There is a reason that each class learns different things. You should spend the summer time outside with friends, and not be cooped up in the house, studying and setting tests for her."

June looked unconvinced, but Grace's voice was kind as she went on. "She needs to breathe. And so do you, little one. Next year is a big jump for you—you'll be learning foreign languages and sciences, and Anna will not be able to keep up with you. She just wouldn't be able to. Not at six."

June thought about this and grudgingly decided that her mother might be right. She let Anna know that they would be taking a break for the summer and that in the autumn—when she was going on to the big school—she would fill her in on anything that she thought Anna might need to know. Anna was disappointed, but asked June whether she would still read to her at night. June said she would. . . but she didn't.

That summer, June discovered friends and boys. She spent entire days hanging around at the local shopping precinct with other teenagers, laughing, and joking. Anna missed her deeply.

When June came home, Anna would show her what she had been reading or writing during the day, but June was no longer interested. She made only vague, non-committal noises by way of response to Anna's excited rambles, and gave her younger sister the impression that she was tired of speaking to her. It was as if a light switch had been turned off. Anna began to fear that June didn't care about her anymore.

Grace saw what was happening and tried to talk to June about it. But over the course of that summer, June had changed. She had lost interest in what was going on at home, and only wanted to be out with her friends.

Jim told Grace not to worry about it. He commented that Anna was still a child, while June was growing up. Some parting of the ways was inevitable, but they would come back together in time. As parents, they just had to let their daughters get on with it. It had been happening since time immemorial, and they weren't going to be able to change it, he said.

Grace would sit with Anna, read to her, and draw pictures with her, but she knew it wasn't her company that Anna was craving. She noticed during this time that Anna was a lovely artist—she could draw horses and dogs in perfect proportion, and was extremely talented. She praised her and tried to encourage her away from books and into creative play; she hung Anna's pictures on the fridge and on the walls and framed a few to try to convince her how beautiful she believed the drawings and paintings to be, but Anna didn't seem to notice.

Over the next few years, June became something of a problematic teenager. She was caught smoking in school, was apprehended by security guards for shoplifting, and stole alcohol from her parents' drink cabinet. She often sneaked out of her bedroom window to meet her friends, and was brought home by the police on more than one occasion.

One night when she was sixteen years old, she tried to steal her parents' car and crashed it into the pillar at the gateway. Her parents were at a loss as to how to control her. She was always in trouble at school, and with neighbours and she was barred from the shopping precinct at which she loved to hang out.

Anna noticed that her mother would often cry, and knew that she was crying over June. Jim often lectured June about her behavior in the living room, while Anna sat in the kitchen with her mother, wondering what had happened. During that turbulent year, Grace taught Anna how to bake and cook.

June completely stopped talking to Anna after a while. Anna felt very rejected and unloved by her sister, and couldn't understand what she'd done wrong.

She continued to stay at the top of her class in school, and would go to the library on the way home to gather books on things that she knew June was learning. She still hoped that June would reengage with her one day soon, and wanted to make sure she would be ready to have an informed conversation with her when that time came.

When June entered her senior years in school, she began to apply herself more seriously to getting good grades, as she still wanted to become a teacher. However, she held the house to ransom in the evenings, banging doors and loudly bemoaning how stressed she was, how difficult her exams were, and how nobody understood her. Anna, Jim, and Grace walked around on tiptoes around her, and when she went to teacher training college at eighteen, the whole house seemed to exhale an enormous sigh of relief.

By then, Anna had started secondary school. She was the total opposite of June. She didn't find puberty as stressful as June had, and held a deeply earnest desire never to make her mother cry. She was quiet and reserved, with few friends, and was very studious.

Her grades were never as good as they should have been, given how devoted she was to her studies. During exams, she would often freeze, feel sick, and forget everything she'd learned. It was as if there was a trap door in her mind that would snap open and devour all of the information that she had so diligently acquired. Grace worried that she was putting far too much strain on herself. She thought about the child she'd lost and sadly reflected on how different things would have been, had her other daughter survived and provided that vital bridge in the age gap between her two living daughters.

A spiral of fear had taken hold within Anna. She absorbed information with ease, but she couldn't recall what she had studied under any kind of pressure. It wasn't just exams now. Even in class, if she was asked a question, the answers would run away from her and she would freeze. This worried her hugely, and she began to fret that she was inherently defective in some way. She didn't realise that the pressure she felt was coming only from within herself.

She began to get very superstitious, imagining that if certain innocuous things happened to her during the day, she would fail her exam. If she stepped on a crack in the pavement, something bad would happen to her parents.

She set impossible goals, setting herself up to fail, then took the blame for the failure. It was a vicious circle.

She told herself one evening, for example, that if she didn't complete a history essay that night, June wouldn't come home for the midterm break. She was so tired after some previous work she had done that she didn't manage to finish the essay. When June opted to stay at college for midterm, Anna blamed herself.

Things like this happened to her many times a week, and she always found a way to take the blame for them. If it looked like she would successfully reach a particular target, she would move the goalposts, challenging herself to do more. She was constantly in a race with herself. A race to fail.

She managed to contain the stress of this internal battle within her own mind and body for many years—she concealed the full extent of what was going on inside from everyone around her. Her teachers just thought she was shy when put on the spot and stopped asking her questions, sure that they were just embarrassing her.

During June's first Christmas break from the teacher training college, she came home for two weeks, and was a changed woman: more relaxed, serene, and agreeable. Anna could see her parents breathe a sigh of relief when they realised that June was out of the 'teenage angst phase', as they called it. Anna wondered whether this was the phase she was now enduring.

They had a wonderful Christmas together that year. June had brought home lovely gifts for her parents and Anna. She and Anna never discussed how their relationship had changed—Anna had no idea how to broach the subject—but they gradually found a new way of relating to one another.

When June finished college, she got a job in a school about two hours' drive away, and one day phoned Anna to ask whether she would like to come and stay for a long weekend at her flat during the Halloween break.

Anna was sixteen years old, and was very excited at the prospect. Her mother dropped her to the train station, and Anna felt very grown-up as she headed into the city with her weekend bag.

June picked her up and brought her to the flat. She shared this flat with another girl, but had set up her own bedroom to accommodate Anna, saying she didn't mind sleeping on the couch for that weekend. Tomorrow, she declared enthusiastically, she would take Anna to the city's main gallery and museum, and they would visit a restaurant where she loved to lunch.

June noticed that Anna seemed very nervous: not the happy, clever child she remembered from her youth. She asked her whether anything was wrong, or whether she wanted to talk. She apologised for her 'raggle-taggle teens', as she called them, and asked Anna whether it had been very hard to be her little sister while she had been out causing so much trouble.

Anna didn't know how to describe what she was feeling inside. She thought that everyone would think her weird, or broken, if she told them about the anxious, shame-laden conversations she constantly had with herself. She didn't know what to say in response to June's apology, either, so she just muttered that it was okay, no problem, not to worry about it.

The two sisters had a wonderful weekend, despite Anna's suppressed unease. June revelled in being a tour guide and playing the role of loving big sister once more. Anna took her cues from June and tried to react to everything in the way she felt June would want her to. When June brought Anna to the train station on Sunday for her return trip home, she told her to work hard, concentrate on her exams, and assured her that she, too, would land a professional job and get her own place and that life would be great.

Anna felt desperately lonely on the return journey. She wished she'd had the courage to ask June what she had done wrong during June's teenage years, and why they had missed out on nearly ten years of sister-hood. Anna always assumed that things were her fault.

Her dad picked her up from the train and asked her how she'd got-ten on. Anna smiled brightly, determined not to reveal the worries that were silently plaguing her. "It was great, Dad. June is so happy there. She has a lovely place and she showed me the outside of her school and everything and it seems lovely."

Jim smiled broadly and nodded. "Thank God for that. She's a wild one, our June. A firebrand—full of excitement. Just like my aunties! You're much more like your mother, Anna. You're different; you're kind and loving."

He patted her hand, and Anna felt like she could cry.

During her final year in school, Anna could no longer keep a lid on her anxiety. Grace knew for a long time that she hadn't been getting the

grades she deserved, and saw that she had become increasingly with-
drawn. She asked June to intervene and help Anna with her studies, but
June thought her mother was overreacting and told her that all students
handled things differently.

Grace asked Anna whether she would like to go and talk to someone
about how she was feeling and Anna refused, saying that she was feeling
like she always felt and she'd be okay. She was appalled by the idea of
being sent to a therapist—this seemed, to her, like the ultimate admis-
sion of failure. She was determined to handle everything alone.

Then, on the night before her first exam, she broke down and had
what could only be described as an emotional meltdown.

Sobbing so hard she could barely get the words out, she told her
mother that she couldn't do the exams: that she felt very guilty about
this, and she knew she was letting them down. She would never forgive
herself for what she was saying now. She described feeling frayed at the
edges, unable to cope with the pressure to perform and remember everything she'd learnt.

She confessed that she hadn't slept properly in weeks, and couldn't
bear to go through the coming weeks of pretence around her school
friends. She said that every time she looked at a question from an old
exam paper, she would see the answer in her mind, fully formed, but
when she went to write it down, the words ran away from her and
wouldn't come out on paper. She tearfully told her parents that she felt
completely overwhelmed and helpless.

Grace was open-mouthed and lost for words when she heard all this.

Jim was the first to speak. Immediately, he told Anna that she'd do
no exam. There was no need at all for her to do them. He had long felt
that it was ridiculous for the school system to put so much pressure on
young people. What in the name of God were they at anyway, teaching
children ridiculous things they'd never need to know? No piece of paper
would define whether or not she'd be a valuable member of any workforce or any community.

He urged her not to worry one bit about it: to forget about the whole
thing. She'd get a fine job and find the perfect place for herself in life.

She needn't think, ever again, about any ludicrous exam. The neck of the people who had decided that this was a way to treat children! If he were in charge, there'd be none of this! He'd organise a system where each child was valued for their unique talents and urged to develop them. How dare they do this to his daughter?

Grace thought she had never loved him more than she did during this rant. Jim had a habit of pacing when he made declarations like this and it forced everyone to watch him. When Grace was sure he'd finished, she reached out to her daughter and hugged her, to confirm that she felt the same.

Anna cried and cried until her parents thought she couldn't possibly have any more tears to cry. She tried to explain to them that everyone else in her school was doing the exams no problem—so what was wrong with her?

Her parents had no answer to that, other than to say that every child was different, and she might be surprised at how many other students were feeling just like her. Her mother told her that she needed to rest. They would find someone who could help her to organize her thoughts and feelings. They would get through this together, as a family, and she was not to worry one bit about anything other than getting back to feeling good about herself.

But Anna couldn't remember ever feeling good about herself.

That night in bed, she did feel hugely relieved at having finally told her parents how she felt. She was deeply appreciative of their reactions, but she couldn't shake her niggling concern that they could do without this. They deserved a daughter who would have no problem doing exams, and wasn't the anxious mess that she was. She stayed up late, thinking that maybe she would feel better in the morning and would, in fact, be able to face her English paper.

However, she ended up sleeping right through the exam. Her mother had phoned the school to explain that she wouldn't be attending for the final examinations.

So, after all of her sleepless nights, and the fears that had almost torn her apart, Anna didn't do her final exams.

The world didn't spin off its axis. The sky didn't fall in. Nobody excommunicated her.

She started seeing a counsellor instead, who was recommended by a friend of her dad at work. At first, she needed some medication to help her sleep; they told her that this was to get her normal body rhythms back, and rebalance the chemicals in her brain. Then, when she felt better, the work with the counsellor would be so much more meaningful for her.

The counsellor was a kind lady who helped Anna to see that if she could quieten her mind and see herself as the only one who actually had control of her mind—the only one who thought in her mind—then she could take back the reins of control over her anxious thoughts.

It was a very slow process. Anna had to identify for herself where she had mixed up other people's good opinion of her with success in exams. Her problems clearly stemmed from childhood, but the lady explained that what had happened wasn't her sister's fault or her own fault. Her habit of associating success in exams with her own self-worth was just an erroneous assertion that had gotten into her mind as a fact.

The woman showed her that the 'rejection' Anna had experienced from June had nothing to do with her own actions, and everything to do with the two stages the sisters had occupied in their development. June had clearly been struggling in her own way throughout her teens, and when Anna saw this truth, she found a way to forgive herself.

Anna saw how she had allowed herself to be brought to a place in her mind where she felt that if she failed her exams, she would lose everyone.

"What we resist persists," the counsellor had said to her, "and we end up bringing about exactly what we were trying to avoid."

Anna also had to deal with a sense of having missed out on an important initiation into the next phase of her life. University was now out of the question. The very thought of that made her feel sick. Her parents wanted her to take a year out and told her she could decide, when she felt better, what she wanted to do.

She had her whole life ahead of her, they told her.

She got a job in the reception of a local hotel and was efficient and friendly. She loved the feeling of freedom of being able to handle everything that would happen throughout the day. She loved welcoming the new guests, watching families sitting together having treats and days away together. She loved the restaurant staff and the maintenance men, who could fix everything from a leaky shower to broken heaters. She loved the gardeners and the housekeepers. She loved feeling useful and able to manage. She wondered at the fact that so many of these great people had never finished school or gone to university either, but were so vital to their community and so integral now to her own happiness. They appreciated her and never asked her a question about anything she'd learnt in school.

She began to truly believe that there was life after her perceived failure and she settled into her new life.

When her school friends came home from college, they told her how envious they were of her independence and her earning ability. She felt proud of herself for the first time since she'd been a little girl getting top marks in June's tests.

Grace and Jim too began to trust her—trust that she was becoming happier in herself and they saw emerging a very bright and beautiful young woman who was clever and capable. They sometimes wondered if they could have helped her earlier, but they were experienced enough to know that everyone blossomed in their own time and in their own way.

Anna's twenties were when she truly discovered the many different facets of herself. She had enormous fun with friends, occasionally staying out all night partying, going home for a shower, and heading straight into work. She had a few relationships that lasted a year or two but she never fell in love until she met Daniel.

She was transfixed by him when she first saw him. Tall and well built, she joked to her friend that he could carry her. He was talking to a mutual friend and she wasn't sure what really attracted her to him. Daniel was ordinary enough to look at, but something about the way he was paying such attention to the friend he was talking to just struck her as being very decent and she watched him for a while. When he turned in her direction, they caught eyes and smiled immediately at one another. The mutual friend caught the look that passed between them straight away, and beckoned her over. She walked across the bar and they were introduced.

After that night they became very close, very quickly. Although getting to know one another was obviously new, there was something very comfortable about how they interacted. There were no games, no power plays, no dramas.

Her new life had begun.

Chapter Nine

Dawn was six years old and growing up rapidly. Her relationship with the fairies was beginning to fade. She still brought them lemonade and chocolate on occasion, but she was beginning to notice that other children in her class at school didn't have fairy friends, and they seemed to be fine. It began to change for her when her best friend Debbie first started coming over to her house to play, after school. Debbie and Dawn had decided that they were going to be best friends and when they grew up, they were going to be one another's bridesmaids.

Debbie pretended that she too could see the fairies and went along with the conversations that Dawn was having. After a few days, it became clear to Dawn that Debbie was not hearing and seeing the same things as she was. Debbie spoke out of sequence and about things that weren't happening at all! Dawn knew for certain that Debbie was pretending, when she put the sandwiches for the fairies in a part of the garden that they would never go to eat. At first, Dawn was cross with Debbie for pretending, but soon she began to doubt herself and her own vision. On cue, the fairies receded into the greenery.

Debbie was a very vivacious and popular child and Dawn was glad to be her best friend. She did not want to fall out with her and she did not want to feel odd or foolish. One day, she said to Debbie that she couldn't really see fairies and Debbie replied that she knew that but that it was great fun pretending. Dawn got her first lesson in denying her truth in order to fit in with others.

However, she still maintained a very strong relationship with a being named Sylvia. She perceived Sylvia as a very long and tall lady who lived in the wood of the trees and wore a silver scarf around her head. She communicated with Dawn all the time. Room had to be made for Sylvia in the car every time the family embarked on a road trip, but not at the dinner table. Sylvia didn't eat, apparently. Dawn felt safe with her family and they had never pretended to see Sylvia, so she was happy to continue that relationship. Sylvia could travel, unlike the fairies, who never left their garden.

Daniel and Anna had managed to go on a three-week holiday every year since Dawn had turned one. They had been to lovely resorts and child-friendly campsites, but nowhere had captured their imagination or their hearts quite like the old vineyard outside Elba's town. Anna asked Daniel whether he thought they should go back.

During the previous year's holiday, they had travelled to different places each week, and Anna had found it stressful to pack and unpack every few days. She told her husband that this year, she wanted to go somewhere familiar, plonk herself down for a few weeks, and just chill out.

"Would the cabins not be a bit small for us, now we have Dawn?" Daniel asked. After all, Cal was soon to become a teenager, while Blu would be turning twelve on his next birthday.

Anna waved away his concerns. "Not at all. The boys would still go in together, and the cabin had a spare room, if you remember. We lived outside anyway, Dan. We ate on the deck and only used the cabin for cooking and sleeping."

Seeing that his wife had her heart set on visiting Elba's town again, Daniel smiled at her and declared, "It's settled, then. Back to the vineyard we go!"

Anna was delighted. She could already feel those sunny afternoons on the deck calling to her: her entire body began to relax deeply at the very thought.

Her mother, Grace, had passed away just before Christmas the previous year, leaving an enormous hole in Anna's life.

Grace's death had happened very suddenly. She hadn't been complaining about feeling unwell, and had given her daughters no indication that anything was wrong with her. Both Anna and June thought that she was simply getting on in years and slowing down a bit. They didn't expect her to still be able to do the same things she had been able to do five years prior.

She had been forgetting things more often, but this was normal and to be expected, as far as the girls were concerned. It gave them the opportunity to take care of her for a little while—repaying her many kindnesses towards them—for times when she had gone above and beyond the call of duty.

Every week, they took turns to provide Grace and Jim with home-cooked dinners. Neither parent was driving any longer, so the girls traveled to them.

One fateful morning, Anna arrived to see her parents as usual, and immediately knew that something was very wrong. Grace was still in bed, which was very out of character for her. She was very breathless, even as she lay perfectly still. She told Anna that she just couldn't get up today.

Anna's father was beside himself, pacing the kitchen with his hands clasped together. "She's been much worse than she's been telling you all, Anna," he repeated bleakly, over and over again.

Anna phoned June—who was at work—and asked her to come as quickly as possible, as she thought their mother might need an ambulance. June said she would leave immediately, but urged her not to hang around waiting for her. "Do whatever you feel is right, Anna. I'll be there as soon as I can."

Their father was 89 years old by this time, so Anna told him that she didn't think it would be a good idea for him to go into hospital with Grace until they knew more.

Jim's eyes filled with tears. "But Anna, I've been by her side for sixty years. What if she doesn't come home?"

"Oh, Dad. . ." Anna sighed. "It'll just be a matter of my getting her settled in. Dan will bring you in to see her later. I know it feels wrong to watch her go into hospital without you, but I think it would be for the best. I'll call Dan and ask him to try and get here to be with you. As soon as I know anything, I'll be straight on to you, and Dan can bring you in."

"I don't need a babysitter, Anna," her father retorted. "I'm perfectly well able to look after myself." He sat down at the kitchen table and began to weep. Anna thought her heart would break. Part of the desperately high price you paid for having beautiful parents who lived so long was that you had to see them in states that they never would have wanted you to see them, she thought.

Her shoulders drooped. "Oh Dad, I'm sorry—I'm being insensitive. I'm just trying to think about what's best for Mum right now. I'm sorry. I didn't take your feelings into account."

Jim sniffed and wiped away his tears. "You're right though, Anna. That's my problem, really. You're right! Yes, please ask Daniel to come, if he's able. Maybe June will want to be with her mother, too. But if Dan's not able to come over, I'll be okay. I'll wait beside the phone until you ring me and tell me what is going on. You're right. I'm too old to be going with her. I'd only be in the way at the hospital. It's a tragedy."

Anna couldn't stay in the house much longer—she knew time was of the essence, if she were to get Grace the care she needed—but she longed to sit down beside her father. She longed to wrap her arms around him and tell him everything was going to be alright.

She called the ambulance, then Daniel. She quickly told him what was wrong, and he said he would be with Jim as soon as he could. Anna then texted June, telling her to go straight to the hospital. She and Grace would meet her there.

The ambulance came. The paramedics were so kind and efficient, they put everyone—including Grace and Jim—at ease. One of them even had the wherewithal to make Jim a cup of tea. They helped calm down the situation immensely, and Anna was so thankful for that.

June was awaiting the ambulance's arrival at the hospital. She and Anna accompanied their mother as she was checked in through A&E. While Grace waited to see the geriatrician, the medical team took her away to perform some tests and ultrasounds.

The girls continued on into the main body of the hospital, as it was clear that their mother was being admitted. They signed the relevant forms, gave a nurse their details, and were then called up to the ward.

Anna's phone beeped with a message from Daniel, telling her that he was with Jim and would hold tight for further updates. He would have to collect the children from school soon, but would bring them back to be with Jim. The children! Anna couldn't believe it, but she had somehow forgotten all about the children.

The news wasn't good. Grace had a massive inoperable tumor on her abdomen. The mass was so big that the doctor couldn't tell from where it had originated. He feared that what was happening now was that Grace's organs were shutting down. He told them to prepare for the worst, and that he would be recommending immediate palliative care.

The girls were gobsmacked by this. They literally could not form a sentence. The doctor put his head down, muttered that he was very sorry, and walked away. June reached out and took Anna's hand. They stared at one another, wide-eyed and open-mouthed, searching each other's faces for what they should do or think or say.

A nurse came straight over to them and gently asked them whether they were Grace's children, as she was looking for her girls. They nodded and followed the nurse. They were holding hands like two young children following an adult.

"We have her nice and settled and comfortable up here in her own room," the nurse said congenially. "She is very calm and is looking for you both."

They took a moment to gather themselves before they approached the room, then went in and sat on either side of Grace's bed, trying their best to smile.

"Now, Mum, you must rest and gather some strength," June remarked brightly. "It's a very cold afternoon, and you're in the ideal place for someone who's not feeling the best. You look snug as a bug in a rug."

She smiled at Grace and moved her hair to the side, kissing her forehead. "Anna and I are here for you, and once Daniel gets the children home, I will go get Dad and bring him in to see you."

Their mother didn't seem able to respond verbally, but she weakly squeezed June's hand to show her that she understood. She had been placed on a drip for fluids, and had an oxygen tube going into her nostrils too. The effort of keeping her eyes open seemed to be too much for her.

"It's alright, Mum," June whispered. "You can rest."

With an air of relief, Grace closed her eyes. Her breathing was a little labored, but reasonably steady.

Anna didn't know how June had been able to keep her voice so warm and gentle, but she thanked God for her presence. June turned to her and said, "I'll stay with Dad tonight, Anna. Your kids are young. It's best if you're at home with them."

"Who'll stay with Mum?"

"Mum really is in the best place. Aren't you, Mum?"

The sisters glanced at Grace, who seemed to be fast asleep.

June came around the bed to Anna and whispered, "Anna, I think we're in for a long week. It's best if you go home tonight and make plans and talk to your children. Prepare them."

The reality of what was happening hit Anna then and she nodded to her sister and they gave one another a long hug.

Jim kept a vigil beside Grace's bed for days as she slipped away. He barely spoke to the medical team other than to smile and greet them but he didn't want any information.

"After sixty years, I wouldn't be anywhere else but here, beside her," he insisted every time his daughters tried to get him to leave and go home to rest in his own bed. "I don't want to be anywhere else, girls. I mean it. Leave me to it."

The hospital provided them with a family room where he sometimes went to rest. Most of the time, however, he was by his wife's side, murmuring to her, holding and rubbing her hand, sometimes snoozing in the bedside chair. He kept telling her that he wouldn't be long after her, and that he loved her to beyond the borders of infinity.

His clear and infectious love for her drew out the tenderness of the nursing staff. The girls were sure that the nurses, who were no stranger to these scenes, were very touched by what they witnessed.

"She must be a great woman, Jim, for you to be so devoted to her," they'd say to him.

"She's the best," confirmed Jim. "The very best."

One night, less than a week after she was admitted, Grace quietly slipped away in her sleep. The three of them were with her at the time. Jim was silent for a long time after Grace had taken her last breath, before finally saying, "she's with the baby now. I just have to wait for my turn now to go and be with them."

June and Anna were devastated by their mother's death. Just a week ago, this was the last thing they had been expecting.

Jim confided in them that evening that as couples got old, they talked about these things together: where they'd be buried, what one of them would do if the other of them went first, and other such things. The girls were shocked to hear this. They had never imagined their parents discussing such things. And yet, when they thought about it, it seemed like such an obvious thing for a loving couple like their parents to do.

"But that doesn't make it any easier now, of course," Jim added, his eyes misting over. "I'm still going to miss her and wish I was with her. We were lucky, girls. We had a great life together."

Anna and June were consoled by the fact that during Grace's lifetime, they had found a record of their sister's burial and had discovered exactly where her body was buried, along with many other stillborn babies from those years.

No registration of the baby's birth existed, since she had not been born alive, but the registration of her burial was held in a large graveyard that served the surrounding town.

June and Anna had both gone to the graveyard without their parents first, just to stand in the plot where their sister had been buried many years before. The burial ground was a large, bleak three-acre field. The records at the graveyard office were good though, so they easily found the approximate area where their sister's remains lay.

They asked the cemetery staff about the possibility of creating a memorial to the lost babies who had never been properly honored in life. Anna and June were not the first siblings to come searching for their sisters and brothers—the cemetery staff gave them the number of a local campaigning group of affected families.

This group was well established, and had already asked the local council whether they could set up more amenable visiting conditions on the Angels' Plot, where families—especially mothers who were by now quite aged—could sit and spend time with their deceased children. It took some tenacity to pressurise councillors to accede to the families' request. June was a particularly adamant and strong member of the group, adding much-needed impetus to their campaign.

In no time, they had reached an agreement. The council arranged for a new entranceway to be erected between the graveyard proper and the Angels' Plot.

The campaigning group also secured adequate signage, a number of newly planted trees around the perimeter, plaques on the outer walls of the ground that were inscribed with the babies' family names, and benches spaced throughout the plot, so that families could sit down together and honor their own children and the others who were buried together in this space.

While this was in the works, Jim had—quite out of the blue—spoken to June about his experience at the time, and how helpless he had felt.

"Men didn't know whether it was best to just not mention the whole thing at all or whether they should try to talk about it," Jim told her. "We didn't know what was best for the woman. The advice was that it was best to ignore it, but Grace and I are close, so we have spoken about it, just between the two of us."

June was fuming at the thought of her parents having to whisper their grief quietly to one another, but she sat quietly, smiling encouragement to her father as he told his story.

It was during this conversation that Jim revealed that they had privately named their daughter Emma. He told June that he wanted Emma's name to be inscribed on their gravestone after he and Grace died. He wanted the stone to read: "In Loving Memory of Jim and Grace and their dear departed daughter Emma."

June didn't tell him then about the ongoing negotiations with the other families over the Angels' Plot, but she gave the name Emma to the campaigning group for the records department at the graveyard.

Anna viewed it as a sign from the other side, that her father would talk about Emma out of the blue. They felt confident that they were doing the right thing, but the girls were unsure how they would prepare their elderly parents to bring them to the burial place of their stillborn daughter. What would be the appropriate way to prepare two old people for such an event?

Anna decided that they should take them out to lunch and tell them about the work they, and the other families, had been doing at the cemetery. Then they would propose that the four of them might go and view the improvements that had been made there, where Emma's body had been laid to rest. On the appointed day, the sun shone, the lunch was perfect and Grace and Jim couldn't finish their dessert quickly enough, once they had grasped the enormity of what they were hearing from their daughters.

They were overwhelmed with emotion—mostly gratitude and joy—as they held hands and followed their daughters through the old cemetery, right down to the newly tended and cared-for Angels' Plot at the back. Here, their little girl's body was buried.

The four of them sat together on the bench closest to where Emma lay: smiling at one another when their eyes met, looking out into the vastness of the space, and thinking of all of the babies who lay there.

They walked over to the nearest plaque, and Grace gave a little gasp when she saw Emma's name engraved.

Finally, her very own acknowledged spot, on Earth, that acknowledged that her perfect baby Emma had been real!

That memory served as a great consolation to June and Anna after Grace's death, but their hearts broke for their father.

During the funeral, and at a family gathering that Christmas, Jim seemed to have shrunk. He was milder, meeker, less strong, and barely spoke a word to anyone. Who knew where he was going in his mind, and what he was thinking?

In truth, Jim had by now given up. He was finished with life now, he thought. There was no point in being here anymore, without Grace. He loved his daughters with all his heart and soul, but they had their own lives.

Grace was his life. Grace was his partner. It was Grace's company he longed for.

Anna and June tried their best to talk to him about practical matters, in a vain attempt to keep him occupied with the here and now. They worried that he would keep slipping further and further into his sorrow, and they would no longer be able to help him. They had spent the last few Christmases at Anna and Daniel's house—Christmas was all about children, and this was where the children of the family were.

On Christmas Day, they decided to leave an empty chair for Grace at their family table, so that Jim and the children could feel as though her spirit was with them. Dawn watched, bemused, as she saw Sylvia clearly converse and laugh with somebody in the empty seat. She later told this to Anna, when she was putting her to bed, and she watched her mother's face flush with emotion and happiness.

"Dawn, you are such a gift. You have a lovely way of saying exactly the right thing at the right time, and I love you all the more for it." She tucked Dawn down, put her magic star under her pillow, as she did every night, and went downstairs to tell her father.

"Dad, Dawn has an imaginary friend who she tells me was talking to the empty chair earlier at dinner."

June looked around at her, startled. "Really?" she asked.

"Yes, she said that all during dinner, her friend Sylvia was talking and joking with a presence in the empty chair."

In unison, Jim, Daniel, Anna and June looked back over at the table at which they'd spent their afternoon, the candles that were still burning on the table flickered and they all instantly felt a deep sense of peace.

"Nonsense," said Jim and smiled at his daughters.

But now, by the time Daniel was booking the holiday, Anna really needed to plan some time away. She didn't want to spend too much time on the road this year—hence, her request to Daniel that they spend some time just relaxing on the campsite in the much-loved old vineyard. She checked with June whether it would be okay for her to go away for three weeks.

June replied that this would be fine. She had decided, by this time, to move in with their father. She knew he would just shrivel up and die if they put him into a nursing home, and she had always been better able to manage him than Anna was. Jim tended to act up and complain when Anna was with him, whereas June was better able to move him along and keep him focused. June's apartment didn't need much maintenance: she dropped by every few days to pick up post and check on things.

Anna visited Jim every day while June was at work and her own children were in school. This arrangement suited everyone, and served to carry them through the winter and spring.

Anna felt very self-indulgent about asking June for three weeks off "Dad duty", as they had begun to call it, but June absolutely insisted it was the right thing to do. She laughed that she would get her back by disappearing somewhere warm and sunny in August.

Anna then asked Daniel whether Laura would like to accompany them on the holidays for a few days—or a week, even. She suggested that

Laura could join them towards the end of the holiday. If she traveled over to them alone, they could all travel back together. She knew that Dawn's room in the cabin would be fitted with a bunk bed, and was sure that Dawn would love having her grandma in the bottom bunk for a few nights.

Daniel's eyes lit up when he heard Anna's suggestion. He had already been looking forward to seeing Elba again, and now he could introduce her to Laura!

Laura was thrilled by the invitation. She was 77 years old by this time, and feeling every year of it, but she was very touched by her son's excitement. As soon as she agreed to accompany them for the final few days of their holiday, he began to send her pictures of the area: urging her to have a look at all of them and decide where she'd like to go on day trips. He told her that there was a wonderful traveling market that often visited the town near the vineyard, and they'd have to make sure her visit overlapped with a market day.

Daniel called Elba to tell her about their plans. She expressed great pleasure at their impending visit, but Daniel also detected some tiredness in her voice. He could hear that she was failing in her strength. This concerned him slightly. Grace's death had brought home to him that no one was immortal. Presumably, not even Elba.

After Grace's death, Daniel had been thinking about all she had given to their family. He was going to miss his mother-in-law so much. All of the wisdom she had imparted to his family, all of the love she had showered on his children, all of the understanding she had of life and its ups and downs. Her presence would be sorely missed. This focused him more on the value of still having his own mother with him. This would almost certainly be his last opportunity to see Elba. He decided to record this holiday, frame by frame.

With all of the arrangements agreed, Daniel booked the cabin.

The family arrived on a Saturday. Daniel and Anna noticed that a number of renovations and upgrades had been made to the campsite since their last visit. They were delighted with their decision to come back.

Three glorious weeks stretched out before them, promising relief, enjoyment, and adventure. They planned to make the most of every minute.

At this time, Anna had some nascent plans to start a small business. She wanted to begin by creating cards and prints of her artwork. She thought there was a possibility for her to launch a range of giftware items: beautiful writing paper, little crystals, unusual presents for babies, and pretty decorative pieces for the home and garden.

She wanted the boys and Dawn to see that she was capable of earning money and starting her own business, as well as doing everything she did at home. She was very happy with the decision she had made, before Cal was born, to stay at home and care for her children during the earliest years of their lives, but now, she felt a stirring to create something new. Her boys would soon be entering their teenage years, and she felt that a new phase was beginning for them all.

She would be able to show her children—and learn, herself—how to create a business out of nothing: how to order stock, supply a shop, take a margin, and pay the bills. If they saw how this could be done while they were young, it might open up some thought processes in their minds. It might free them to consider a broader range of options for their own futures. As Anna knew all too well, exams weren't everything. Life was a great teacher.

Her mum had left both her and June a significant amount of money that would cover her expenses until she got a business stocked and up and running. The money hadn't come through probate yet, but it would within the next few months. Anna was going to spend this time on holiday blue-skying her ideas and seeing where her dreams took her.

They spent the first few days of their trip settling in, and didn't leave the campsite as a family until the Tuesday morning market.

The day after they arrived, Daniel went to see Elba on his own. He was mindful of how tired her voice had been during their phone conversation, so he wanted to gauge how she was and whether she would be up to meeting his family.

He found her in fine fettle and very pleased to see him. She was a little less sure on her feet as she walked around her room, getting him some food, but apart from that, he could see very little difference in her since the last time they had met. He supposed that the pace of life in this little town lent itself to people staying healthier for longer.

They enjoyed a good catch up. As always, Elba was very interested in how he had been getting on. She told him that she loved receiving his Christmas cards, with their family photos and updates. She said she was looking forward to seeing how the boys had grown, and most of all, she was looking forward to meeting Dawn.

She clapped her hands together when she heard that Laura would be joining the family during the last week of their holiday. "Well, I would love to meet your mother, Daniel! She must be a wonderful woman. It will be an honour to meet her."

"I was hoping you'd say that," Daniel replied, smiling from ear to ear. "She'd love to meet you, too. I was thinking of bringing the whole family out to the field and the nun's chapel, Elba, if you think that would be alright? Would you like to come with us? I have a seven-seater car hired. There would be plenty of room. But this would all happen in our last week. I'll let you think about it."

Elba chuckled. "It's not for me to tell you whether you can or can't go up to that special site. I don't own it, Daniel." She thought back to the silent initiation he'd had there some years earlier, and knew he was more than capable of holding the space for his family. "I do happen to think it would be a brilliant idea. . . but it's something you should do with just your family. There's no need for me to go with you. I'd slow you down, besides anything else. . . oh, bring a picnic! It would be great to think of your children walking through those fields, picking flowers, having fun. The land would sing."

She smiled radiantly at him. "I am so looking forward to having you around for the next few weeks. The markets are back, the tourists are back, and there'll be lots of activity in the area. I love this time of year, when the outside world comes here to see us."

The boys would always remember this holiday as their favourite one ever. They were like two peas in a pod. Their personalities were different, but they gelled together very well and were great friends. Cal was quieter than Blu. He thought very deeply about things, but didn't share his thoughts, whereas Blu seemed to have no filter. He just spoke his mind, without pausing to reflect on what he was saying.

The family had hired bicycles, and the boys often used them to meet up with other kids on the site. Together, the kids spent the evenings cycling around to one another's tents, chalets, and caravans, getting treats wherever they could and checking in with their families.

The campsite had opened up a new zipline circuit, allowing children to fly through the trees. They went down to this area multiple times a day, where they played at being Tarzan and making jungle noises as they zipped through the woods. Daniel loved watching them, shouting encouragement and urging greater competition between them. Anna watched them, peeping through her hands, fearing one of them would end up smacking into a tree. After a day or two, she designated Daniel as the one to go to the zipline with them. She would avoid it like the plague. The dreams of the father and the fears of the mother. Wasn't it ever thus?

They spent a great deal of the time in the pool, sliding down the water chutes, and playing table tennis with other children. After they had spent the day playing together, Daniel would take the three children down to the poolside bar for a treat. These were blissful days.

Anna was enjoying her afternoons sunbathing and allowing her mind to wander. She often thought about her mother and about death, and how shocking it was that somebody who had been such a vital presence in her life could just be gone in a matter of days. It didn't seem fair.

Life was very cruel sometimes. What was it all about, she wondered? She knew that the shattering grief she felt was in direct proportion to how deeply she had loved her mother, but somehow, knowing that grief was the price we paid for love wasn't always enough for her to accept this pain.

All she could do was hope that time was the healer everyone had told her it was, and that she would soon start feeling better. She and June both knew that it wouldn't be long before they were back at that graveside to bury their father. She shuddered as she thought about what lay ahead.

During the first week of the holiday, she and Daniel made lunches and dinners together, but on Friday evening, they got ready to head into the market and meet Elba, as Daniel had booked the large round table at the back of Rolo's restaurant. When they got there, Elba was already seated.

Elba expressed her condolences for the death of Grace, and Anna was grateful. Her eyes filled with tears and she said, "Elba, I know it's not a tragedy. I mean, I know it's the way things are meant to go. Our parents are meant to die before us. But it's just so hard!"

Elba replied, "Anna—my darling Anna. Oh no, don't think that! It is a tragedy, for you and your family. Of course it is! If you listen carefully to people's stories, woven into them will be these heart-breaking tales of grief and loss. It's the toughest experience we can ever go through. It doesn't matter what age... There are other tough experiences, of course, like fail- ure and disappointment. But in the long run, people will contextualise their successes and the stories of their lives, giving due regard to what they learned, how they gained, how they were shaped and made braver by their painful experiences. Made humble and powerless, in the face of death, brought low by life's trials, we learn true humility, true power and true heart. We reach great heights within ourselves. The jewels on the tapestry of a life well-lived are those of resilience, effort, grace, acceptance and sur- render. Death of a loved one brings them all home to us. Be gentle with yourself during these times. Give yourself whatever you need."

She fondly patted the younger woman's hand and leant her head over to touch the younger woman's head, as Rolo came to take their order.

Anna was touched by how Elba had acknowledged the depth of her grief. Sometimes, she felt as though people just didn't know what to say to her. Some people just didn't understand how devastating a parents' death could be... not until it happened to them.

Her business ideas had been on her mind over the last week, too. She had been looking for inspiration in the little craft shops of Elba's town, and hoped she would get a chance to tell Elba about her ideas. She knew that the shops in town were catering for tourists, and were full of pretty things that you would never buy at home, but she was questioning why that was. Maybe she could appeal to people to buy these beautiful things for themselves or others when they were at home.

The town's shops and the stalls on the market had little keychains with people's names written on them, as well as angels, little crystal tumble stones, craftwork, incense, wind chimes, soaps, and natural beauty products. Anna's hometown didn't have anything like these little Aladdin's caves. All of the products she was seeing here could easily be transferred into her own town for her to sell, alongside her little prints and cards.

Anna was very open to new stock ideas. She wanted her shop to be an inspirational place where people came to get gifts for special people and special events. During this holiday, she was spending a lot of time observing the evening market and watching people's shopping habits. She took note of what they were buying, what they would just pick up and put down again, and what they would ignore.

She was particularly interested in what women were drawn to. She wanted to be able to reach women and give them what they wanted, as she knew that women always tended to put themselves last. Her eyes filled with tears again as she thought about Grace, and how much she would miss her.

The crystals in the market seemed to attract a lot of women. They appeared to be especially drawn to rose quartz and amethyst stones, but Anna made a note to do more research and find out more about these crystals' properties, and what they were supposed to be good for. Wasn't it quartz crystals that kept clocks ticking? Hadn't she heard that somewhere? She would have to learn more about the things she was selling.

Anna was quite excited about diving head-first into her business research. She could feel her studious mind kicking into gear again—this time, motivated not by the terror of failing an exam, but by the joy of providing people with products they would love. She would be able to offer quick consultations to people, helping them with whatever they were looking for.

Over dinner, she eagerly told Elba about her plans, and commented that it was normally only while she was painting that she entered the meditative state she had been in throughout this holiday. Elba smiled and told her that this must be happening because her soul was busy.

Ever since Anna had dreamed about the lady in the cloak, she had found that she often revisited that mysterious castle in her mind. She told Elba about it now, explaining that she had wondered about the meaning of the dream and tried to understand the metaphor from her subconscious about drawing her energy back into her own inner sanctuary, ignoring the outside forces that would have her engaged in futile battles.

That much, she understood. . . but she was still a little puzzled by the connection she had felt between herself and the woman in the cloak. The connection had been so strong, as if she had somehow already known this woman very well. She understood that she'd seen her image in the mirror, but she also felt that this other aspect of herself—or whoever this woman was or signified—knew an awful lot more than Anna currently did.

Elba suggested that it might be a sign that she was growing into this beautiful woman, or she already was within her, waiting to shine out. That made Anna smile, as the woman in her dream had been completely free of worries, and full of love. Elba told her how the subconscious likes to communicate with us using images to evoke emotions, hoping we'll get the message. She told her how the moon represented the feminine; the beautiful woman, with whom she felt so safe, was almost certainly an aspect of her own Divine Self and she considered it a very portentous dream indeed.

Anna then spoke with Elba about what her commitment to opening a shop would entail, in practical terms. She would have to get some help in the shop; hire someone for the afternoons, or maybe only open up in the mornings? These were all decisions she would have to mull over and talk about with Daniel.

Daniel just nodded and said he was sure that whatever Anna wanted would be a great idea. Anna flashed a look at Elba and threw her eyes up to heaven.

Elba chuckled and quipped, "Well, at least you've no battle to fight there!"

It would be very trying, Anna thought aloud, to have to be there every weekend for Saturday shoppers. She had a lot to weigh up before she made any firm decisions. When dinner had ended, she continued to talk to Elba over coffee, as the boys accompanied Daniel on a walk around the market. They had spotted some sports hats and jerseys on their way in, and were eager to get a closer look.

Dawn decided to stay with her mother and this 'majory-star woman, Elba, who was now encouraging Anna not to over-complicate things in her own mind, but to simply go with her heart. Plans, strategies, and a list of pros and cons were all very well, she went on, but nothing beat answering the call of the heart.

"How do you feel when you think of the shop?" she asked the younger woman.

"I feel. . . excited and hopeful," Anna replied slowly, feeling her heart soar as she said it.

"Well then, you can't not open it," Elba responded in a matter-of-fact tone. "What'll you call it?"

The answer came to Anna at once. "I'll call it Love, Grace. . . in honour of my mother."

"I think you've decided." Elba sat back in her seat and looked very pleased with herself.

Dawn had been looking up at the two women, wide-eyed, as they carried out their conversation. Now, she chimed in to agree with Elba. "Yes, Mum, I think you've already decided."

"Sometimes, we're further along the process of making a decision than we think we are," Elba commented. "Things are unseen, falling into place all around us. I often use the analogy of the caterpillar's evolution into a butterfly to talk about transformation that we go through."

"I know this! I do! I always tell the caterpillars that one day they'll fly," Dawn burst out excitedly. "I want them to keep going."

"You do," agreed Anna, as she ruffled her daughter's hair and gave her a big smile. "And I always tell you not to spoil the surprise." She grinned at Elba, thinking to herself that it was some surprise for the poor caterpillar—all he'd go through to get his wings.

"Well, that's just it isn't it?" Elba remarked, winking at Dawn. "Caterpillars don't know what it even is to fly. They couldn't even conceive of what that might be like. It must seem so outrageously out of the question for them. They're crawling along on their bellies and a little girl tells them that one day, they'll fly. They must think you're joking with them, sweetheart."

"Yes, but something in them knows I'm right," Dawn insisted with great confidence. She leant forward towards the two women, for effect. "I can see it in their eyes. They mightn't know how though. . . or why. . ." She trailed off, frowning a little.

"Did you know," Elba said to Dawn, "that if you lined up all of the cleverest people on Earth, they wouldn't be able to tell you why a caterpillar goes through this process at all? They will bore you to tears explaining the process, and what happens. But they don't know the *why*."

"I know what happens; I know; they shed their skin a few times and then they spin a cocoon and then they go into the cocoon and then they come out as a butterfly." Dawn was very pleased that she was able to tell Elba what happened, but then furrowed her brow as she considered what the old lady had said. "But, no, I don't know why. . ."

She screwed up her eyes tightly in concentration, before they sprang open again. "But I do know that they help make flowers bloom. They go around and visit the flowers and smell them. They bring seeds with them that way, and make more flowers grow. . . oh but we have bees for that, so I don't know why we need butterflies as well."

Elba smiled at her. "Very good. That's a very good description of what happens. And now, think about all the stages of that, and how the little caterpillar just knows what to do. What I sometimes wonder about is, while he's in the cocoon, does he think 'oooh, there's something happening in my back?' Imagine, as he's disintegrating and dying to his old self. . . he's all locked up in this prison and his life has changed so much. . . it must feel very stressful to the poor little thing."

"But Elba, that's why I tell him that one day he'll fly! Because I know he's going to go through really hard times and I want him to remember that a little girl told him that one day he'll fly and then he'll be happy; that he'll carry seeds from flower to flower and make the place beautiful and colourful," Dawn interrupted, eager to get the caterpillar to the best bit of his life cycle, as she saw it.

Elba chuckled, delighting in the young girl's enthusiasm. "Yes. You are such a darling girl to think of him that way. His whole life up until then, think about it. . . he'd been travelling around on his tummy. Now, there's something happening in his back! But, you know what? He has the imaginal discs with him! He just doesn't know it as he's experiencing it."

"Oh. What are the 'maginal discs, Elba?" asked Dawn.

"They're the magic things that the caterpillar had all the time. They are the cells that hold the memory of what to do to become a butterfly. Every caterpillar has them, but they just don't know it! He just had to form this soup of his tired old body to let them do their magic thing."

Elba moved seats to sit beside Dawn. Dawn turned her chair towards the old lady so that they were both facing one another. Anna watched the magic spell that Elba seemed to cast on her little girl. "Dawn if you remember nothing else, please remember this: You have the empathy within you to try to help the caterpillars by telling them that one day they'll fly."

Dawn nodded. "Yes, I do. I love the caterpillars," she said earnestly.

Elba continued, "Now imagine the impact it would have on them if a butterfly told them the same thing. The butterfly could relay stories to them that he remembers about the times that he was a caterpillar and the trials he went through. He might be able to tell them that he knows and remembers what it feels like to have grit stuck on his little belly and how uncomfortable that feeling was. Don't you think that the caterpillar might really get a true sense of what he will become, if a butterfly tells him?"

"Yes. That would be wonderful if the butterflies would come back to help the caterpillars understand their journey, wouldn't it?" Dawn nodded and fixed her gaze back on Elba.

"Dawn, you will be a butterfly to so many caterpillars on your life's journey. Sometimes you'll be the caterpillar and somebody else will be the butterfly to you. What's important is that we share our stories and experiences, to help others and stay true to ourselves. That's the best example we can ever be; helping people go through their difficult times. Tell our own truth in order to help others. And then you will be true to the process of evolution, knowing that you have the magic inside you to become who you truly are."

A light went on inside Anna as she listened to the conversation. Elba looked directly at her, sensing this. "We do know what we're doing, Anna," she said softly. "We truly do. At every point in the process, the imaginal discs are just waiting to do their magic."

Anna nodded slowly as her understanding of this fell into place.

"There's something happening in your back," Elba joked, "and soon it will be time to fly!"

"I love you, Elba," Anna said warmly. She deeply appreciated this wonderful, wise old lady.

"I love you too, Anna."

"I love everyone," Dawn chipped in, determined not to be left out.

Chapter Ten

On the Monday of the final week of their holiday, Laura arrived.

Daniel and Dawn traveled to the small regional airport to pick her up. On the way back to the campsite, they passed through acres of sunlit countryside. Laura was enchanted. She had never been to the area, and was revelling in every moment of it.

Everywhere she looked, the landscape seemed so vast and expansive in comparison to home. The motorway was just part of the landscape itself. On either side of it, she could see life happening, across the flat-lands. She saw towns in the distance that were like little enclaves of humanity and community.

"I saw all this as the plane was coming in to land," she remarked. "It's a stunning view. How lovely it is to be right in the midst of this beauty now, having viewed it from the airplane."

Daniel nodded agreement. "It is amazing, isn't it?"

The boys were delighted to see Laura when they arrived back at the campsite, and Anna hugged her warmly. Laura noticed that her daughter-in-law looked tanned and rested. She was glad to see this, as she knew how the previous year had taken its toll on her.

The chalet was cool and secluded: a welcome refuge from the mid-day heat. Dawn—eager to show her their shared room—pulled at her sleeve. "Come on, Grandma, you have to see!"

Dawn excitedly pulled Laura in the direction of their room, explaining as she did that Laura wouldn't be allowed to sleep on the top bunk in case she fell out and broke her hip: Dawn had heard her parents say so a few nights earlier.

Laura laughed and frowned pointedly at Daniel, who shook his head ruefully and commented, "No one can have any private conversations around here."

"So, Grandma, I will sleep in the top bunk," Dawn informed her in a business-like tone, then brightened up. "But we can still talk! I can look over the side and you'll still be able to see me. We'll have so much fun! Maybe we'll have a midnight feast when everyone else is asleep."

Laura chuckled and winked conspiratorially at her. "Maybe we will, darling."

The next day, they went to the early market and had lunch in town. Anna told Laura about the plans she was developing for her shop. They ambled around the market stalls and little shops, looking for inspiration. Every now and then, Laura picked things up and showed them to Anna, asking her whether she would think of stocking them back at home. Anna gave her verdict to each item with a simple gesture.

They looked forward to the Friday night market when—Anna told Laura—the whole town took on a magical air. The stalls had lights hanging from them that couldn't be seen during the day, and it was very special.

On Wednesday, Daniel brought them out of town, to the field that housed the Nun's Chapel. He had gone through the directions with Elba, to be sure he would remember the way.

Dawn was the first one to climb into the back of the car: telling the rest of the family, as she so often did, that her woodland friend Sylvia would need to have a space set aside for her. She'd sit in the back with her. The six of them, accompanied by the invisible Sylvia, made their way out of the campsite, through the town, and to this special place that Daniel had told them about.

Dawn was in charge of the picnic, and kept everything upright as they meandered through the country roads. She took her job very seriously, glaring at any flask that dared to tilt too much for her liking.

Daniel spotted the familiar little left turn up ahead and told the rest of the family to hold onto their hats. They turned, and he parked in the exact same spot where he had parked some years earlier with Elba.

A silence descended on the group as everyone got out of the car. Daniel offered his mother his arm to hold onto, but she shooed him away, insisting that she was fine. He did help her over the stile though, just as he had done for Elba, and she gratefully accepted this help.

The children started running the instant they got over the stile and into the field. Daniel pointed at the hillock where he had previously stood to behold the view and shouted at the children to go that way. They disappeared over the brow of the hill as the three adults walked behind them. Daniel was now carrying the picnic box—he planned to sit in the little grove where he and Elba had once shared their lunch.

"This is exciting," Anna commented, her eyes alight with intrigue. "You've talked so much about how special this place is, I can't wait to see it."

Daniel smiled at her and thought to himself how he loved this woman: the mother of his children, his soulmate. He was the luckiest man on earth.

A gentle breeze moved through Anna's hair, lifting it from her face, as she closed her eyes and looked upwards. She breathed in the air, laced with the scent of summer meadow flowers and freedom. Daniel felt a sudden rush of emotion and thanked the heavens above that they were together, on this life journey.

They soon arrived at the top of the hill. Daniel couldn't wait to see the beautiful vista again, and to watch his mother and his wife's reactions too. The children were now rolling around in the meadow before them. Cal had been keeping an anxious eye on the brow of the hill, to make sure the grown-ups arrived. As soon as he was satisfied that they had caught up with them, he relaxed and jumped straight into playtime with his brother and sister.

Anna suddenly stopped dead in her tracks. She could not believe her eyes.

"I've dreamt of this place," she breathed, awestruck. "I've been here before. . . I know this place. . ."

Laura and Daniel stopped abruptly, looked at one another, surprised.

"It is the exact same place. But there should be a rock right there." She pointed out into the distance. "Right in the centre of this place, there should be a rock with a castle on top of it. What is happening? Can you take some photos, Dan? Did you bring the camera? I want photos of this place. I want to paint it. I want photos of the children here. I want to remember this place forever."

She stopped short. How could this be? Her brow was furrowed and her eyes were brimming with tears. Neither Daniel nor Laura knew what was happening to her.

"The beauty is intoxicating," Laura ventured. "I've never seen such a stunning view."

"No. I mean, yes, I know. I know it's beautiful. It's not just that. . . I've seen this place in a dream, Laura," Anna blurted out, in a rush of excitement. Her eyes were wide open and her head was nodding, as if making what was happening truly real to her.

"You lucky thing," Laura said. "I wish I had dreams like yours." She put her arm around Anna's shoulder, and the two women stood in silence for a few minutes, watching the children.

After a while, Daniel called to the children and indicated that they were going over to the little grove to sit and eat.

"You know, Anna," he said then, suddenly remembering, "Elba said that there used to be a big basilica or cathedral in the centre of this field. She said that people used to go there to be healed, but that it was razed to the ground many centuries ago. You should talk to her about this dream you had of this place."

Anna nodded, not trusting herself to speak at first. "I mentioned the dream to her, when we had dinner. . ."

Cal, Blu and Dawn arrived, giggling and out of breath. They had picked some flowers, which they now placed in the centre of the picnic blanket. They ate hungrily, then sped off to run races between the trees. The adults watched and smiled and remembered.

"There's more," Daniel went on, after they had cleared away their lunch. "We are about to behold the Nun's Chapel, which Elba seems to think was a maternity hospital or something."

Laura and Anna smiled quizzically at him, before Anna got up and strolled back to the brow of the hill, to feast her eyes on the incredible view once again. She tried to remember where the trees had been and where she had taken shelter in her dream. . . and sure enough, they were all positioned exactly where she was expecting them to be. She was mystified. She just could not understand how she had visited this place in her dream, and was now—somehow—standing here in real life. It was an astounding sequence of events that she would never make sense of, even if she lived to be a thousand years old.

When they got to the Nun's Chapel, Daniel noticed that it was no more overgrown than he remembered from his last visit. Its interior was still emitting the same low, barely perceptible hum. The children naturally fell silent as they entered, and walked carefully around the old building, touching the ancient stones as they went.

Laura and Anna were instinctively drawn to the altar stone, Daniel noted. They headed straight for it and sat down, looking around at the ancient structure. They, too, could hear something, but they weren't sure what.

The six of them stayed in the roofless building for almost an hour. Dawn hummed a little tune to herself, and had a snooze on Laura's knee. The boys also snoozed, with their backs and heads up against the ivied walls. Daniel took photographs. Anna was far, far away in her mind. She sat with her eyes closed and listened to the air around her. She made a silent prayer to heaven that she could always have access to this feeling of deep peace and completion.

They walked silently back to the car, and no one at all spoke for the duration of their journey back to the campsite. Not even Sylvia.

On the last day of the holiday, Daniel went into town to collect Elba and bring her up to the vineyard, so she could meet Laura and spend some time with the family. They would then go to the evening market and bring Elba back to her home.

As soon as Laura saw Daniel's car pull up outside the chalet, she walked out to meet it. She stopped at the passenger door and opened it, smiling heartily at the woman in the passenger seat.

"Hello, Elba," she said warmly, as Dawn came running around the side of the chalet.

The two women clasped one another's hands tightly and engaged with happy eyes and beautiful smiles.

"It's so wonderful to meet you at last," Laura went on, "after hearing about you for so many years."

"The feeling is mutual, Laura," Elba replied. "It is my pleasure." The two women embraced and Dawn smiled happily up at Daniel.

Anna beckoned them to a shady spot at the bottom of their pitch where she had set out a little table, water, and seats for the ladies to sit and chat. She said she would go and prepare something for them to eat, but would join them shortly. The ladies thanked her and settled down, while Daniel took the children to the pool for their last swim of the day.

Elba radiated a smile and reached out to squeeze Laura's hand. "I have admired you for the longest time, Laura. I first met your son nearly twenty years ago and was lucky to spend a lot of time getting to know him."

"You shaped him, too, Elba," Laura replied graciously. "You had a massive influence on him. I remember when he stopped meeting you, he missed you so much. He often talked to me about your conversations—I could see that you really got him thinking at times. You got me thinking too! The Bridge of Now has helped me more than once throughout my life. If only I'd had it to help me in my youth. I was so grateful you gave it to Daniel."

"That's very kind of you to say, but to be honest, he was already shaped and moulded before I met him. I enjoyed my time with him so much. I tried to help him understand the length of life. How life is important, whether you're a twenty-five-year-old young man or a seventy or eighty-year-old woman. He had an innate understanding of this, and had great compassion for his fellow man. And woman." Elba smiled gently. "You went through a lot, didn't you—as a woman—to help him be such a good man."

Laura nodded. "He was my only focus for many years. My life was all about trying to make a real and true person of him. Our children are tomorrow's adults, and I think parents can forget this. The most important thing to me was that he would never put a woman through what his father had put me through. Well. . . me, and the other women he abused." She shook her head. "His father had at least two other children, you know, with two other women. Two daughters. Those girls are out there, and their father gave them a very bad grounding and example of what was acceptable from men."

She sighed a little sadly. "I hope, for their sakes, that their mothers have been able to show them otherwise, and that they don't accept the same things in their lives as I did. . . or as their mothers did. I wish women could be safe with men, could feel safe walking the streets; it's only right, when we think about it. We have to raise good men. It's a simplistic generalisation, I know, but if a boy respects his mother, his sisters, his female classmates. . . well, it gives him the best chance of respecting girls and women as he grows."

Elba nodded. She poured a glass of water each for them from the tumbler Anna had left on the table.

Laura continued, "I was delighted when Daniel met Anna. She's a real, true person, isn't she? She cares about the real things. She never cut me off from Daniel. I had decided many years ago that I would do my best to get along with whichever girl Daniel brought home. I was never going to compete with anyone. He needed to move on with his life, and I understood that it was in my best interest, personally, to find common ground with that girl. Whatever girl." She gave a knowing look to Elba, who was nodding her agreement. "But Anna made it easy. It's tough for boys now, isn't it? You know: the peer pressure, the technology, the objectifying of women. . . everything they're exposed to."

Elba nodded her agreement and remarked that every generation had their issues to deal with and decisions to make about the future. She congratulated Laura on being mother and father to Daniel, adding that sometimes she felt a lot fell to mothers in the raising of children.

"My mum wasn't there when I was a child," Laura said. "I grew up placating my father: not demanding anything from him, just fitting into his timetable and his expectations. I think I was ill-prepared for Daniel's father. He was an addict and a narcissist. Nowadays, the psychologists have named all of these patterns, so it gives people somewhere to start when you're dealing with these relationships. But I was too young and too naive to take on the big challenge that was Peter."

Elba nodded at this, understanding, then carefully ventured, "I've gathered a little about Peter, over my time talking to Daniel. What happened to him in the end, Laura? I've never really felt it was okay to ask Daniel about the details."

"He was an actor." Laura flamboyantly threw out one of her hands and rolled her eyes. Both women grinned.

"An actoooooor," chimed Elba.

They both laughed for a moment, and Laura shook her head. "He was starring in a very successful run of a play at the other end of the country. I always kept tabs on him—as much as I could. I suppose I felt that if I knew where he was, I would know he wouldn't be around me and Daniel! I felt safer from Peter, the further away he was. Even though Daniel was twenty years old by this time. . . and really, Peter couldn't have done any more harm to him."

She laughed a little ruefully. Elba nodded her agreement and tipped her glass towards her.

"There were rave reviews in the local media up there and he was riding a wave," Laura continued. "That was always a dangerous time for him. If he was doing well, it went to his head. Because he got a standing ovation every night, and people congratulated him everywhere he went, the comedown for him was very difficult—he never liked coming home to a humdrum reality. So, he would stay out as long as he could, feeding his addictions. I saw that behavior from him very early on, and I can only imagine that it got worse as he got older."

"He wanted the partying and the adulation to go on all night. He wanted to regale people in the pubs about how he'd got the part, how he'd worked for it, how he was the best man for it. I heard him tell the same stories over and over to anyone who'd listen. I'd say he was insufferable to anyone who loved him around this time."

Laura shook her head and gazed into the distance as she thought about him. Elba looked down at her hands.

"He was always adamant he'd make it big," Laura said, after a few moments of reflective silence had passed. "But he never did, because he didn't want to work for it. He had no love for his craft, his art, his ability: for all his talk, he had no real respect for his talent. He was undoubtedly extremely gifted, but he had no grounding in what that should mean: how he should mind himself and grow it."

She shook her head again, continuing, "Then he would almost take on the roles he was playing. It was like he didn't understand that he was just calling on an archetype of humanity, and he was free to take it off when he removed his costume. It was like he was possessed by the different characters."

"Of course, he played the macho hero best. It's a pity none of the idealistic natures of these characters ever rubbed off on him in real life. He was really very difficult to deal with. When he came back to get our divorce and claim his settlement, he'd just been through a low point in his career. His ego had taken a battering. Another dangerous time for him. Come to think of it, any time was a dangerous time for Peter. But he was always on to the next thing. Everything and everyone were a means to an end for him."

"This period, when he died, was probably the closest he'd ever come to really cracking it. He was staying in a boarding house, away from the woman and the daughter he had been living with. About 100 miles away, I think. He came back to his lodgings one night and accidentally overdosed on either too much—or perhaps a very bad batch—of party drugs."

"The post mortem showed huge toxicity levels in his body and a blood alcohol level of over five times the legal driving limit. So, he was totally psychedelic before he took any drugs. There were rumours that some other people had been with him at the time, but the boarding house management shut all of that talk down, and we were left with a skeletal truth. I didn't really care. The writing had been on the wall for me many years before. But I did care for Daniel. His death brought about the end of any chance of reconciliation for them as adults."

Laura sighed again as she finished her sad tale and reached out for her water.

Elba spoke gently. "I know what you're saying, but it sounds to me like Peter was not the kind of man who was likely to change. Do you think he could ever have changed?"

"Changed? No." Laura looked out into the distance again. "When he came back when Daniel was about ten, he called for him at the appointed time every week, like the perfect father. But do you know what he did with him? He took him around the corner to the pub. This was what he thought of time spent with his young son."

Elba scrunched up her face and nodded her head from side to side slowly.

"I didn't find all of this out until a few years later. A friend of Daniel's mother told me. She saw them there often; our hero, Peter, winning pool and darts and being the big man, while young Daniel sat cheering him on, looking for his love. My heart broke for my child when I heard that.

It disgusted me, but it never surprised me. If I had seen Peter around the time that I heard that story, I would have gladly shot him on sight." She looked at Elba ruefully. "Does that make me a bad person?"

"No. I think it makes you a human person, Laura." Elba snorted, then reached out and patted Laura's hand.

Laura shook herself. "Ah, I'm a worrier, Elba. I have a tendency to overthink sometimes. I plot my ways out of imagined or potential emergencies, think of Plan B and C, think of worst-case scenarios. I probably put myself under too much stress sometimes. I've read that the body doesn't know which thoughts are real and which are imaginary. So, the brain sends the signal to the body to produce fight or flight hormones, irrespective of whether the trauma is truly happening or not. I probably have high levels of this... this cortisol... all the time."

"No matter how I talk to myself about this, it still happens... and then I'm blaming myself for putting myself under all this stress." She laughed and glanced a little sheepishly at Elba. "It's a vicious circle. And I feel I have so much judgment in my heart. So many desires for different things to have happened to me on my journey... and yet, I'm also largely happy with where I've ended up. Isn't it strange?"

"It's one of the scourges of having been through trauma, I suppose," Elba answered. "You've been through hell—you've mastered that experience. But you also know, all too well, what can happen. The mind remembers. I suppose the body does, too. We humans do things when we're in pain that we never meant to do. But we react because the wound has been touched. We should never lead with the wound, as we go into battle. It devastates us."

She smiled kindly. "I think being aware of this process within you is the first step to managing it, Laura. When you first feel that familiar sense of foreboding or dread creep up on you, you recognise what's happening. You have the power within you to stop the process then and come back to the present moment—where, of course, you're always safe and in control. On the Bridge of Now, remember? If you learn to master this, it almost makes the trauma worth it!"

"Does it?" Laura laughed, then reached for another sip of her drink. "Oh, I understand what you're saying, Elba, but it's easier said than done."

"I know that, Laura—I really do." Elba leaned a little closer—she had decided to confide in her about a traumatic incident of her own. "Years ago, when I first went to the city, I was mugged by a young man. He was a scrawny little boy, only a few years older than your grandsons are now. I'll never forget the shock of it. I knew he was behind me—I even stopped and turned to look at him. Why, I don't know. I suppose I thought that would be enough to dissuade him from what he did next, but it wasn't. When I turned back in the direction I had been going, he just came at me. He had decided he wanted my handbag, and didn't care that I was aware of him.

"I was ready, and put up a bit of a struggle. I fell to the pavement and instinctively gathered my handbag under my body. He pulled me around a little bit trying to get it, and after a few short moments, he pulled out a knife and cut the strap. This enabled him to just drag the bag and run. He went off down the back streets with it. I had heard the slicing of the strap—just beside my ear—and at that moment, I let go of everything and let him take it."

Laura stared at her, wide-eyed. "Oh my God, Elba—what a horrible experience."

"Yes, it was horrible. My knees were badly scuffed, and I was in a lot of shock and pain for almost a week. I was very rattled emotionally. I'd never experienced anything so violent in my childhood here in this place. For the next number of years, I was always very aware of who was on the street with me. I was very vigilant. I didn't like being out alone. Even though I was a young, strong woman, this little teenager had made short work of me. I had to be cognizant of that. Men are stronger: even scrawny young men."

"Do I wish it hadn't happened to me? Yes, of course I do. But am I really in a position to judge that young man? How do I know what had led him to survive by mugging women on the sidewalk? But, anyway. . . the reason I'm telling you this story is because years later—maybe even thirty years later—I was aware that something was bothering me: brewing and niggling in the back of my mind. I was worried about something, but I wasn't sure what."

"It was just before I met your Daniel. I was staying in my sister's house at the time, in an unfamiliar country. So maybe it was that? When I sat with myself and deliberately asked myself to listen to what was really wrong with me, it was indeed that I feared for my safety in these unfamiliar streets. I knew nothing about the crime levels. Knew nothing about deprivation levels or social issues, or whether young men were likely to be roaming the streets looking for little old women to rob. . ." she smiled over at Laura. "When I stopped to listen to myself, a lot of my anxieties came out. I felt a lot better for having done that listening to myself."

"It probably would do nothing to lessen my chances of being mugged, but at least I'd been heard by myself. I had acknowledged the creeping fear within me. I was able to reflect on what I'd do to protect myself and lessen my chances of being attacked again. I listened to the fears I had, about how I mightn't bounce back as quickly as I had done in my early twenties. I listened to my vulnerability. No, it didn't mean I knew what was around every corner, or that I could prevent ever being mugged again. But it did mean that I'd acknowledged the fear within me, so it no longer had the power to run that low-level humming anxiety within me. It was going to negatively impact my life if I didn't address it."

"I also made some decisions to keep myself as safe as I could—I would take a well-worn route to the train station, at busy times, and try to get home before dark. Not out of fear, but out of respect for myself. To honor myself. Some things we won't change in our lifetimes, Laura. Some things will be left to our granddaughters and great granddaughters."

"That's so very powerful," Laura mused. "Just acknowledging the fear and doing what you can is half the battle."

"Yes. Name it. Explore it. Listen to yourself. It was around this time that I met Daniel. He reminded me that the city was also inhabited by safe young men, who didn't look at me and wonder what was in my bag. My fear, unexplored and unexpressed, might have made me fearful of all young men. And Laura, we would not be sitting here now having this conversation in that case."

The two women smiled at one another, and Laura clasped Elba's hand once again. "I really am so thankful to have met you, Elba."

"And I you."

Daniel soon returned from the pool with the boys and Dawn. Dawn crawled up on Laura's knee and snuggled into her chest. "Oh, my tired baby," Laura crooned, stroking her hair. Anna called out a minute later, so they all moved towards the chalet to have dinner.

During dinner, Daniel told Elba that Anna's dream had been about the place they'd been to up at the Nun's Chapel.

"Oh, that's unusual," Elba commented, "but not unheard of. You may have spent many lifetimes up there, Anna." She winked at the younger woman. "It is a very potent and powerful spiritual place; they say it's a vortex into another time and sphere." Elba wiggled her eyebrows at Dawn, who was open-mouthed at her description of a place where she herself had been!

"Didn't you say something about there being a basilica in that field once, in olden times, that was destroyed?" Daniel prompted her, trying to remember the story himself.

"Yes, in olden times. . ." Elba said dreamily, then smiled at her enthralled audience. "Didn't Einstein prove to us that time and space are but an illusion? It is not absolute; this construct of time and space is probably a mental construct. But we don't talk about that because it doesn't suit the agenda that keeps the world turning in the way our societal structures want it to. Time not existing won't pay the mortgage!"

Elba giggled to herself and continued. "There is nothing in the laws of physics to state that time moves in the forward direction we perceive, you know. Therefore, the basilica—if it ever was there—still is there. It's certainly a very special field, and the spirit of the place is very healing. There are said to be many treasures buried in the fields around there. I'm not surprised to hear that you've seen it in your mind's eye Anna." She smiled at her. "Were you in a magical place when you connected to it?"

"Yes, actually," Anna replied. "I was in Dawn's fairy garden; I fell asleep there. And I saw that field as clearly in my dream as I saw it standing on that hillock."

"This fairy garden must be a bit of a power place then too," Elba said.

"It is, it is!" Dawn perked up at this mention of a subject she could speak about with great authority. She would not be left out of any story involving her beloved fairy garden. "It's full of 'majory friends, Elba. But I don't think they're really 'majory—I think some people just can't see them properly. They're mostly for small children. They fade as you get older. I'm getting older now."

"Well, yes indeed, there are some things we cannot explain." Elba smiled at Dawn and raised her eyebrows expectantly. Dawn nodded knowingly, and they both giggled.

"Do you really believe in past lives, Elba?" Anna asked suddenly. The old woman's earlier suggestion was playing on her mind: she had been startled by it at first, but on a deeper level, she was unsurprised by the idea that she could once have lived in the place that had housed the ancient basilica. "Do you really think that I could have been in that place before? In another time?"

"I don't know. I believe we have imagination that can be construed as memory. Or we could have a memory that could be construed as imagination. We have no way of knowing which it is when it comes to talking about past lives. I believe that as far as we're aware, our consciousness is here—in this moment. This moment is our point of power, then. So, I don't worry about the rest of it, as I'll never find the answer. At my age, you pick your battles!" Elba chuckled, then turned back to Anna. "Why do you ask?"

"I was just thinking about karma. What is the force that draws people to one another and to places and such like? I was just following thought through my mind," Anna said. "I meet people at yoga who are very spiritual and always going off on weekends to explore these aspects. Past lives, healing, karma. . ."

"Ah now, I believe karma gets a bad rap," Elba said briskly. "Like it's used by some punitive deity to teach you lessons. I see karma as the universal law of balance. Just balance—that's all. Equal and opposite actions and reactions, bringing the pendulum back to balance. For example, if I owe you money, I can repay the money to you, or give you my car, or my rings and earrings, or something of the same monetary value. There are many ways in which I can repay you. Can you imagine a deity waiting around the corner to jump out and trip you up because of something you did in the Middle Ages that you have no conscious memory of? That doesn't make any sense to me. I don't believe that the universe believes in punishment. Just experience and lessons. We are just experiencing life on the tapestry that's been formed by our collective experience."

"Say in a lifetime—if different lifetimes even exist—I were to kill you. What would be achieved in the next lifetime by your killing me? Our souls would be just caught in a never-ending spiral of death and revenge. What good would that do?" Elba shook her head and Dawn— eager to align herself with this enchanting woman—joined in with her. Dawn thought it was probably a good idea to listen carefully to everything the 'majory star woman said. She decided to mirror her, nod when she nodded, raise her eyebrows when Elba did and agree sagely and authoritatively with everything she said.

Elba smiled at Dawn, as if she could read her mind, and gave her a little wink. Then she looked back at Anna. "It is better for us to transcend and grow and find healthier ways to rebalance this karma, if it exists. As they say, an eye for an eye makes us both blind."

"If there are many lives, I would like this to be my last life," Laura declared, in an exhausted tone, out of the blue.

"What?" asked Elba, mock-horrified, and swept her arm around the table. "To never eat with these people again? To never witness the budding of a summer rose? Smell its scent? Never taste a ripe orange? Are you sure?"

"Well. . . no!" laughed Laura. "No. I'm not sure at all. . . when you put it that way. No. I'm just tired." She started to giggle to herself. Why would she even think such a thing?

"I agree," Elba said amiably, as she settled back in her chair. "We should leave the decisions like that for another time and place. I sometimes think I'm finished here—I'm getting weaker and older, but life hasn't finished with me yet. If I do go tonight, though, I'm happy with my legacy—the little sprinklings of courage I've been blessed to leave on people's lives. I'm honoured to have witnessed such beauty. And strength. Whatever is waiting for us on the other side, we will have to do our best with it. But the work we've done doesn't belong to us. The work stands alone. God has no hands on earth but ours, remember."

"That's a lovely thought, Elba," said Anna with a smile.

"Yes. And apply it to your creations, too, Anna," Elba urged her. "If you were to stop painting now. Say you were to go on an anti-painting rampage, become anti-painting. . ."

Dawn giggled at the thought of her mother going on such an anti-painting campaign and Laura reached out and tickled her.

". . . it would in no way affect the beauty of the creations that adorn the walls of those who've bought your lovely paintings to date," Elba finished. "The work stands. And what's of benefit to one is of benefit to all."

Daniel was washing up the dinner dishes and relishing eavesdropping on the female conversation. Why didn't men talk like this? The two boys were chatting and laughing in their room, no doubt planning the last morning of their holiday. Daniel decided that he had never, ever been happier than he was at this moment. This was what life was all about.

The market was warm and full of tourists and locals mixing amiably, when they dropped Elba home and took a last stroll around this beautiful town. As Daniel walked Elba up the steps to her home, he got a pang in his heart as he realised that this was probably the last time he would ever see her.

It was dark, so she turned on the lamp as soon as they got inside and she said to him, "Daniel, thank you. It has been a huge honor for me to spend time with the people that you love most in the world. I will never, ever forget you all." Daniel wondered, not for the first time, had she read his mind. He blushed slightly and said earnestly to her, "Elba, the honor is mine. I am indebted to you in numerous ways."

"There are no debts in Love, darling boy. And I love you very much. Be very proud of what you have created in your life. Go and enjoy it. Raise great children—for they will be needed. The Earth is changing. Love is taking over. We will all need to stand up for Love, when we are called."

Daniel did not know what she meant, but as their eyes locked, he nodded to her and said, "Love is all there is."

Chapter Eleven

During her teenage years, Dawn grew into an impassioned yet contradictory young woman. She was committed to activism and making things better, but was also very accepting of the way some things were. She tried to pick her battles, but sometimes her emotions got her tangled in things she couldn't change and this caused her hurt and pain.

She often worked in her mother's shop. Her creative spirit soon led her to start making crystal bead earrings, pendants, and rings, using craft wire and stones from her mother's stock. They sold well, so Anna put that money aside to ensure that Dawn would have it available to her when she went away to college.

The back wall of the 'Love, Grace' shop was adorned with a special canvas that Daniel had made for Anna, using one of his photographs of the wonderful day the family had shared during their vacation. The canvas displayed the enchanted valley they had visited that had also appeared in Anna's dream.

Daniel's photographs from that day had acquired a very special place in the family's hearts. They had set aside a particular photo album for those pictures. Anna often sat with this album and leafed through it, recalling each treasured memory in detail as she did so. The boys sleeping against the ivy walls of the Nun's Chapel. The women sitting on the table. The children running through the fields.

Anna had no idea how Daniel had found the wherewithal to capture everything. She herself had spent that entire day in a haze!

When she was establishing her shop, Anna made sure to set up the phone and till desk beneath the exact spot on the canvas where she imagined the rock and its blooming castle would have been. She firmly believed that this gave her strength and protection. She also made sure to paint each one of her little cards with the three stars in this spot, and always felt more connected to what she was painting.

She loved the days when Dawn was in the shop with her. They were both focused on what they were doing, and conversation flowed more naturally between them. She got to know the true character of her daughter during these days spent together, when both of them were in their own creative space.

One day, she watched from a chair beside the desk that Daniel called "her little perch", as Dawn crossed the street to the local supermarket to get some lunch rolls for them. She noticed Dawn lean down to talk to a homeless man who was often seated outside the supermarket, begging for money.

She saw her put some notes into the cup he was using to collect cash. They were smiling and chatting easily together, and Anna was proud of her.

On her way back out of the shop, Anna noticed that she'd gotten him a roll and a drink as well, and had laid them down beside him. She searched her pockets for what Anna soon saw were salt and pepper sachets for the man. The two exchanged another few pleasantries before Dawn made her way back across the road.

As soon as she was back, they hungrily started into their own lunches. Anna asked her why she had given the man food and money, too. "I hate to say this, but he'll probably only drink it, Dawn. . ."

Dawn looked up at her with great annoyance. "So what if he does buy drink with it?"

"I'm just saying, Dawn. . ."

"Maybe that's all he has to look forward to!" Dawn burst out. "A few drinks. He's not the problem, Mum. Don't you think that a person would rather do almost anything else with their day than sit on a cold pavement, hoping that one out of every hundred people might care a little bit about them? I would! I could think of nothing I'd rather do less than sit over there begging. How much lower do you think he has to go to plead for our help? He is baring his soul over there, mum. He's not the problem. The system that allows him to exist in that space is the problem. Where are the supports for that man, whatever he needs? Whatever he's done or not done in the past? Where is his hope? Why should we deny him a few drinks or his drugs or whatever, when we've nothing else to offer him? We won't solve the drug problem by denying him his few spliffs or whatever else he might need to ease his pain. Drug barons on their yachts. . . drinks companies running their big-shot marketing campaigns. . ."

She was getting upset now. Anna said gently, "You're right, Dawn. He is not the problem. He's actually a very nice man. I often talk to him, too. It is society that's let him down. Of course it is. I didn't mean to upset you and you're right. You've made me think. I agree that by denying him his fix—whatever it might be—is actually a cruel thing to do, in the absence of offering him hope to create something different for himself. Yes, I'm sorry. I didn't think before I spoke."

Dawn relaxed slightly. "It's okay, Mum. It's not your fault. I see what you're saying. I just get so upset by things I see sometimes. I'm so frustrated by things like this, that could be so easily fixed. Life should be much easier than this shambolic system we have in place."

"I know, my love." Anna wanted her to stop now. The pioneering, warrior spirit that Dawn possessed could go from her just feeling something in her heart, to her being consumed by overreaching sorrow and anger, in no time at all. Anna wished her daughter was able to find the balance within herself.

But Anna was as proud of her daughter as she could be; she looked across at the man eating his roll and reached across to rub Dawn's shoulder. She had learned something very important from her daughter's compassion.

Anna's father, Jim, had fought the good fight and lived for two more years after Grace's death.

June had been an absolute godsend, as she had lived with him for that entire time. She acquired a home help assistant for his meals, washing, and personal care, but sat with him every night: answering the same questions again and again; giving him his medication; and putting him to bed. She was a saint, as far as Anna was concerned.

During the weeks leading up to his death, Jim constantly asked his daughters who was that man and that woman and those people, and what did they all want. . . it was clear that he was seeing things.

This upset Anna greatly, but June just pretended that she, too, could see whoever he was talking about, and replied that it was just a friend who'd popped in to see him. He always seemed satisfied with that—cheered by it, even—and would smile and raise his eyebrows in the direction of whatever he was looking at.

"What's he seeing, June? Who is he seeing?" Anna would often ask in a fretful tone.

"God knows, Anna. God alone knows, but I'm sick of it now. If these people are here to take him, why doesn't he just go?" June would laugh.

The sisters drank copious amounts of tea each evening. It was a healing time for them both, to sit together at the kitchen table, in the house where they had grown up, connecting with one another in a deeper way than they had previously been able to achieve. Each of the sisters learned more about who the other really was.

There were a number of questions that Anna had always wanted to ask June—not out of nosiness, but out of a desire to understand June and be there for her, just as June had been there for her when she was feeling low after Cal's birth.

She wanted to know why June had never met someone or gotten married. What were her wishes now? Was she looking for a relationship or was she happy to be single?

Anna wasn't really sure how to approach these questions. She didn't want to be insensitive to her sister, or make her feel as though she thought there was something wrong with her, or that there was something missing from her life. In fact, Anna had often thought that it might be nice to be a single professional, with no one to worry about but yourself. She knew that June often traveled abroad, or embarked upon interesting day trips, with a number of walking and hiking groups.

Her older sister's life was very full. Anna had no doubt about that, but she sometimes wondered why June had never introduced the family to a partner, or spoken to them about any special person in her life.

She danced around the subject for some time—uncertain whether or not she should broach it—but one night, she decided to just take the plunge and asked June, straight out, whether she would like to meet somebody and have a relationship with them.

June answered her question with equal directness.

"Yes," she said simply. "I would, Anna, actually. I've been thinking about it recently. Thinking maybe it's time I settled down! I've been happy on my own up until now. . . but I think I've come to a stage in life where I'm more mellow. Less selfish. Better able to share my time and my life, maybe. Every decision I've made up until now was entirely my own, and I have enjoyed that."

Anna smiled. "You were always so independent, June. A firebrand, Dad called you. Why don't you join an agency? Lots of people find men online. Some are on their second go around—with marriages that haven't worked, or whatever—but they're wonderful guys, just waiting for the perfect match."

Anna thought she was being helpful, and was surprised to see a glint of amusement in her sister's eye.

"Anna," June chuckled, shaking her head, "you do know that I'm gay, don't you?"

"Gay?"

"Yes. I'm gay. . . so that would make me. . . not looking for a man."

"Oh, of course not, no. If you're gay. . . well then, a man is the last thing you'd be looking for." Anna started to giggle, and June soon joined in. They laughed together for a few moments, letting the air between them fill with humor.

"June. . . seriously, though. . . I never knew you were gay. Why didn't you tell me?" Anna asked, when the mirth had finally settled down.

She could remember Daniel asking her, many years ago, whether June was gay, as he had noticed that she never mentioned having any man in her life. But Anna could recall June dating a few boys during her younger years, so she told Daniel that no, June wasn't gay. She had never really thought about it since.

June shrugged. "I didn't see any reason to make a big deal of it, to be honest. I never got to a point in my life where it was going to impact Mum and Dad, or involve having to tell them. I was never on the verge of marriage—or even in very serious relationships, where I'd be bringing anyone to dinner to meet them. I know they would have accepted it: they were great parents. . . but I was aware that I'd put them through a lot as a teen. I didn't want to continue making them stretch themselves to accept this as well, and feel obliged to tell the family and the aunties and the cousins. . . and then if I had told you, well then, you'd have to be hiding it or pretending you didn't know. To me, there just never seemed to be any point in telling people about it. I was fine. It would be different these days. If I were young now, starting out. . . yes, I would tell them. I did think you knew, though, Anna, I have to say. I'm not sure why—perhaps because I know how intuitive you are—but I had a feeling you'd picked up on it. I was sure you knew."

June started laughing again, and Anna suddenly felt indescribably stupid. Her sister's orientation had always been obvious, now that she thought about it.

"Well, I'm sorry I never asked," she said gently. "You know, there must have been times when you needed someone to talk to."

"Not really, Anna. I knew by the time I got to teacher training college that I was gay. I suppose I spent my teens rebelling against it and trying not to be, if you can do such a thing. I was so angry when I was a teenager, and I think a lot of that was because I was angry with myself. I wanted to be like the other girls I hung out with: only interested in guys. I wanted to be different. I thought I was bisexual for a while. You might remember a few boyfriends from my early twenties, but I wasn't bisexual. I am not, rather. I'm just plain old gay."

"Plain old gay is fine, so long as you're happy, June. Did you ever think about whether you wanted children? Is that too personal a question to ask?" Anna asked, narrowing her eyes as she wondered how June would react.

"No, it's not too personal, Anna. . . and obviously, I have thought about it over the years. Especially when Cal was born and I became his godmother. I was 41 then and I really, really loved him so much that I wondered whether it was my own biological clock giving me a nudge. But no, Blu arrived and I was certain then that my nephews were enough for me. Dawn was the icing on all our cakes, I think."

The two sisters sat back on their chairs, lost in their own thoughts for a few moments.

Then June leaned across to Anna and whispered, "To be honest, I don't know how you coped when they were small. Mayhem! I've never regretted not having my own children. Not for a moment. Mothers probably find that hard to believe. The amount of my friends who've said, 'You'll regret it.' But I haven't. Never. I've taught kids at school. That was more than enough for me!"

"Some mothers probably just don't understand where you're coming from June. But I do. I've never felt you were missing anything in not having children," Anna said, meaning every word.

"I got sick of having to explain myself to the women at work, then taking on their fears and torturing myself—searching underneath my soul, nearly," June laughed, "for the place where I must have been hiding my unhappiness at not being a mother. I thought I had to find this elusive part of me that was supposed to be so unfulfilled.

"Of course, some of the women I would explain this to would just nod and smile, and I'd see in their eyes that they thought I was deluding myself. That would irritate me; it irritated me for years. Then I looked at the reality. These were only their opinions. I had to let them have those opinions. I'd only waste my energy trying to argue my point; how and when would I know I'd convinced them, and why was I even going to waste my time trying to vindicate myself?"

Anna nodded, understanding

"My God, it's still so hard for women, isn't it?" June exclaimed. "Always trying to excuse ourselves and apologise for ourselves. Sick of it. And sometimes it seems it's the women are hardest on other women. Who is the perfect woman, anyway?"

"All of that is nearly the total opposite of what I went through, when you think about it," Anna mused. "Strange, isn't it? There must be a balance."

"Yeah, the balance is to leave women alone and let them get on with doing whatever they want to do!" June grinned.

"Totally agree, June," Anna said firmly. "So, tell me: you've said you would be interested in a relationship, but are you actively looking for one at the moment? And I know you've never met anyone serious enough to bring home to our parents, but has there ever been anyone... semi-serious, perhaps?"

"Not really. There've been a couple of women I loved spending time with over the years, but when it came to making things serious..." June grimaced. "You said it yourself, Anna—I'm fiercely independent. Set in my ways, I suppose. I like my own company, but I am thinking... you know... once Dad passes, and I go home... I'll put more thought into meeting someone I can really be myself with. Then I'll start looking. Sending out a request to the universe not to make that too difficult!" June threw her arms up in the air and smiled.

"That'd be lovely," Anna said with great sincerity. "I could see you in a relationship, June. I think it would suit you."

"Hm. Time will tell, I suppose." June got up to take their empty teacups to the sink and glanced at her sister with another flash of mirth in her eyes. "We'll see how it goes!"

This was her cue to leave, Anna thought. She rose from her chair, hugged her sister, and thanked her for confiding in her. They gave one another a huge smile that reached right to their eyes. All of the old pain and misunderstanding melted in the warmth of the love between them.

The following week, they got a call from the carer, telling them that Jim had fallen and hit his head. He was very dazed, and didn't know who she was, or where he was. She was going to ring an ambulance.

Anna closed the shop. June left the school. The girls met at A&E again, and were overcome by a sense of deja-vu.

"Here we are again," June remarked sadly.

Then they saw their father being rushed past them. He'd had an enormous aneurysm, and he was gone. Just like that. The doctor explained that they'd never have known when it was going to burst, and they couldn't have prevented it. It was just one of those things.

"One of those things." The girls felt this sentence running around their heads on an endless loop over the following few days, as they tried to deal with the practicalities of funeral planning. They often repeated it to one another as they moved about the house, numb with shock.

They felt as though they had been cheated of the closing part of Jim's life. Their big, strong father who had the biggest heart of any man they had ever met. Just gone, without either of them having had a chance to be with him in his final hours and moments. They'd always assumed they would be chatting to him and holding his hand as they watched him gradually slip away from this world, just as they had done with Grace.

But it wasn't to be. One of those things.

Anna's children came together solemnly during the funeral service and honored their grandfather—the only grandfather they had known. Daniel, Anna, and Laura were so proud of them. Their conduct was impeccable; mature, reflective, and loving. They spoke so movingly of Jim that there was not a dry eye in the church.

The family remained together for a few days after the funeral. They reminisced, told stories, went through all of the old photos, and celebrated Jim's life. When June and Anna ordered the lettering on the headstone of his grave, they made sure to include their sister's name, Emma. Just as Jim had always wanted.

The 'majory people of Dawn's childhood had receded into the foliage—all, that is, except for her dear friend, Sylvia. Sylvia often visited Dawn in her dreams and spoke to her of a time to come, when she would be needed. Dawn still spent time under the trees of her childhood fairy garden, reading and writing. It was there that she felt Sylvia's presence most strongly.

For the most part, Dawn felt that life was intended to flow smoothly, and that it was all about following your path. She seldom worried about her future, as she had always believed that life had a plan in store for her, even if she wasn't consciously aware of it yet. She was dedicated to simply enjoying the journey.

She knew she had been lucky so far: blessed with a loving home and family. She had an innate understanding that she would be supported in the future, too, when she left home and embarked upon her own independent life. She had a sense that she was on a mission of some kind. There were many inequalities she could see around her in society, and they irritated her immensely, but she had decided that she would do her very best to change them, within her own sphere of influence. She had decided not to rage at life if she didn't have to—she would try to pick her battles.

In one of her dreams, Sylvia had told her clearly that she was a warrior of light, and that this was her time. The women in her blood line, Sylvia said, went back to a tradition of ancient priestesses who had existed in a civilization that humanity no longer remembered. All of the women who had gone before her had held a part of the jigsaw, and it wouldn't be until Dawn's piece was put into its allotted place that everything would fall into place for her and the true picture would form.

Sylvia told Dawn that her life—formed, as it was, from the lineage of these powerful women—was perfectly encoded for her to be able to make a startling impression on the future of the planet. "The time is upon us for the truths to be told," she said with great solemnity.

Sylvia unfurled the entire back story of Dawn's female lineage during one very long dream she had one night.

Dawn was shown the female healers and the warrior women of her ancestry. She saw the leaders of communities and women on thrones; she saw queens and princesses and presidents, some of whom had existed in eras that were never recorded in modern history. She saw the truth tellers, the way seers, and the witches. She saw the urchin girls, the prostitutes, the scientists, the alchemists and midwives. She saw the professors, the holy women, the doctors, and the teachers.

Then she saw the mothers and the daughters who had acted in a perfect relay, to hand to her the life mission that was now hers. She knew each woman—each face, each set of eyes—on an intimate level. She could read their souls. She thanked them for what they had contributed to her life and consciousness today.

The timelines of each woman spread out, from a beautiful bridge on which she stood in the dream. They formed an enormous tapestry behind her, like a cloak that had been laid out over millennia. She could see the life of her mother, as well as the lives of her two grandmothers, Laura and Grace, knitting the tapestry into her own timeline. She was in awe at the intricacies of this mysterious cloak's design.

Dawn felt a very special responsibility as she wrapped this cloak around herself. She wondered whether she could have carried the burdens that her ancestors had, but Sylvia told her she didn't have to compare herself in any way to them. The ancient women in her family timeline had borne what was theirs to bear, and that was all Dawn needed, in order to achieve what she had come to this planet to do.

Dawn could feel that these women were alive within her. Their achievements, loves, teachings, losses, suppression, persecution, and demonization were a part of her story, too. She was deeply honored and grateful to have been shown the stories of the women who had gone into making her.

Sylvia told her that it was important that she take this legacy seriously, but carry it lightly. Dawn asked Sylvia for a guarantee that she would live up to her task, but Sylvia would not give it. She told her that she had free will at all times, and that her humanness had to be taken into consideration—most of all, by herself.

She was not here, Sylvia told her, to act out a pre-ordained script written by another hand. She was a creator herself—or more precisely, a co-creator—with Spirit and with all other beings on the planet, alive and dead, in spirit and on earth. As with life itself, every dream and idea had its own energy and intelligence.

Opportunities would be plentiful to make great progress at this time, but there would be no judgment. The times in which Dawn lived were very auspicious for a massive leap in consciousness, and she was one of many who would help to bring humanity over a very large bridge.

Dawn was awed by what Sylvia told her, and accepted her message gratefully.

The previous week, she had decided that she wanted to study English literature, social studies, and psychology, and be of service to people in the future. She wanted to find a language that would help people to understand that life was never meant to be complicated.

Now, she added that she also wanted to contribute to the lineage and legacy of the women from her dream: to hold and use the power of what they had so carefully cultivated. She would hand on their gifts as deeply as she could to those who would come after her. She would be a link in this beautiful chain.

Dawn often watched the news in disbelief. She couldn't understand why humans made everything so complicated. Was it not in everybody's interest for all people to be treated equally? It seemed to her that throughout the world, there were riots over the treatment of one oppressed group after another. She saw the riots as an expression of different strands of humanity trying to be heard and to heal.

The race riots caught her attention: she couldn't believe that people had to fight so hard for basic human rights that she knew should have been a given. She saw how oppressed groups were met with resistance and force by people who had no right to withhold these basic rights from another human being in the first place.

Racism was easily defined in Dawn's mind as simple fear. She saw it as a belief system built by centuries of injustice, intolerance, and fear of backlash. She felt that the oppressors were assuming that their historical victims would be merciless in seeking revenge for themselves and their forefathers.

Dawn knew that the oppressors were just ascribing their own natures to the people they'd oppressed, and that this would never provide the opportunity for all races to come together and live peacefully.

At its heart, Dawn felt that the solution was simple: we were all One. She had been born with little ego or greed, and she was naturally expansive and inclusive in her views.

There had to be enough people in the world who felt the same way she did. She wanted to dedicate her life to getting that message out there. Perhaps she should start by finding other people who felt like she did, and then growing that group.

Dawn's school friends loved her empathy, and found her advice and counsel to be invaluable. Among her peer group, Dawn encountered very little resistance to her outlook on life. Her friends came to her with many of their own stories and backgrounds, but Dawn was always able to help them see things from a different perspective and ease the pain of what they were feeling. Her best friend, Debbie, was the person that she herself relied on. They shared everything and went everywhere together. They'd seen one another through all of the teen dramas and had accompanied one another through all the teenage initiations.

Having seen and met the characters in her ancestral line during that momentous dream, she had come to understand the greater tapestry of life. Her beloved friend, Sylvia, had gone silent since then, as Dawn was now preparing to finish school and all of her attention was going to her studies. But she had seen and understood enough during that amazing dream to know that she was completely safe and protected. Her future would be bright.

Dawn's optimistic attitude rubbed off on her friends. They were a great bunch of people, and she enjoyed hanging out with them, laughing and joking together. She had had a few boyfriends during her early teens, but it wasn't until she was seventeen years old—and met a boy named Mark—that she understood what it was to have strong feelings for someone.

Mark had moved to their town from another part of the country. He was different to some of the other boys she'd met. He was quiet, and usually chose to stand in the background of their crowd of friends. He seemed to watch rather than react. As the new boy in school, she presumed that he was still finding his feet.

She was very interested in him, and liked to imagine that he was equally fascinated by her. She often found herself daydreaming about him, but it took her some time to work up the courage to do anything about it.

Right before their final exams, they would be having an end-of-year ball event. Dawn hoped that Mark would ask her to go with him. Everyone was allowed to bring a date from another school, and she hoped that Mark didn't have a girlfriend from his old school—she had never dared to ask him. She discussed and planned what to do with Debbie. Debbie urged her to take the bull by the horns and ask him out straight.

One day, after much dithering, she finally decided to take matters into her own hands. She asked him whether he would like to go to the ball with her, and he smiled broadly and told her that he would love to. From that moment on, they were inseparable.

Mark wanted to study medicine and travel to parts of the world that were enduring war and strife, so he could help people there. He was very serious about his studies, which inspired Dawn to work extra hard to get good grades, so that they could go to university together.

Dawn often spoke to him about the many problems in their own society, pointing out that he wouldn't have to go far to see the homelessness and the disenfranchised in towns and cities close to home. She didn't feel the need to travel to help people: she wanted to work within her own sphere of influence.

Mark, however, felt that their own people owed those from other continents, because of the centuries of colonization and brutality that had been visited upon those far-flung places.

"Someone needs to take the world and turn it upside down," he commented. "Deconstruct what has been erected, implement a new ideal, and then we'll have something approaching the way it should be for all humans."

She couldn't disagree with that.

They had great plans for where they would go and what they would do together. They both agreed that they would need a whole battalion of people with similar motives and ethics.

They knew their parents wouldn't approve of them moving in together so young, and they didn't really want to start living together so soon anyway. Once they left school, they had plans for Dawn to live with Debbie and some other girlfriends, while he would be with some guys. They'd make sure they were close to one another.

Within their group, they soon became known as the stable couple. This didn't mean they were boring or staid. They knew how to have fun and be young and carefree. They just had an air about them that made them right together. There was never any storming off or drama between them.

When the time came for the end-of-year ball, Mark arrived at Dawn's home to pick her up. He came bearing chocolates and flowers, and his parents accompanied him. Daniel and Anna welcomed them in for drinks, and they all sat out in the back garden, enjoying the evening sun.

Dawn's brothers Cal and Blu were home for the weekend, eager to see their sister off on her first real adult night out. They had never met Mark until tonight, and wanted to get a sense of him and how he would treat their sister. They joked with him that he and Dawn would be up to all sorts that night, and Mark looked at them, aghast. This seemed to settle the boys. They were sure that Dawn would be safe.

Mark knew he was being set up, but he didn't know how to deal with these two young men.

The brothers were both working in the city by this time, and lived in an apartment, along with another friend of theirs. They had only been apart for one year—after Cal had gone to university and Blu was still at school—but Blu soon followed his older brother, and they had spent the majority of their college years together on campus, becoming known as The Brothers.

They both had plans to travel, and were working in jobs that they didn't feel were their 'forever' jobs. Cal was still the more cautious of the two, but Blu's enthusiasm for life and new experiences was infectious.

Blu wanted to head east to Tibet and India soon, followed by Australia and New Zealand. The brothers were saving up for this trip of a lifetime. It would take them a full year to complete, but the sensible Cal already had the entire itinerary planned out, almost down to the hostels they'd stay in and the train timetables they'd need.

Dawn loved the two of them with all her heart—she smiled as she watched them teasing Mark. She would have to talk to them about that tomorrow, but she felt happy that they had come home to check him out. In their eyes, she would always be their baby sister, and they would always be protective of her. She understood that.

Daniel—who had acquired a solid reputation as the family's photographer by this time—took some lovely pictures of the young couple before they headed off on their night out.

Mark's parents left soon afterwards, and the boys soon headed into town to meet some friends.

Anna and Daniel sat alone at the kitchen table for a while before deciding that they would rather go to bed than wait up all night for Dawn to come home. They trusted their daughter, and wanted her to have fun and let her hair down.

They both slept like logs. The following morning, they found Dawn fast asleep in her bed, with her gown hanging up on her wardrobe door.

"I don't know what we did to deserve her," Anna said fondly, then glanced at Daniel. "What were you like at her age?"

"I never gave my mother a second's trouble," he assured her, with a grin.

"I'll have to check the veracity of that statement with Laura," she teased him, then shook her head. "I remember Dawn's Aunty June! My poor parents used to be worn out, looking for her and trying to keep her on the straight and narrow. It was very stressful for everyone. But I understand now that things were hard for her during those years." She squeezed Daniel's hand and smiled at him. "We're lucky to have Dawn."

"Yes, we are," he agreed, and hugged his wife fondly.

After completing her exams, Dawn spent the summer working in the shop and making plans for her time in university. She was sure she had done well enough to get the call she was hoping for.

When the results came out, it looked like both she and Mark had gotten their first choice. They were ecstatic. Debbie too, and the whole group were heading on their next big adventure.

It was a time of great celebration in Dawn's life, but during her quiet moments—when she was alone with her own thoughts and visions—she was starting to receive premonitions that she didn't fully understand.

She often felt that she could see a future in which everything would be easier, but before that, a time was coming that would test them all. She knew that the path of least resistance was to accept whatever was coming exactly as it unfolded: to recognise fear, and not to punish it. She didn't want to waste time obsessing over why things happened in the way that they did: she had too much life to live.

Despite that, she could feel an ill wind approaching that foretold a time of darkness and panic. One night, she dreamed that her society was about to make many mistakes, and that many would drown or perish. It would be a moment of reckoning for humanity. She didn't know whether this was a foretelling. Sylvia did not appear in the dream, so she pondered that it might be a reflection of her own subconscious fears surfacing.

She needed help. She wanted to understand what she was seeing.

She asked for Sylvia to come and talk to her, even going so far as to light candles and intoning her guide's name. There was no response. She tried to remain lucid and alert during her dreams, to ensure she heard Sylvia's every word. But Sylvia didn't speak. She went out to her fairy garden and knocked on trees for the Wood Queen to come and assist her, but the leaves seemed to laugh at her.

She shook wind chimes to attract her 'majory people, and left out chocolate and lemonade. She went through all of her normal rituals. Nothing.

Where were they all gone? All of her fairies and guides and her constant companion, Sylvia?

In the end, her eyes had to be drawn to beauty and faith. She knew that she was being asked to hold onto the vision she had been born with. By the time the coming decade was over, society at large would be ready, she felt, to admit to its mistakes and embrace the change that was required. It was time for her to accept whatever was to come.

In the end, her generation would help vindicate her foremothers— the brave women whose witch wounds had oozed septic, sacrificial blood that had taken so many generations to heal, in order for it to now flow as clearly as it did in her own veins.

In the end, she knew she would ready herself for the sacred battle of love for which prior generations had prepared her.

In the end, she would wait for her name to be called.

In the end, the song of the Divine Matriarch would sing in her heart.

Chapter Twelve

Laura managed to continue living independently until quite late into her 80s. After her eightieth birthday, she came to live near Daniel and Anna. She wanted to make this move while she was still in good health, rather than placing Daniel into a difficult position at a later date.

She had decided, long ago, that she would talk to Daniel and Anna about her plans before she became too old or frail to look after herself. She didn't want Daniel to feel responsible for minding her, to constantly travel to see her, or God forbid, to be placed under pressure to suddenly move her in with his family, if something were to happen to her.

They all chose Laura's new house together. Anna kept an eye on any new properties that were listed for sale in the area. She viewed many houses alone, and some with Daniel. Every few weeks, Laura would come to visit and they would get some viewings done together. Laura greatly enjoyed these trips, as she could well remember walking around the area with the boys and Dawn when they were babies. She had always loved the atmosphere of their neighborhood.

One day, they all decided to check out a little cottage bungalow two streets away from Daniel and Anna's home. The instant they walked up the little driveway, they knew this was the one. It had a beautiful south facing back garden and a pebbled front garden with railings and a small path. It was perfect.

Laura had plenty of money put aside for residential care, should that ever be needed. She told this to Daniel and Anna—adding, as she did so, that it was her wish to never be a burden to them living their lives freely. Her instruction was that if she were ever to 'lose it', they were to lose her! In the meantime, she would try her best to mind herself and keep herself healthy.

Daniel and Anna silently prayed they would never have to make that decision.

Dawn was the grandchild with whom Laura had always had the best relationship. The boys had been thick as thieves growing up, looking to one another for their support and company. They seemed to communicate in a secret language of their own. Dawn was more outward looking and inclined to seek out the company of others, including her grandmother. She spent many holidays and long weekends with Laura, and their relationship was deep and easy: a friendship, even.

The boys had grown up and left for college by the time Laura arrived in the area, but they loved the fact that she was now nearby any time they visited home.

Dawn began to make a habit of getting off the school bus one stop early, to drop in and see her. She had a key to Laura's front door and would often let herself in to sit down for an hour, drinking tea and talking about anything that was on mind: her memories of the past; her hopes for the future; her philosophy on life and the world at large. She was delighted to have her grandmother all to herself.

Laura was always honest with her. She told her the truth any time she asked questions about Daniel's childhood, or about how things had been for her when she was younger.

Dawn was able to ask questions of Laura that Daniel never had. Sometimes, Dawn would talk to Daniel about some event that had happened in his mother's life, only for Daniel to exclaim, "I never knew that!"

"Men!" Dawn would roll her eyes and smile at Anna. "Well, did you ever ask her, Dad?"

"No," Daniel would concede a little sheepishly.

Laura was proud of her life achievements, but she knew she had led a quiet, solitary kind of life. She sometimes wished she had made more of an impact in the world—studied to be a teacher maybe, or been a more vital presence in her community.

She knew that she possessed an innate ability to understand people, but had never really used this gift to its fullest. She was pleased to see that Dawn had inherited this gift, and seemed poised to make great use of it.

Laura, however, had always been shy. Hurt. Wounded from early on in her life. Betrayed in love, she had never sought another life partner and she knew now as she got older that this was because she had been afraid to open up again. There were no guarantees in relationships; people shifted and changed and she hadn't been prepared to risk it. The 'love' she experienced with Peter had been anything but love, and she had never yearned for another relationship after that. She was too afraid to put her hopes for the future into the hands of another man. She had never wanted another child, either. She didn't want anything other than what she had.

The ones who mattered to her the most were Daniel, Anna, Cal, Blu, and Dawn. They were her people. She knew who she was when she was with them. She had never felt truly necessary or wanted in this world until they came into her life. Instead, she had felt like a nomad: wandering, waiting, and feeling strangely distant from those around her. Her heart had only fully connected to the planet once Daniel was born.

During the early stages of her life with Daniel, she had felt that if she could just maintain her health and her safety from Peter, and ensure that Daniel would be successfully educated and launched into his own life and career, that was all that mattered. The latter part of her life had been devoted to enjoying time with her family. There was no urge or desire within her to seek out another relationship.

Now that she had entered her own twilight years, she often looked back on her father's death and remembered how angry and indignant she had been over the fact that he had hoarded so much wealth, but never used it to improve their quality of life. Over the years, she had mellowed somewhat in her views.

She had come to understand that it just wasn't in her father to be extravagant. He had been born during a world war, at a time of immense lack, and she could now understand that he just didn't have it in him to be frivolous or showy.

And then there was his own experience of early married life. After leaving the village in which he had been born, he'd moved to the bigger town close by, and met and married her mother, Emily. He had worked in a large factory for many years, until the great school tragedy had struck the village of his birth.

Laura could remember him speaking to her—just once, and very briefly—about how his mother had begged and pleaded with him to come back home with his wife and help the village to heal. Everyone there was deeply traumatised. It was as if all of the lights had gone out, and Laura thought now that it must have been a very selfless act for her parents to go back there. They had sold their house in the big town and bought her childhood home.

If her father had made wise investments, that was his own business. He was probably ashamed of how much money he'd accrued, and had no desire to show it off in front of his more impoverished neighbors. Their village was not a place of affluence. Laura also knew that he and her mother had had no children for a long time. He could have been earnestly saving for years, in the hope that they would have a large family. After Laura's birth and Emily's death, maybe he had felt that there was no point in spending or seeking joy in material things.

When she thought about what had happened in this way, she was able to let go of her resentment towards her father. The choices he had made were his to make, and he'd made them in a completely different time. Her poor father, who had lived out his life alone in that damaged and judgmental place; whose only peace was his fishing; who never asked anything of anyone; who was so unable to verbally express his love.

Her previous anger had melted away and now, Laura could see how she had brought a great deal of unnecessary stress upon herself around the time of his death.

She herself was not yet ready to die. She really didn't want to miss out on her grandchildren growing up. She supposed that this wasn't really a valid reason to avoid death—an inevitable event for every person on this planet—because if she ever got to meet her great-grandchildren, she would want to see them grow up too. It could go on forever.

She smiled to herself one day, as she sat in her favorite chair in her new cottage, and reflected on all this. Love—it was what made the world go around!

Something stirred outside. It was a robin. Laura watched him as he put his head from side to side and looked straight at her. Had she put out the crumbs from her breakfast? She couldn't remember. Oh God, her memory was really tricking her these days.

She snoozed for a little while, and when she awoke, Dawn had arrived. The kettle was whistling on the gas ring.

"Oh, hello darling," Laura said with a smile, beginning to stretch in her chair. "I dozed off for a while. How are you?"

"I'm annoyed today, Grandma," Dawn fumed. "We discussed the witch burnings today in class. Did you know that somewhere between 35,000 and 100,000 women were killed? For being labeled witches? Can you believe it? The history books don't even know how many. As if you can just lose track of 65,000 people! You can if they're women, apparently."

"Oh dear. I didn't know it was that amount, Dawn."

"Well, they don't know the exact amount. They lost count, obviously. I'm very annoyed about that."

"Yes, it is very annoying."

"It was just a way of getting rid of women," Dawn snapped as she rooted around in Laura's cupboard for a couple of mugs. "I'm furious about that, too."

"Yes. . . but they're not allowed to do it anymore, Dawn."

Dawn snorted as she placed the mugs down on the countertop with a great degree of force. "That's just it—they have other ways now, don't they? And there are places where it's still going on."

"They're afraid of us, Dawn," Laura remarked, a little sadly. "They always were. They're afraid of what we know. They don't want to know what we know, but they sure don't want us to know what we know." She laughed at her own jumble of words.

"I suppose," Dawn reflected, as she brought the tea over to the kitchen table. "Dad told me that Elba once said to him that it's not women that men are afraid of. It's themselves. The feminine within them. The lower three chakras or something? The being side of their nature. They think women are the scary enemy. But they're not. It's their own inner child, their own inner feeling, their own inner knowing."

Remembering what Mark had said, she added, "Anyone with half a brain would see that we need to take the world and turn it upside down and then we might have something approaching equality. . . ." She trailed off as she looked at her grandmother. She could see that Laura was tired, and in no mood to talk about witches.

Dawn lowered her voice. "I'm glad you rested, Grandma. You need rest. You work hard."

"I've no work, Dawn. I've done my work," Laura said wearily.

Dawn smiled at her and got up to cut some brown bread she could see on the sideboard. "Well, you've made bread," she quipped. "That's work! Let's have our tea."

Laura moved in her chair. It took a while for her whole body to align properly, and for her strength to even out throughout her body. She rose carefully and went to the table as Dawn brought the bread over, together with some jam and butter knives.

"It'll be spring soon," Laura remarked brightly, as she took a slice and began to apply some jam to it. "The daffodils will be blossoming like they always do. I love the colours of spring. Purple and yellow. And buds on trees. And then the long nights of brightness. I'm tired of this winter now."

"Yes. Me, too." Dawn smiled a little shyly. "Grandma... you know, I've met a boy, and he's absolutely gorgeous."

"I'm sure he is," her grandmother laughed softly.

"And kind," Dawn added.

"Oh good. Kind is good. Talk to him, Dawn. Find out who he is. Meet his family. And his friends. See how he treats them. See that he's kind to everyone. Listen to what he says about them to you."

Dawn glanced appreciatively at her. "That's good advice. Can I bring him to see you?"

"Yes. I'd like that. What's his name?"

"Mark."

Daniel came by to visit his mother the next day. They sat in the little conservatory at the back of the house, enjoying the sun.

"It'll soon be time to do the first grass cutting of the season, Mum," he commented, looking out at her garden. "I'll bring the lawnmower around."

"Thanks, Daniel," Laura said gratefully. "You could do without the hassle of that, I'm sure."

"No. It's no problem at all, Mum," Daniel assured her, then smiled. "I heard Dawn was with you yesterday."

"Yes. She was upset about the witches." Laura chuckled a little wryly.

"Well, you didn't make her feel any better about them, because she was still giving out hell last night about it all. I eventually had to remind her that I hadn't burnt anybody, and neither had her brothers or her poor boyfriend," he laughed. "Anna eventually talked her down from her soap box, but she was very upset."

"I love her spirit, Daniel. The fight in her. She's so true and gutsy and clued in to what's important. She knows what she's doing. I trust her implicitly."

"Like you, Mum. She's like you." He smiled across at her, and they held their gaze for a few moments.

"The boys are coming home this weekend," he went on. "Come around on Sunday and we'll have dinner if you'd like to do Sunday with us?"

"I'd love that, Daniel. Thank you."

That night, something wasn't feeling quite right within Laura. She was feeling frightened for a reason she couldn't explain, and she really didn't know what was happening to her. She remembered Elba's advice on how to listen to yourself, talk to yourself, to get to the root of what was troubling you at the back of the mind.

She didn't want Daniel to be walking lawn mowers around to her indefinitely. Why was life so cruel? Yes, she knew she was 89 and wouldn't live forever. She was grateful to still be able to live alone, but she knew it couldn't go on for much longer.

Something was really irritating her inside because of this. Could she not just ask to die? Would the Lord, in His mercy, not just take her gently in the night, and she wouldn't know what had happened to her? She had prayed for that many times, but each morning she woke up in the same bed and faced the same monotonous day, thinking the same thoughts and feeling another little bit of her physical and cognitive ability slip away.

She was so tired of everything. People patronising her in the shops and talking loudly to her, because they knew she couldn't hear them. She was sick of it all. So cranky and judgmental. It was all because she was tired. In one way, she didn't want to die, but in another way, she did.

She also wondered whether there really was life after death. She had always believed in life beyond the veil—that there was something out there—but now, she wondered whether everyone was just kidding themselves, afraid to face up to the fact that they were nothing. She certainly felt like nothing sometimes.

She also saw how religion and religious rules had been used to subjugate the masses and keep people afraid. Her own religion had caused her to be afraid of a father in the sky with many rooms, with an exacting doorman called Saint Peter—oh, the irony of that—who would decide whether your life had made you a fit person to enter the kingdom.

Did people really believe that? If so, why would they believe such a crazy thing? If not, why would they pretend to?

It was time to gather all her courage and decide what to do.

She decided, then and there, that she would talk to Daniel this weekend about looking for residential care for herself and just getting out of everyone's hair. She was sure they worried about her, but just didn't say anything, and she felt she was a nuisance. Even for her to be thinking of herself this way revealed just how exhausted she was.

That Sunday, over dinner, she announced to the table that she was going to look at going into a home somewhere, in which she would be given her breakfast and dinner and tea, and avoid becoming a burden on everybody. She was careful to make it clear to them that they hadn't made her feel this way. This was how she felt about herself.

She hadn't meant to tell them of her plans like this—she'd been planning a quiet word with Daniel alone—but the words had fallen out of her. Once she'd blurted them out, she couldn't take them back.

Her family were shocked.

"What's brought this on, Grandma?" asked a flabbergasted Cal. "Where would you go? Like an old folks' home?"

"Yes. A retirement home, I think they call them now." She smiled at Cal as Dawn kicked him under the table. "To be honest, I just don't feel safe anymore. Something has changed. I've thought about nothing else for weeks now. I don't want you all to have to be worrying about me, or what you might find when you come in. Even though my father was younger than I am now, I've never been able to get rid of the image of finding him dead, on his own, sitting in his chair. I wondered for years whether he'd suffered, dying alone like that. I don't want you to find me that way."

"I'd prefer if there was a Nurse Manager or someone to break news to you at some stage over the next few years that I was slipping away. I don't want to be carted off to hospital in the dead of night, never to be seen again, and for you to all be running around saying 'Why didn't I go to see her on my way home or ring her? How long was she on her own?' To be honest, to be really honest, I just don't feel safe being alone anymore."

"My body is very unsure of itself and I don't want to suffer any pain that I don't have to. I don't want to have panic buttons hanging around my neck that are linked to some bell here that alerts you all that I'm in trouble. I just don't want any of that. I really have decided.

I want some dignity and safety and . . ." Her voice trailed off, as she was overcome by a sudden wave of emotion. She struggled to hold back tears of frustration and anger. She was not looking for pity from the people she loved most in the world. She would stop talking now and regain her composure.

Anna looked at Daniel, startled. Daniel was open mouthed. He didn't know what to say. Finally, Anna broke the silence. "It sounds like you've really been thinking about this a lot, Laura."

"I have, Anna," Laura said firmly. "You could all still come and visit me, of course."

Dawn began to cry. She was deeply touched by her grandmother's courage, to have come to all of these conclusions by herself and to have thought everything through like this: she thought it was the most courageous thing she'd ever witnessed. She couldn't imagine what it must feel like to be so honest about your own vulnerability and death that you were able to bring this conversation to your family, with all of your decisions made.

"Oh, Grandma, I'm sorry for crying," Dawn choked out. "It's just. . . I would so miss our chats and everything, in your house. But we could just have them wherever you live. I'm being selfish. Expecting you to stay where you are just so that I can call in two or three times a week to chat."

"Is there any way to talk you out of this?" asked Daniel. "Maybe convince you to come live here for a while?" He flashed a quick look at Anna, to see whether he'd spoken out of turn. It suddenly occurred to him that he couldn't just move his mother into their home without asking his wife. But Anna nodded to him to continue.

"Thank you, Daniel. And Anna." Laura smiled at Anna, acknowledging her response to Daniel. "But I don't think that that's in any way what I or you would need.

My world is getting smaller and I don't want to confine you all to it. Just as your children are leaving, I'm not going to lock you in here, minding me." She laughed. "I mean it. I've thought about it; I just need help with the planning and execution of it, if you would be good enough to help me with that. It doesn't have to be too far away."

And so it was that for another three years, Laura lived in a retirement home about a twenty-minute drive away from her only son and his family.

The moment she arrived in her new home, she made new friends, had interesting conversations, and enjoyed plenty of life, music, card games, and company.

The staff did some crazy things for them. They tried to get them to do yoga in their chairs, brought dogs in to visit them, had a hairdresser brought into the home once a week so they could get their hair done, and held movie nights and pizza nights. Laura thought they were all cracked, but she appreciated their efforts nevertheless.

There was always someone visiting someone, and she soon found that she was quite nosy. She was usually able to guess what everybody's children and grandchildren did for a living, and people-watching passed the days nicely for her. It was perfect. She thought this was the best decision she ever could have made.

She didn't miss her independence. It had been causing her too much stress for too long and, like everything else in life, it wasn't until she faced her problems that she could change them.

Dawn called to see her on the weekends she came home from college. Sometimes she brought Mark and sometimes she came alone. Laura liked Mark. He was clever and strong, and it was clear he was besotted with Dawn.

When she thought of all of the years and decades that Dawn had in front of her to live, she was weary. She didn't know how Dawn was going to have the strength to face it all. Times had certainly changed for the better for women, but there was still such glaring work to be done.

She remembered how Elba had once told her that there was work for the granddaughters and great-granddaughters to do. Maybe this was to be their work for their time?

Cal and Blu always came to visit her as a twosome, just like they always had. They entertained her with stories from the city, what their plans were, and how they were going to take on the world and enjoy every moment of it.

They showed her pictures of their nights out, their friends, and places they'd visited. They brought her little gifts. They told her how much they loved her and how great they thought she was. She was always cheered and amused by the boys. They were a breath of fresh air.

Her favourite nurse was a Filipina woman who regaled her with stories about her homeland every day. Laura was sure she made up half the stories she told her. How could cultures be that different?

The nurse's name was Jean, but she confided in Laura that this wasn't her real name. Her real name would be too difficult for most Western-ers to pronounce, so she had taken on the name Jean to fit in with the culture of her new home. Laura was startled by this. Imagine having to change your name to suit the people you served and helped!

Jean told her that she sent money home to her family to help them to survive. After she had paid her rent, bills, and food, everything else went back to her family. How mad was that? Laura often reflected on how quickly her own people had forgotten that, for generations, so many races and nationalities had had to do the very same thing.

The thought saddened her. Had we learned nothing about displacing people and then exploiting them in their loneliness? Paying them a pit-tance and expecting them to do the jobs we didn't want to do? Had the white, northern European race still not faced up to the reality that they were not superior in any way to anyone else? Oh God, it was exhausting. Laura couldn't think about it anymore.

She asked Jean whether she would like to go home. Jean said yes, she would; that her parents would be getting old, and she would like to be with them. This made Laura feel desperately sad. To her, Jean's story was clear proof that society had failed.

Maybe Dawn and her generation would do something about that. She would ask Dawn to watch out for immigrants. They were giving so much of themselves to a society that didn't treat them very well.

She asked Daniel whether he could get a solicitor from her solicitors' firm to visit her. She wanted to finalise her will, and she told him that she was keen to include a gift in it for Jean, who had been kindness itself. "Money is Love, Daniel. I've come to that conclusion. It can be used for such good. It won't change her life, but she will know that I loved her."

Daniel acceded immediately to her request. He accompanied the solicitor to the retirement home and listened as his mother outlined her plans for providing Jean with a gift that would help ease her financial burden. After witnessing this conversation, he went out to his car and sat and cried for half an hour, overcome by the beauty of his mother's heart. He thanked the heavens above to have been raised by such a woman.

Daniel often visited her, sometimes alone and sometimes with Anna. Anna spent a lot of time talking to Laura about the children's antics and plans. They also reminisced about the past.

They remembered Grace and the special time they had shared together when the boys were small: the healing and friendship that their circle had brought them. They talked about their magical holiday and the enchanted valley from Anna's dream. They talked about Elba, and how her wisdom and humor had added so much to their lives. They remembered both good and bad times.

Both Daniel and Anna marvelled at Laura's memory—she could recall events in precise, startling detail—but they were aware that her energy levels weren't strong. Whenever she suddenly became very tired in the middle of a conversation, they knew it was time to go.

One afternoon, during Laura's third year in the home, Daniel came alone. He sat beside her bed and said to her, "Mum, I cannot honor or thank you enough for everything you've done. For me, for my family, for all you've carried selflessly for years."

Laura was very hard of hearing now, but she found it easy to lipread Daniel. The medical staff at the home had fitted her with a hearing aid, but she hated it with a passion, and spent hours planning how she could break it. She could roll over it in her wheelchair. Smash it with her walking frame. She could drop it in a glass of water. Roll it up in her towels and let them take it to the laundry. She had never actually done any of these things, but a girl could dream! Tomorrow, she'd come up with an ingenious plan on how to get rid of it forever.

She didn't need the hearing aid for Daniel. She knew every curve of his face, how his hands would gesture, how his eyes would light up, how his facial muscles would move when he'd say certain words. She had been studying his features for 62 years.

She was watching him now and marvelling over how beautiful he was to her, after all these years. What was he saying?

"For all the work you did, making it acceptable for a woman to raise a child alone. You snubbed your face at them all and just gave us the best life you could. I'm so very thankful. It must have been very difficult. . . with your father and the older generation of that time. . . you know. . . to have fought so hard for yourself and me and your independence."

Laura smiled as he went on. "When I think back on the people of your village, and the things they said. . . it must have been tough for you to keep your head up on our behalf. I'm just in awe of what you achieved, and how the work you did makes it so much easier for kids now, especially girls like Dawn. . ."

His voice trailed off, heavy with emotion, but Laura had understood every word. She replied, "Daniel, I did what I had to do. It wasn't hard. I can't even remember most of it now. I thought it was the right thing for both of us. For your safety. For my safety. For our future. It was tough on you. None of the decisions were made by you. It wasn't your mess. My father made that clear to me. I'm so proud of everything you've achieved! You are the real inspiration. Not me."

"Well, I think I like this mutual admiration society we've got going here, Mum," he laughed. "I just want you to know that you mean the world to me and I'm very proud to be your son. I love you so much."

"I love you too, with all my heart, my beautiful son."

Daniel could not have said anything that would have meant more to Laura during this final stage of her life. She was so moved by his expression of love and appreciation, it kept her going throughout the next painful days. She had begun running a high fever.

A few nights later, after receiving her pain medication from Jean, Laura fell away from this life quietly and slowly, alone in her room. During her last moments, she clearly saw in front of her the beautiful old face of Daniel's friend, Elba.

"Laura, Laura. . ." she heard Elba calling out, as though from a great distance. She beckoned her over a bridge of light, nodding her head encouragingly as she began to take her first tentative steps. "I have many people for you to meet. Those you love, and are a part of, are waiting for you to release your body and join us."

Release her body? How?

She wasn't certain, but over Elba's shoulder, at the other side of the bridge, she was sure she could see the essence of Daniel, Anna, Cal, Blu and Dawn. Then she saw the essence of a young woman whom she knew to be her mother, Emily. She saw the essence of her father and many, many more essences of different people she couldn't place—all of whom she loved deeply. The presence of her living family members startled her.

"But how could that be?" she asked Elba, gesturing at the essences of Daniel, Anna, Cal, Blu, and Dawn. "My family are alive! Dawn is away at College."

Elba smiled warmly at her and said, "Yes. Your family are alive. And they're alive here, too. Don't worry about how they're on earth, but also here. This is not the appropriate moment to discuss multidimensionality." She winked at her.

Elba was joking with her? Was she hallucinating? This was wonderful. There was humor here in this place. And Elba. Laura's heart gave a jump of joy, swelled and suddenly burst open: fizzing, first of all, and then exploding in love, filling the space that was between them. This closed the distance between her and this vision she was seeing.

"That's right. Come with me," Elba coaxed. "All is well. We are all here to meet you."

Daniel jolted awake. A few seconds later, his phone lit up and started ringing. He sat up in bed. This woke Anna up with a start; she looked around at his phone and immediately whispered, "Laura."

Daniel answered the phone, spoke quietly to Jean, thanked her, and said they would come immediately. He turned to Anna, who could see in his face that Laura had indeed passed away. They didn't need to say a word to one another. They stood up, walked around the bed, and hugged for a long time. Then they left to be with Laura.

Laura had been clear to Daniel in her funeral instructions the previous year. She wanted her body to return, in death, to the little town that had raised her. She wanted her remains to lay beside her father and mother, and rest there eternally.

The following day, Daniel asked the boys and Dawn whether they would like to spend a week together as a family, bringing his mother to her final resting place. They were all home within hours. Anna and Dawn made all of the arrangements with the undertaker, while Cal booked them into a hotel just outside Laura's old village for three nights.

They travelled down together in the same car. The hotel that Cal had picked was set in its own grounds and gardens, and must have been a beautiful stately home in its day. On the evening they arrived, they enjoyed a delicious dinner together in the formal dining room, then had an early night.

After the funeral service in the church the following day, the family followed Laura's coffin around to the back of the church and walked in silent procession through the churchyard to her final resting place, alongside her parents. Daniel recalled taking the exact same journey with Laura, after his grandfather had died. He couldn't have conceived then, as a 17-year-old boy, that he would make the exact same journey for his mother.

The birds were singing brightly. Daniel could hear the priest praying over the coffin, saying, "As we take leave of our sister, Laura. . ."

His family all stepped forward in turn and dropped a single rose into the grave. He looked down into the grave, memories flashing through his mind. Laura sitting at the table with him, helping him to do his homework. The comforting smell of her beside him. The two of them eating some delicious baking she'd made, with her saying, "Eat up—you've earned this treat." Walking through woods together, playfully laughing with nature's fairies. Watching her cry over some letter she'd received from his father. Seeing her clap and sing "happy birthday" on his 21st. The amazing cake she'd made for the occasion which fed the many guests. Her face beaming up at him as she held her grandchildren in her arms for the first time. Her standing with Anna on the raised hillock in the enchanted valley.

Beautiful images of their life together comforted him now. Yes, they would take leave of Laura's physical remains, but they would always carry their love for her in their hearts. She would live on through them.

Daniel shook the priest's hand as he left the family standing at the grave of Laura and her parents. They stayed there together for a long time, saying no words.

After some minutes, Daniel spoke:

"I wasn't born here. I was born about half an hour's drive away. But I lived here for a few years. First, we rented, then when my grandfather died, we moved into his house for a couple of years. My teen years were difficult for me here, but Mum was my constant. She never pried, but she'd be there, making just enough noise to ensure that I knew I had support."

"It was lonely. Look around. This place hasn't changed in forty years. The nearest second level school was twenty kilometers away. It was grim—all of it. Black and white. No color. When you live in a town like this, you spend your life dreaming. Mostly of escape."

He looked around at each of his family members before going on. "At least, I certainly did. I couldn't wait to leave. But I really didn't want to leave Mum here on her own. Turned out she was just waiting for me to finish school. We ran out of here together!" He chuckled. "I do understand why she wanted to come back though—come full circle, return to her parents. She was a special lady. Unselfish and undemanding of others. I loved her deeply."

His head dropped and he looked down at the grave. Anna reached out and held his left hand. Dawn walked over to him and wrapped her arms around his waist, laying her head on his shoulder. He wrapped his right arm around her. His two sons, who were standing on the opposite side of the grave, were silent until Blu spoke. "She set the tone, Dad. She was a special lady."

They walked together back to the car and travelled back to the hotel.

They each went to their rooms to freshen up and decided to meet at six o'clock for an early dinner.

A few hours later, Anna looked out the bay window of the bedroom as she was getting dressed. She and Daniel had both had a snooze, and she had just enjoyed a long, warm shower.

She saw her three children sitting below them on the patio of the gardens, all laughing at some story Blu was telling them. He was acting something out for his brother and sister. Cal and Dawn were in hysterics laughing, and this was egging Blu on with whatever story he was telling. She called to Daniel, who was brushing his teeth, and he came over to take in the scene.

They both started giggling like exhilarated children.

They didn't know what had come over them. Maybe it was the release of the stress of the last week? Maybe it was the joy of seeing their children together and so healthy and happy? Whatever it was, they laughed for a few minutes, before wrapping their arms around one another. "What a sight to behold from the Bridge of Now, Dan," Anna said happily. "Let's go and join them."

They gathered their things and made their way downstairs to spend the evening with their family. The future stretched out ahead of them, and they were going to meet it.

Chapter Thirteen

Before we close, I know you will want to hear about what Peter found at the gates of heaven. You remember Peter? Peter was Daniel's father. Dawn's grandfather.

Peter had carried an important thread of the lineage of the coercive and destructive masculine that could not abide intimacy or equality. This group had maintained control for millennia by stripping the rights of those over whom they sought power and control. If they couldn't break people's spirits, they maintained order with guns and outrageous rules that they could change whenever it suited them.

It was a very effective system that had allowed them to create hierarchy, competition, and division within their own spheres of influence, however big or small. They could run a continent, a country, a town, or a household with the same tactics.

Might was right, and they had might.

They also had strength in numbers for the longest time. As they banded together as a group, their version of law and order had enslaved billions of people and ensured material success for the chosen few.

But that system was falling out of power, as people had been through enough abuse and were ready to empower themselves. The existing system was toxic to growth: a stifling malignancy to creativity and joy.

At the peak of its power, the people who had fallen foul of its sanctimonious laws were hidden in institutions behind high walls, where they were abused by this system that required the submission of the oppressed and the supreme dominance of the regime.

Laura and many others who had struggled and persevered to get out of its grasp—and who had subsequently thrived independently—had weakened its grip. Everyone who now disagreed with it helped to loosen its hold on power. Every person who told their story divulged some of its secrets. Every person who cared for someone else's plight—especially those who could do nothing for them in return—tilted the scales in favour of Love.

Some time after Peter had left the earth, he was waiting outside the gates of heaven for Saint Peter. The religion he had been raised within had led him to believe that Saint Peter was the figure who would meet him at the gates, to deliver his judgment.

Peter was alone here and felt quite powerless: an unusual and uncomfortable position for him, as he generally liked to be in control. He was wondering how this might go, and was thinking of how he might explain his recently-lived life. He wasn't sure what the rules were here, or if he'd fit in.

Foremost on his mind was returning to the place he'd just been, and continuing with his rise to fame and acclaim for his talent. More than anything, he wanted to know what was coming next in the life he seemingly could no longer access.

He felt as though he was being held back on an elastic band, like a stone on a catapult, and could at any moment be propelled into God knows where.

Since leaving his earthly life, he had been travelling, weightless, in the mists of time. There didn't seem to be any clock time or great white light or tunnels; everything just was. He slept, mostly. He saw no other people. No angels or clouds. He just felt that he was waiting for something, but he had no idea what.

After a while, he started seeing faces. He saw his son's and his daughters' beseeching eyes, looking at him for his approval and his love. He couldn't meet their gaze, since he had abhorred their mothers: those weak and restricting women who had been so jealous and unsupportive of his great talent and ability. They didn't understand his need for expression, nor did they care about his efforts. Nothing he ever did was ever going to be good enough for them. Why even try?

Peter's antipathy towards women had begun with his own mother. He could see this clearly now, as he floated about in this formless mist, waiting for Saint Peter. If it looked as though Saint Peter was going to be difficult, he would explain exactly how awful it had been for him.

Peter's mother had told him—from the moment he could understand the spoken word—that she was the most beautiful woman who had ever been born in the whole county. She told him that she'd had blonde curls as a child that naturally fell about her face, and she grew into the most beautiful woman.

Peter wondered whether she had always felt that men were fools, who could be manipulated at will. Her beauty seemed intoxicating to them. When he was a little boy, Peter often watched her as she wound up men and left them spinning. She didn't care much for him either, he thought. He made a vow that he would be wary of women in the future.

She was still very young, and Peter only four, when she married his stepfather. His mother and this man went on to have three girls together, who soon took over everything, as far as Peter was concerned: commandeering all of his mother's attention, all of her conversations, all of her money, and all of her time. Peter felt like an outsider. He often begged his mother to go back to the time when it had been just them. It hadn't been any great shakes then; they had been poor, and she always had lots of men coming and going, but at least she hadn't beaten him. She told him they couldn't go back.

His stepfather frequently told him that he was going to be no good, just like his father. He slapped Peter hard across the legs and head if he ever talked back to him. Peter could still feel the sensation of his stepfather's wedding band cracking on his skull.

He would tell Saint Peter about that.

He would be glad whenever he'd hear his half-sisters getting a few slaps too, but this rarely happened. He wouldn't mention to Saint Peter that he'd enjoyed that. He sometimes heard his mother intervene on her daughters' behalf, but never on his—and this slight caused him to burn with shame and indignation. How dare she sacrifice him like that?

He never asked any questions about his own father. He had been told that his stepfather was good enough to give him his surname, and that should be enough for him. Anyway, he didn't care who his father had been. His only desire was to escape and never look back.

Schooldays were a revelation to him—all this time during the day, when he could be whoever he wanted to be! He created a persona of an under-loved and undernourished waif for the teachers and adults, and the persona of a tough guy, who cared about nothing, to his peers and friends.

During his teens, Peter unexpectedly fell in love with the writings of Shakespeare. He memorized the entire text of Hamlet, The Merchant of Venice, and King Lear in no time at all. He had an insatiable appetite for the plays, and often saw himself acting out the key parts on stage in the future. He loved the tragedy, the dramatization, how every character acted on instinct, and was so utterly consumed by their own personal plight.

He left school and home when he was sixteen years old and went straight to the city. He started working in theaters as a backstage hand, and so impressed a travelling Shakespearean actor with his innate grasp of the Shakespearean archetypes that this actor took him travelling with him for a year.

The actor mentored Peter and taught him some of the key skills of holding the audience enraptured, by always holding a little bit back. He explained that this would let the audience know that you knew more than they did, which would keep them paying attention. Holding an audience in the palm of your hand was intoxicating, the actor told him.

Peter had already seen from the stage wings just how empowering it must be to perform. He was already decided in his mind that this was the only job he would ever want to do.

He never had any formal training, but the actor helped him to secure some understudy roles. Peter's career soon began to take off. He started to be noticed on the theater circuit, and his natural chameleon ability helped him to become a very compelling actor.

His mentor tried to instill a sense of discipline within him, to no avail. He encouraged him to unwind after a performance: go to his dressing room, sit in silence for a while, and let the night and the performance go. To return to himself.

Old timer. Do-gooder. Peter knew a better way. He didn't want to return to himself anyway! He knew a faster way to make it big. Peter knew that one day, he'd get his big break. It was only a matter of time.

But he didn't get his big break; he was a fool, he fumed now, as he stared at the mists swirling around him. He'd always had a weakness for women and song and dancing the night away. His job easily lent itself to his having plenty of opportunities. He loved the sense of freedom he had. The sensations.

Then he met Laura. He was getting on a bit by then, and she was a safe port in any storm. She was dull and impressionable—an only child, with no family to speak of. Just that father of hers, who lived in a sad, miserable village that life itself seemed to have forgotten about. The old man's biggest thrill was fishing at weekends with no-hopers like himself, standing in rivers for days, hoping to catch a fish. Peter couldn't think of anything more life-draining.

Laura had her own house, which was a huge advantage in Peter's eyes, as he often struggled to find a consistent place to stay. She adored him and seemed to appreciate the attention he lavished upon her in the beginning. He had enjoyed the game of flattering her for a while—as

THE BRIDGE OF NOW

he often did, when he had just started seeing a new woman—but her neediness began to grate on him.

Soon after they were married, he grew to despise her. She was impossibly dull: making her own curtains and then making matching cushions; then making other people's curtains and cushions. Who would bother? Cushions on a chair that matched the curtains. Seriously? She was no fun. She always wanted to stay at home and get him home earlier than he wanted.

Laura had wanted him by her side for the birth of their son, Daniel. What an absolutely dreadful experience that was. All that lowing like a cow or farm animal, the other-worldly noises she was making, her clenched face. The huffing and puffing and howling. It was all about her; the midwife and nurses making a fuss of her. He was just standing there like a spare wheel.

He remembered the total disgust he had felt when Daniel was handed to her, still covered in after-birth fluids, and she looked up at Peter with pleading eyes of joy and hope. Was she a complete fool? Did she really think he was going to tell her how great she was?

The child was the ugliest thing he had ever seen. He was like an old man—bald and red-faced, silent at first, then squawking like a little piglet. Vile. Covered in blood and slime. Laura smelling him and sniffing him and kissing him. It was horrific.

This was not a place for real men. Unless you were a doctor and could direct proceedings.

Peter had made sure he was far, far away when the other two women he'd gotten pregnant were about to put on that particular performance. It was not something he wanted to witness again. Ever.

He hated those women for trying to tame him. They were all the same. Their child. Their house. Their bloody curtains and cushions. He was growing furious now, even thinking about it. Did they really think they could seduce and own him with babies and curtains and cushions?

He loved the women that met him at his after-parties. They were the best fun. They didn't expect anything of him and he could be himself for a while. But they always went down the same road sooner or later—looking for something from him, trying to own him. He would never be owned.

He had had some amazing nights, though, and he had no regrets. If he were to do it all again, he would still have fought for his right to freedom and independence. He could see that people really admired him and were afraid of his power.

He wondered to himself, suddenly, what his son would go on to do. The instant this thought occurred to him, he saw a screen suddenly materialize in front of him. The screen showed him that Daniel would have a family himself and would be devoted to them. He saw two boys, who would be his grandsons. He saw a little girl, who would be his granddaughter.

He felt a pang at the back of his chest as he watched the children running through a field of wildflowers on a massive expanse of sunlit land, somewhere foreign. They looked so carefree—so loved and cared for. They were clean and well-dressed. They appeared to get on so well.

There were a few adults watching them. Oh, one of the adults was Laura. So, Daniel would turn out to be the mommy's boy she had always wanted him to be, Peter scoffed to himself. A son of his, completely emasculated by his mother. The shame of it!

When he'd first met Daniel after being away, he hadn't thought much of him. He was weak: looking for love, looking for something Peter couldn't give, looking for him to be something he wasn't. There was nothing of him in his son. He couldn't even see a flicker of himself.

This boy was ten years old, and had all of the weakness of a mol-ly-coddled kid who couldn't make a decision. When Peter was ten, he himself had been a feared kid, respected by his classmates. He'd been through a lot. This little child Daniel was probably the laughingstock at his school. Weak and insipid.

Peter then thought about how he'd died. Why was his body alone in his boarding house bedroom? He couldn't remember the exact hour leading up to it. Earlier that evening, they'd had a great show—he'd put on a spectacular performance and was about to really make it big this time. He could feel it. It was a feeling of invincibility.

Then they'd had a great night's partying, went back to his boarding house and then... nothing. A total blank. All he could see now was his body on the floor beside his bed, vomit coming out of his mouth. Where were all the friends he'd been with earlier?

Maybe he'd been murdered? He was strong and healthy, so it couldn't have been anything to do with him.

Maybe when Saint Peter showed up, he could fill in the blanks. He'd ask him what had happened at the party and where all his friends had gone. Even the woman who owned the boarding house had joined in the fun when they all came back. It was very odd. Someone would tell him.

Suddenly, a woman appeared. Well, this was the last thing he was expecting. It might be harder to convince this woman than it would have been Saint Peter. He wondered whether she had seen his file. Did they have files here?

"Hello, Peter," she said, with a warm smile.

Okay. She knew his name. Someone had briefed her.

"Em, hello there," he answered, wondering whether she was a secretary of some kind. She was a bit old to be a secretary. Did they have secretaries here?

"I am here to meet you and to help you," she said, "to help you to decide, you know... what you'd like to do next."

"Oh, well, em ... yes... thank you, that's very nice. The real problem is that I don't really know where I am." Peter felt uncomfortable now. He wasn't going to hang around making chitchat with this woman for a moment longer than he had to.

"I know where you are; we have no problem so long as one of us knows," the lady answered. She smiled at him as if slightly amused, and he felt his face flush. Could his face flush here?

"You are on the Bridge of Now," she continued. "From here, you decide your future."

The Bridge of Now? He looked down, and sure enough, they were standing on a bridge. He hadn't noticed his feet landing on anything. He turned his head and looked behind him. He could instantly see the trail of the life he had lived—the trail he had only been getting snippets of, up until the woman had appeared. He turned back to the woman, then tried to see over her shoulder, in the direction of where his future would most likely be. There was nothing at all that he could decipher. He tried to compose himself again.

"I was going to ask Saint Peter how I died," Peter explained. "I think there might have been a mistake, you see. I wasn't finished. I was about to become very famous and successful and my life was about to change forever."

"Well, I think we can agree your life has changed, Peter," the lady said mildly.

"Yes, yes, I see that. . . it's just. . . except that. . . you see, I have a play tonight, and I'm the lead, and it's getting very good reviews. So really, I would like to go back to where I was. Everything was fine." He nodded his head and tried to move back in the direction of his old life, but found that he was still held back by that strange feeling of the catapult at his back. He decided not to show the woman that he was struggling to break free.

"That play finished many moons ago, Peter," the lady said softly to him. "I'm afraid we cannot go back to where you were. We must decide on the next act, so to speak. Where you'd like to go next. Of course, we don't have to decide this very moment. You can take your time and see if anything comes to you about what you might like to do next. You have many supreme talents and abilities. There is a myriad of things you could do. I can show you some options, if you would like that, or you could wait and see what you decide yourself."

"Like a brochure or something?" Peter asked. He was thinking that this mightn't be as bad as he had first imagined. Perhaps this woman had something that would suit him even better than the last play. She seemed to like his acting. Maybe he'd ask to see this brochure.

"Well, I suppose a little bit like a brochure in many ways." She smiled at him, but he thought she also gave a little laugh. "I was just wondering how do you feel? Here. Now."

Feel? Was this woman mocking him? What was so funny? She clearly wasn't grasping the gravity of his situation. This was one of the most annoying things about women, Peter raged inwardly. Always going on about feelings. Feel? How did he feel? He didn't have time for this. All he felt was a rising panic within him.

"Feel?" he replied harshly, narrowing his eyes in disbelief. "Well, I don't feel anything at all, really. I just want to do something to get out of here and stop wasting my time. If you can't do something for me, could you just go and get Saint Peter? He'll sort this whole misunderstanding out."

He wondered whether he could slap the annoying woman, but his arms wouldn't move in his shoulder sockets. The damned catapult thing, holding him back again.

He looked down quickly to see whether there was a clasp or something that he could undo at his sternum. That would stop the restriction, and then he could escape from this woman with her mock-kind eyes. Where would he run to? Surely there was an exit somewhere from this place.

Oh! Maybe he was in a dream. Of course. Why hadn't this occurred to him before? He blinked his eyes several times to rouse his conscious mind out of dream state. The longer he tried without success, the stronger the panic within him surfaced.

The woman saw the flash of pure rage and evil that was forming within him, but she didn't flinch. She looked straight into the abyss of darkness and loathing that fed the furnace of hatred within his soul: right down to the root where it had seeded and seduced him with its power.

You see, darkness had Peter down as one of its finest warriors. As Peter was unwilling to feel anything real—neither pain nor joy—his addictions had kept him focused on sensation instead. His love for altered states of consciousness had provided fertile ground for darkness to do its work through him. Just as Light had no hands on earth but ours, neither had darkness. It was all just the interplay of the light, shadow, and darkness of humans, with the earth as its stage.

The woman knew she was not at risk from Peter as he became more and more angry, but from her vantage point, she got a clear view of Laura and many other women—all of whom she knew intimately—who had taken the brunt of his viciousness.

This went on for some time until Peter looked away, defeated. He stopped blinking and stopped trying to awaken. He could do nothing but surrender.

"Is Saint Peter coming to meet me?" he snapped at last, completely exasperated.

"No. Saint Peter isn't coming."

"So, who are you?"

"I am Elba. Eusebia Sylvia Elba."

With that, a soft violet wing touched Peter's cheek. As it did, he turned his head towards it and the wing wrapped itself around him, drawing him inward towards its centre. The catapult restriction released from around his heart and he felt himself being engulfed in a feeling of softness that he hadn't experienced ever before.

An irresistible move inward to the inner planes was upon him, and he glimpsed a hazy outline of a rich story that could potentially be told within him. He saw his many gifts, his ability to transcend, to be able to access the archetypes that the good actor can, and he understood for the first time ever that this was a true talent. He felt a feeling of pride in himself and gratitude to the giver of gifts—whoever that might be.

Then he looked and he suddenly saw that the flip side—the shadow side of that gift—was what darkness had depended on with him. His realisation made him feel cheated, because on the flip side of his enormous ability to transcend, was the propensity for escapism and addiction. He saw clearly now how what was his prized possession, his true gift and ability, had the power to destroy him, or rather for him to destroy himself. What he could not transcend was the earthly, human, emotional parts of his being. He saw how he could not acknowledge or even address, much less resolve, the conflicts within himself.

His gift was his strength.

His strength was his weakness.

If he were to have it to live all over again, would he be able to find the balance to fulfil the maximum potential of his talent? He began to wonder. His gift had the power to destroy him? But there was no destruction, he saw. Only creation. He again began to ponder. To dream.

So please, dear reader, do not worry for Peter, for I know how your compassionate heart aches for him. The next part of his evolution is a story of realisation, awakening, atonement, and redemption, and is currently being written. Its telling is for another day.

Afterword

Eusebia Sylvia Elba is a very old soul indeed. She is a very special Being who has many roles and many duties. She has been around the galaxies for eons, and there is nothing she has not seen. Because of this, she instinctively understands the sufferings and the urges of all of the humans she meets.

Yes, she is an instructor and a teacher; yes, she is the archetype of the wise, old feminine; the catalyst for compassion, forgiveness, and release.

Her transmutational compassion is emitted from her at such high frequency that it cannot be detected by the human eye or heart, at their current vibration. But its violet spray magically enables the release of all judgment of one by another.

Elba doesn't go through the normal human death when she travels between the worlds, for she has no more to experience for herself.

She goes to where she is called, and is instantly there, in whatever guise is most appropriate.

She feels a call to key locations—to where the smallest tweak may be all that is needed—then she travels to that timeline to unravel a knot.

These knots, had they not been unravelled, would almost certainly have catastrophic consequences for humanity down the line.

She serves the One. She links the Divine Masculine and the Divine Feminine within each Being in a perfect union of Heart Love. She promises that this is what will bring about perfection in humanity and a new way of living.

She is willing to put in the hours, travel the train lines, take people to old ruins, live in the wood of fairy trees for children, show them magnificent views, and drink coffee, tea, water, and wine with women and men all over the world in different times and locations at key moments.

She emanates an unconditional love for whomever her companion is at any given time: a love they have often never felt from anyone else in their lives.

Nowadays, she is around more and more often, to see that everyone forgives and is forgiven as we set about embracing a new era. The reward will be greater than she can convey to us at this specific moment in time.

She doesn't always show up in the same human clothes. But she is always a woman. She is the perfect ingredient that has been missing for many, many millennia.

She is here now. Her Presence is knocking on the doors of your life today. Those to whom she gives her magic stars and touch are released of worry from the moment they receive them.

Watch for her today as you go about your daily life. She walks alongside every dream you ever had. She is the germination of every good idea that ever took hold. She is the very abhorrence and antithesis of the notion that some are better or more deserving than another.

When you surrender to her heart (and you will, for that is your destiny), she returns to you the very kernel core of yourself, that was never harmed in any way. She will wait. She cannot and would not leave without you. For she is yours, and she is you.

When you meet her, on the Bridge of Now, you will know.

The Bridge of Now Guidebook

And now to work. . .

If you would like to work with this book on a deeper level, please read through the following pages and do the exercises you feel drawn to do.

The Bridge of Now is a simple tale about a family. It relays how the family develops over generations, and how every generation is pivotal to the next, as each one grows from the experiences of the generations past. What ties all of the generations together is their love for the child of whatever comes next: seeing their own reflections within them, but even more crucial, wanting the new child to be better than they are, to have more opportunities for experience and expression, and to create something better.

As it is within most families, we try to make life as fruitful as possible for whoever is coming next, by doing our own sacred soul work.

To do this work in our own family is to do it for the entire world.

Wanting the next version of humanity to be better, stronger, and freer involves us doing our own soul work to the best of our ability. This is the greatest gift you could give to the evolution of your family, and to the wider human community. It doesn't require us to be the perfect parent or family member; just to do our honest and humble best.

In this book, I have wound a story around concepts that I use in my classes or healings. These concepts became so prevalent that I decided to put them in a book.

The telling of stories in order to help others to learn lessons is ancient and universal, going beyond simple words or language. Philosophers, sages, and seers have always used the medium of the parable in order to evoke emotions within the listener that allow the lesson to be heard.

The lessons of this time are many: trust, faith, love, community, resistance, rebellion, letting go, rebuilding, renewing, second chances, reassessment, trying, trying again, going with the flow.

THE CONCEPTS I INTRODUCE IN THE BOOK ARE:

1. The Bridge of Now Story
2. The Chakra Development Story
3. The Sovereignty and Boundary Story: Castle and 80/20 Stories
4. Caterpillar Transformation Story
5. The Fever Story

CONCEPT 1: THE BRIDGE OF NOW

This is a simple concept that the prevalence of meditation and mindfulness, yoga, and energy healing have made popular in recent years.

"All we have is now."

"Now is where our power is."

We've all heard these expressions.

Mastering the Bridge of Now can offer us a pathway out of judgment: judgment of others, judgment of ourselves, judgment of life and events and history. Judgment does not solve anything. It simply cements our position on things and can make us inflexible. Inflexibility during a rapidly changing time is an impediment to our growth and evolution as a species.

We need to consciously make our Now moments as happy a place as we possibly can, because logic suggests that the happier we are in the Now, the more this becomes our general disposition. It is always Now and it will always be Now.

Having a positive outlook raises our vibration, enabling us to attract more 'good' into our lives. Of course, there will always be life events that strike us out of the blue, and we will have to find a way to cope with those trials. None of us are immune. However, we are more likely to be able to navigate problems from a happier disposition in the Now if our relationship with ourselves in the Now is as healthy as possible.

Applying the Bridge concept can help people to see that nothing lasts forever: this too shall pass, as all things will. We have survived many trials along our life's journey and we will survive many more. A bridge is often seen as a link between the old and the new, or the past and the future. The metaphor is full of hope.

A bridge can also imply height. We can envision a bridge as an arching structure from which we have a good view of the surroundings. This can give us a sense of being firmly anchored in our own awareness; being in the world but not of it. It can lead us to a feeling of safety, from which to assess both our past and our dreams for the future. At each moment in the Now, we can decide to literally breathe through what we are feeling. Life is flowing over us and through us in the Now.

Another analogy I use with people is the 'Train of Consciousness'.

Imagine you are on your own train, called your train of consciousness. We are primed to disembark the train at certain 'destination' spots. . . and common knowledge has it that we will be fine then! Or, as we say in Ireland, we'll be grand then. We will be grand. . .

- After our exams
- When we meet a partner
- When we buy a house
- When we buy a new car
- When we get our tax rebate
- Etc etc. . . ad infinitum

So, we disembark the train. We've reached our destination. We're grand now.

Aren't we?

Oh, we're not?

Okay. Back on the train... next destination please, driver.

On it goes until we feel that we are still not 'grand', we'll never be 'grand', and there must be something wrong with us because everybody else seems 'grand.' We are dizzy from disembarking and re-embarking the train.

The presupposition is that there was something wrong with us in the first place, when of course, there wasn't.

I've disembarked my own train many times, as we all have.

"It's this! I've arrived!"

These are the ego traps. The ego will never be happy. By 'ego', I'm talking about the dysfunctional part of mind, that is never satisfied and always craves more.

Disembarking is part of being human. We all need to let off steam, experience life, make our mistakes, or maybe just enjoy earth's egoic pleasures, and return to the train when we are spent.

The train cannot leave without us. It is our train of consciousness, after all. It waits for us, without judgment. It can't leave without us, for it is ours! Nobody asks us where we've been when we return to the train, battle-weary and scarred. Nobody denies us re-entry. It just takes us aboard and we continue the more conscious journey.

However, when we realise that we are/were perfectly fine all along, that these 'destinations' were just stations we were passing through— milestones, sure, but never destinations—our life becomes easier. We stop struggling to be grand. We know we were grand all along.

I call this concept 'The Train to Grandland'.

In your journal, answer the following questions:

- What am I creating in my Now for my brighter tomorrow?
- What's the view like from my bridge?
- When I look back from my Bridge of Now at my past, what emotions arise within me?

- Do I need help to deal with some of my memories?
- How can I access the help I need from my *Now?*
- Can I identify times in my life when I disembarked my 'Train of Consciousness'?
- What is stopping me from being happy and content now?

Sometimes when we make a breakthrough discovery within ourselves, we can apply it to clear and heal many memories at once, and be less triggered into the future. For example, when Laura gave up her desire to have had a different past, she was able to move on and forgive many people, rather than stay in judgment of them.

Forgiving people does not mean we have to condone their behaviour. It just means finding a way to untangle ourselves from the judgment of that behaviour and give up the desire, deep within us, for it all to have been different.

Affirmations for Forgiveness of Self and Others:

- I finally release my desire to have had a different past, and by doing so I forgive and release... my father, my mother, my teachers, my ex-partners, my former friends, etc... (name whoever you are forgiving and releasing).
- I accept my past and accept that I have everything I need to completely heal.
- With the release of the past, I let go of all disappointments, dysfunctions, burdens, contracts, and negative karma associated with past relationships, across all directions of time and space.
- My past does not define my future.
- I release the old patterns so that I can create the new.
- 'Knowing what I know now, would I have... ?' This is a great question to ask ourselves when reviewing life events in our past. We have the safety of distance in the review and can be more honest with ourselves.

If the answer to the final question is 'Yes, I would have...', then you have nothing to regret. Pat yourself on the back.

If the answer is 'No, I wouldn't have...', then you've learnt a valuable lesson and are less likely to repeat the behaviour in the future. Pat yourself on the back.

Pat yourself on the back anyway.

Always.

CONCEPT 2: THE CHAKRA STORY—CHAPTER FOUR

The Chakra System of the body is well established as 'a thing.' There is a great deal of information available about chakras, from many different sources. The chakra system is not a 'new age' notion—it was mentioned in the ancient Vedas and Upanishad texts. It is believed that the chakra system originated in India between 500 and 1500 BC and the information concerning them was passed down through oral traditions. Chakra means spinning wheel of energy and it is believed we have 7 main energy centers located along the line of the spine.

I recommend Dr. Rima Bonario's *The Seven Queendoms: A SoulMap for Embodying Sacred Feminine Sovereignty*, for a substantial grounding in the meaning of the chakra system, and how to release blockages within the energy body.

Rima introduces us to the concept of the perfect archetype within each chakra and their shadow sides, as the pendulum of life swings. Her book is a powerful but practical aid to all seeking inner peace and understanding of the Self.

I also recommend Barbara Ann Brennan's *Hands of Light* for the more sceptical among us, who might not yet know that we all have healing hands. As a NASA scientist, Barbara explains it better than I could ever hope to.

Our hands are an extension of our heart chakra—and we have two of them: one for giving and one for receiving.

The story that Elba tells in the book about the Chakra system is the explanation I've always used with my Golden Tera Mai™ Reiki students, and it is the one that makes most sense to me.

I don't know where I first heard the story of the seven Chakras developing in seven-year cycles. I now feel as though I've just always known it. I think I worked out the relationship between the lower and upper chakras myself, with the Heart Chakra serving as the communications bridge between the two. This concept has always made sense to me.

My feminine and masculine, working in balance within me, allow me to focus better on the goal I have for whatever work I'm engaged in.

Exercise:

If I can't 'think' of a solution, I unblock the lower sacral chakra, connect the energies of the sacral to the third eye and within a short time, or maybe overnight, I will have a solution.

If I get a shock, or am feeling angry, upset, or hurt, I never know what's going to come out of my mouth. Whenever I remember this, I do well to clear my solar plexus chakra (which was developing during my teenage years—a very difficult time for me), and allow it to heal and get over the shock before I speak.

This has served me well since I started implementing it. Otherwise, my mouth can tend to speak like a teenager and get me into a lot of trouble. I'm smiling as I type that!

It's all about the connection between the two—the feminine and masculine, the yin and the yang—working in harmony together for the whole, i.e. me!

To 'connect', I hold my right hand on my sacral chakra—the lower tummy area—and my left hand on my brow. I close my eyes and allow the two energy centres to 'communicate' through my heart. The intention in my mind is to merge the orange (Sacral Chakra) with the indigo purple (Third Eye Chakra), and allow my fight or flight hormones to relax, knowing all is in hand, that I have recognised a problem and am now setting about fixing the imbalance. This is intended to reduce the cortisol levels in my physical body.

Similarly, this can be done with a right hand on the Solar Plexus (just above the belly button) and the left hand lightly on the throat.

The intention of this exercise is to allow the yellow (Solar Plexus) and the blue (Throat) to merge, make a connection, and relate.

Standing barefoot on the earth (Grounding the Root Chakra to the Divine Mother), and allowing the Crown Chakra at the top of my head to reach upward to the Milky Way and connect to the Divine intelligence allows me to feel safe within my being.

CONCEPT 3: SOVEREIGNTY—CHAPTER SEVEN

Sitting in your own chair, engaged in your own happy pursuits, taking time to consciously be with yourself in your own safe place is very powerful. Find five minutes, even in the midst of a busy day, to do this.

The meditation that I describe Anna experiencing in the book is one that came to me a couple of years ago, when I noticed that a lot of people were coming to me with too much going on in their heads. Too much chatter, too many instructions, too much judgment, too much regret, too many work problems, too many to-do lists, too much pressure and stress.

What I do is lay them on the plinth to receive Golden Tera Mai™ Reiki and quietly talk them through the meditation. It worked so well for people, every time, that I decided it had to be included somewhere in the book. That meditation—and the 'Garden Wall/Kitchen Table/Fireside' story—serve to remind people who truly holds the reins of control in their life: themselves.

We are always our own boundary setter. Sure, we will all have different pre-sets within us, but these two stories are applicable to everyone. Our pre-sets are what make up our character, determining how empathetic we are, or whether we are the people pleaser, the funny one, the helper, the administrator, the driver, the leader, the follower, the carer, the feeder. . . it's just who we are, individually!

However, we all have many people coming in and out of our lives and energy fields daily; we need to be aware of that, and be able to contain and protect our own energy fields and boundaries.

Affirmations:

- I release everybody to their own life lessons.

- I lovingly delegate others' responsibility for their own choices and their own lives back to them.

- I love myself enough to say *No* to other people's demands on my time and energy at this time. This time is for me.

- I keep my unwavering thoughts, actions, emotions and feelings focussed on my wellbeing.

- I am the only Authority in my life.

- I Own and Master a Sovereign Space into which No One Can Intrude. I Am the Beloved Child of an Ancient Peace I Can Never Lose.

CONCEPT 4: THE CATERPILLAR STORY

The caterpillar's story is immense. What he endures, in order to be able to fly, defies all reason. It is an epic journey of heroic proportions. The fact that he is so stunningly beautiful when he emerges must be the poetic justice for him.

It can also be a lesson for us. The process of transformation is hugely painful, yet we are constantly in motion, called to let go of the old in order that the new may enter. The imaginal discs can only work, if we complete the painful part. Every part of the caterpillar's journey is intrinsically linked to where he's coming from and where the innate intelligence within him is reaching for. He trusts. He has no option.

We don't see rolling swarms of caterpillars protesting the unfairness of the chrysalis-time they must enter. No. We only see the caterpillars moving in the formation of a rolling swarm, because they know that together, in community, they will move faster than they would as single caterpillars. They're that clever!

The journey to the chrysalis phase overtakes them and calls them inward, to make the beautiful but devastating transformation that they were destined to make.

Nobody knows why a caterpillar undertakes this herculean journey. Just that they do. I believe it's the same with us. Nobody knows why we are here. Maybe we are not meant to know. Maybe our current consciousness couldn't hold or understand the details of the universal plan.

This is not meant to frighten anybody—rather, it is to communicate that there is nobody on the planet who absolutely knows, with 100% certainty, who we are or what we are doing here. They may think they do. They may even convince others that they do. But I'll take my chances that they don't.

If you were taught that you had to know everything about a given topic in order to put an opinion forward, and that you had to strive to become the greatest living expert on something before proffering your feelings on it, this fact feels uncomfortable at first. Then it liberates you.

So, what do we know? It's all about the process. The experience. The connection. The relationships. The learnings. The stages. The feelings and emotions. The journey. The sharing of personal stories. Being someone else's butterfly. The love. This is where I'm putting my money: on having faith and trusting.

Affirmations:

- I release my desire to know every detail of what is to come in my future.
- I trust the universal plan.
- I spend time with people who nourish my soul and feed my spirit.
- I am the only one who thinks in my mind. I choose all of my thoughts and I decide now to choose thoughts of freedom, possibility, and peace.
- I choose only thoughts that sustain me in my long-term goals.

Unwind the Wound:

This is a very powerful poem by my niece, Aisling Maria Cronin, from her poetry anthology, *The Light Touch of Liberty*.

Unwound
Pass through
Your world of hurt
Unwind your story
Until your wound
Is no more

CONCEPT 5: THE FEVER

Nobody could miss the symbolic references to the Covid-19 pandemic in my Fever Story.

Everything's alright in the end, though, so if it's not alright yet, that's because it's not the end!

Anyone can see that we are in dangerous and unprecedented times. Coming out of a global pandemic is not going to be easy—logistically as well as mentally and emotionally.

We have so much to face. We let our old people down. Our wisdom leaders. We let our minorities and the less developed countries down. "The least among us."

We must face those facts as a humanity. The nations who don't face up to the atrocities of their civil wars seldom heal properly, as has been shown time and time again across the globe. We can't just sweep this pain and misery under the carpet and expect the next generation to continue doing things the way we have been doing them. The Earth herself won't sustain that.

We cannot, any of us, pretend we don't know that the social fabric protects the elites, the monied, and the privileged within our societies. In a global sense, this same social fabric protects the countries who can afford the vaccination programmes that are being rolled out across the world at this time, the countries who have secured the most effective PPE, and the countries with better health infrastructures. We cannot pretend that we do not see the divide in our societies that are emerging, between the unvaccinated and the vaccinated: echoes of the clean and the unclean. Some people allowed indoors, some left outside. We should not allow this to happen to us. Again. Together, we would be much more powerful.

These big, vaccinated countries, we tend to call the 'developed world'. The stakeholders. The societies whose billionaires and millionaires are increasing their wealth exponentially, while our teenagers are suffering a mental health pandemic of their own, while our old people died and were buried alone, while our small business owners went to the wall from lack of supports—their entrepreneurial spirits crashed up against the rocks of rent and commercial rates, out of date stock, and shattered dreams.

Now, what are we going to do about that? We cannot pretend that these moral atrocities did not happen, and are not still happening.

I believe we will want to be able to look ourselves and the generations to come in the eye when we tell our grandchildren the story of what we did to help our societies recover.

Was Covid-19 all bad? Well, yes; although the Earth got a bit of breathing space from our constant consumption for a while. No world forums or summits of our political leaders could have organised anything on such a grand scale, in their wildest eco-dreams.

What we have seen throughout 2020/21 gives us the opening into a new pathway to walk for the next twenty years. Concentrate on generating less urban pollution, less concentrated working environments, more sustainable ways of living that don't cost Mother Earth so dearly, more time on heart-centred family and community work, more quiet time, and more connection to the Self.

We need a personal plan for this, and we need to prepare now for what the next twenty years will look like in our own inner lives. The more we can achieve within ourselves, the more we can bring these new understandings to our own families and communities, then out to the towns and cities. The more we can do this, the easier and fairer the global society can be for all.

I pray that this is the pivotal time for the great awakening of consciousness that so many of us can feel.

It will start with us, and we need to start today.

Affirmations:

- Today, I listen to my body and give it what it needs.
- Today, I reach out to those I love.
- Life is eternal and filled with joyful possibilities.
- I now choose to love and approve of myself.
- Everything is occurring in perfect timing.
- I trust the universal plan as it unfolds and partake to the best of my ability in creating a better world.

About the Author

Alvagh Cronin was born in Dublin, Ireland. She studied Languages in Trinity College, Dublin and Marketing Management in the College of Marketing and Design. She had a career in the Financial Services sector, until having her family.

After having her three children, she embarked on her healing and spiritual journey. She is a Golden Tera Mai™ Reiki and Seichem Master, Practitioner and Teacher.

Alvagh lives in Kildare, Ireland with her family. *The Bridge of Now* is her first novel.

Learn more: **alvaghcronin.com** and **facebook.com/alvaghcronin**

More Flower of Life Press books

  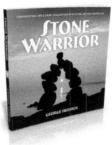 

Check out additional books at **floweroflifepress.com**

Lightning Source UK Ltd.
Milton Keynes UK
UKHW011154030322
399519UK00001B/121